It's All in the Planets

It's All in the Planets

PREETI SHENOY

w

westland ltd

61, II Floor, Silverline Building, Alapakkam Main Road,
Maduravoyal, Chennai 600095
93, I Floor, Sham Lal Road, Daryaganj, New Delhi 110002

First published by westland ltd 2016

Copyright © Preeti Shenoy 2016

10 9 8 7 6 5 4 3 2 1

ISBN: 978-93-86036-45-2

Typeset in Minion Pro by SÜRYA, New Delhi
Printed at Thomson Press (India) Ltd.

The author asserts her moral right to be identified as the author of
this work.

For JB and Figgy,
and the magic of stories

i fear
no fate (for you are my fate, my sweet)
~ e.e. cummings

Tonight I can write the saddest lines.
I loved her, and sometimes she loved me too.
~ Pablo Neruda

Leos, born between July 23 and August 22, is the fifth astrological sign of the zodiac. The Leo is represented by a lion. Self-confident and assertive, full of wit and charm, Leos are generous to a fault. They completely pamper and spoil those they have given their hearts to, and will move heaven and earth to keep them happy. They are fiercely loyal to the ones they love. They are fairly balanced and realistic people. It is not in a Leo's nature to dwell on the past. They want to be admired and appreciated. It is very hard not to like a Leo. Leos are of two kinds. They can either be quiet and confident, or flamboyant and arrogant. But their hearts are pure gold, and if you have a Leo as a friend, they are usually friends for life.

Sagittarius, born between November 22 and December 21, is the ninth astrological sign of the zodiac. The Sagittarius is represented by an archer who is half-human and half-horse. They always speak their minds and are sometimes blunt to the point where it makes your toes curl, embarrasses you and makes you go 'ouch'. Sagittarians are not known for their tact. They are completely unaware of it, though. They would be horrified if they knew they had hurt you. However, their refreshing honesty that is completely free of malice, their childlike demeanour, and their enthusiasm will sweep you along. You want to hear it like it is? Go to a Sagittarian. They love to travel, hate to be tied down and are born explorers. Warm, generous, fun-loving, they are perfect hosts. A Sagittarian can be a very dependable friend.

It's all in the planets—your daily forecast: Darshita Sen

Leo (July 23 to August 22)

*Someone you've known for a while gets into a conflict
with you. You might be feeling low on energy, and this
could be the reason. Stay positive. Focus on coming
to terms with what must be done.*

1

ANIKET

It is only when the train starts moving that I realize how
loud I was being. By then I have been talking at least a
whole fifteen minutes, and I am mid-way through my
life-and-death conversation with Subbu. But my fellow
passengers do not know it and are giving me death glares.
Damn! I feel like such an idiot now as I quickly lower my
voice.

'No. I am *not* okay. How can you tell me to calm down?
She has said she needs time to think about this. Do you

know what it means? How can you? You have never even been in a relationship for you to begin to understand.'

Anyone else in Subbu's place would have hung up on me by now and told me to take a walk. But Subbu? He loves me too much. Subbu, my wingman, my relationship-philosopher, my guide, and now my therapist as well, has been listening patiently to me going on and on about my issues with Trisha. And my last remark was below the belt. I try to make amends.

'I'm sorry, bro. That was uncalled for. I apologize,' I say.

I should not have made that remark. But I was too upset and distraught at Trisha's latest missile.

I had seen it in the auto-rickshaw, on my way to Bangalore Cantonment station.

Ani,

I am really, really, really not dumping you (well, not yet! Just kidding!). Please don't get scared and please don't think of this email as that. But I need time to think about this relationship.

I honestly do. You don't give me space to breathe. You send one mail, then follow it up with a message, then three links, and even before I have had time to check them, you are on the phone calling me. If I don't pick up, there are fifteen WhatsApp messages waiting for me.

I have a life apart from you. I need time on my shoots. I can't respond to you instantly. And I have told you that Vishwa is a friend. Yet you insist on keeping tabs on him. Why in the world did you send him that message asking

*him when he will drop me off? What was that supposed
to mean?*

*I know you love me, Ani. And I have told you that I love
you too. But please understand that you can't bind me like
this. Make me accountable to you for everything. I don't
keep tabs on you, do I?*

*I leave today for Leh. The whole team is travelling with
me—and yes, Vishwa will be there too. Please don't worry if
I don't message you. The Internet, I am told, is intermittent.
I am coming back to you in two weeks. That will give us
both enough time.*

*Please treat this dispassionately and please don't drink
too much.*

*Work out—and lose that gut. Or at least try. Twenty-
seven is no age to have a beer belly—as slight as it is. If
you don't take care, you will soon be a plump overweight
roly-poly-Ani. Heh heh.*

Muaaah.

Trish

What the hell did she mean by this? What does she
mean by she needs time to think? How could she do this?
That too, when I am on my way to Chennai to meet my
parents and tell them about us. That's what we had agreed
on. And now she pulls this stunt on me.

I definitely do not recall flooding her with links. I had
sent her one on anamorphic sculptures, and two xkcd
comics. How can that not be funny? And how long does
it take to read two comic strips anyway? And what did she

mean that I call her and flood her with messages? I think any guy would definitely care about when his girlfriend got home—especially when she was out drinking with a whole bunch of unknown idiots like Vishwa and his gang. And what Trisha conveniently forgot was that she was so drunk that day, she was not even able to stand. I drove all the way to Yelahanka to pick her up and then dropped her at her home in Indiranagar. I drove fifty-five bloody kilometres to ensure she was safe. And she did not even remember that.

This was too much.

I was so lost in my thoughts and consumed by her mail that I was not even aware when the auto-rickshaw reached Cantonment station. The auto-driver said I had to pay one-and-a-half times that of the meter as it was before seven o'clock in the morning—that unwritten rule among auto-drivers of Bangalore. I did not bargain with him. I fished out three hundred rupees and asked him to keep the change. Usually, when I take the Shatabdi, I have a cup of coffee leisurely as I wait for the train to arrive. Today, I had no interest in that either.

I called Subbu to talk to him about Trisha's email but it was too early and he rarely wakes up before eight o'clock. I tried thrice, but there was no reply. By then the train arrived and I boarded it, happy about being in executive class, which has two seats adjacent to each other and not three, like the other coaches. Barely had I settled in when Subbu called and I poured my heart out to him. He listened patiently, despite being woken up at the crack of dawn with my Trish-troubles. Trish-troubles had begun popping up with alarming frequency of late.

And now as a reward for listening to me, I had snapped at Subbu. But he was so good-natured that he brushed it aside.

'No problem. Look, bro—what you have given me is a bug report where you think you know everything about system Trisha, but you don't!'

As upset as I am, it is hard not to laugh at what he has said. It is only Subbu who can come up with such techie jargon when I am telling him that the status of my relationship is in danger. The thing is, I have invested the last one-and-a-half years of my life in this. Well, two, if you count the six months it took me to gather up the courage to approach Trisha for a date.

'No, I haven't. I have given you an accurate report. But we have to admit that what we have here is a Reality 101 failure. I have done exactly what you have told me to, but every single thing I do is misunderstood by her. I wish I hadn't gone on that stupid office trip and instead taken her paragliding, or wherever she wanted to go. Damn.'

'My dear Aniket, what we have here is the mad girlfriend bug. We need to sort out these strange happenings to fix the reality. And it is not failure. This is an experiment. Now we know what works and what doesn't. Give me an hour or so. I will call you right back. It's time for the client call,' he says and hangs up.

Subbu had, in fact, once been completely besotted with a woman. He had watched her for four whole years without once opening up about his feelings. She never got to know how he felt about her. The one-sided four-year love story had a tragic ending when she got married to an NRI chosen by her parents and left for the land where all Indian techies aspire to go—the US of A. The experience had affected him so deeply that he was insistent that my story with Trisha shouldn't meet the same fate as his. In fact, he had been instrumental in pushing me to take it further with Trisha. Since he felt involved from the very start—he had treated my relationship with Trisha as his project—he now wanted to immediately 'fix things' for me. Subbu was like that. Mr. Dependable. I knew he would call me back as soon as his client call got over.

I lean back in my seat, push the button to recline it and sigh, stretching my legs. The Shatabdi Express is one of the nicest trains in the Indian Railways. No sooner have I settled in than attendants bring a bottle of mineral water and newspapers. I pick *The Times of India* and am about to open it, when a female voice next to me asks the attendant, 'Don't you have *The Hindu*?'

It is only then that I even notice her.

It's all in the planets—your daily forecast: Darshita Sen

Sagittarius (November 22 to December 21)

Being put in charge of a new project is a compliment. Focus on staying away from relationships, if single. A new person may enter your life. Treat a cough or cold promptly as this is the time you are susceptible to falling ill. Travel is on the cards.

2

NIDHI

The guy is nice-looking. Slightly plump maybe, but only ever so slightly. He is tall though, and he has a five-day stubble. If he loses a couple of kilos and makes a little more effort with his clothes, he would definitely be attractive. Hell, what am I saying—compared to Manoj, this guy *is* actually attractive. Manoj dresses up well but isn't at all good-looking. This guy at least looks decent, though I must admit that he could have chosen better than a T-shirt on its last legs, knee-length checked shorts and rubber flip-flops. He looks like he has just tumbled out of bed. And, from his conversation, it seems like his girlfriend has dumped him. I wonder if he is overreacting though. It is hard to tell, as he seems genuinely upset. It is rare to find guys this sincere, guys who care this much. This one clearly does. I wonder what his girlfriend looks like. What was their relationship like? She wanted to go paragliding but he had gone on an office trip? Will anyone break up over that?

The attendant brings newspapers and water and he hands me *The Times of India*. I always read *The Hindu*, and so I ask him for it.

'Yes, madam,' he says as he hands me *The Hindu*. The guy whom I have been observing is now looking at me. He looks sheepish and he smiles at me.

I smile back.

'Sorry if I was loud. I didn't mean to be,' he says.

'No worries, you clearly seem to be having girlfriend trouble,' I say. I don't usually pry, but there is something so refreshing about this guy, it makes me want to pat his back and tell him that things will be fine. I don't think Manoj would quite appreciate that, though. I don't want to think of Manoj right now, but it has reached a stage where any interaction of mine with a person of the opposite sex is mentally measured against how Manoj will react.

Stop it—Manoj doesn't own you, though he acts that way. Heck—you aren't even married to him yet.

'Yeah—my girlfriend says she needs space,' he says.

I laugh.

'What is so funny?' he asks.

'I said the same thing to my fiancé! I am Nidhi, by the way.'

'Hi, Nidhi, nice to meet you. Aniket,' he says and extends his hand.

His handshake is firm: a man who is confident, kind and sensitive. You can tell a lot about a guy by the way he shakes a woman's hand. It isn't a bone-crushing grip like most men have, nor is it a weak, wishy-washy, delicate handshake. This one radiates a kind of trustworthiness and confidence. I like this guy! And I have barely met him, nor do I know anything about him. Yet I have surprised myself by revealing something that even my closest friends do not know—that I told my fiancé that I need space. That's the thing about journeys. You open up a lot more to people you do not even know. It's a strange kind of trust. It's something about the anonymity—everyone's a stranger and chances are you'll never see them again—and the sense of adventure that you feel on every journey you embark on. I guess he feels the same way.

'What do you do, Nidhi? And seeing that we are both travelling to the same place, what is your connection with Chennai, if I may ask?' he says. He is looking at me now, and his gaze is direct, honest. I know then that I was right about his trustworthiness. You can always tell from the eyes.

'My dad lives in Chennai and I am going to spend

some time with him. Chennai is my hometown,' I answer. I am usually wary of people I have just met, and never normally reveal details about myself. But this guy seems different. Either that or it is the train-journey effect acting up again.

'Oh, I see. And what about your mother? Where does she live?'

'I lost my mom,' I say.

'I am so sorry,' he says, and for a few seconds there is a pause.

'It was a long time back. It happened when I was fifteen. Besides, I have a step-mom now,' I say, and I can see the relief on his face. It is a familiar look that I've seen with most people when I tell them that I've lost my mother.

'You didn't answer my first question though,' he says.

'What question was that?'

'About what you do for a living.'

'Oh—that. I teach a pottery course at a studio in Bangalore.'

'That's very interesting and unusual. How nice.'

'So I presume your job is the usual and uninteresting?' I quip, and he laughs.

'I wouldn't say it is uninteresting, but yes, the usual. I am a techie.'

'I guess every second person you meet in Bangalore is a techie. And what is your company into? Where do you work?' It is my turn to probe now. Surprisingly, the conversation between us is flowing smoothly.

Well done, Nidhi—for a shy introvert, you are doing well.

'I work for an organization called Connect Technologies.'

'And what does Connect do? Software development?'

'Well, not exactly software development. We are into providing a global business support system for telecom operators. We are pioneers in this field and I think the only company which does this kind of a thing. Right from fraud management, asset assurance, capacity management route optimization, partner settlement and cost management, we give an end-to-end service to our customers,' he says.

God, that sounds so boring. How can anyone want to do such stuff?

I nod and try to appear interested.

The attendants are now serving breakfast, so we keep our seats upright and open the tray tables in front of us, while they ask if we want the vegetarian option or non-vegetarian one. Both of us opt for the vegetarian meal. The tray has a thermos flask with hot water, a cup, a little cutlery packet which has sachets of milk-powder, a tea bag and sugar, apart from the packed parcel containing food. When I open mine, I discover it is khara-bath, a speciality of Karnataka, and I love it. He too seems to be enjoying it. I notice how neatly he has laid out his cutlery, and he eats with his mouth closed. For all the sloppiness of his dressing style, his dining manners are impeccable.

We eat our meal in silence, and then make our tea

with the hot water and tea bags. We sit sipping it, waiting for the attendants to clear our trays.

'And what does your fiancé do?' he asks.

'He's a techie like you. Works at a multinational,' I reply.

'Aaah, I see. Very different from your field, right?'

'You bet.'

'So, do you work with adults or kids? And how long is a typical pottery course? Tell me more about it,' he says.

He seems to be genuinely interested; it doesn't seem like he is making conversation for the sake of passing time. I hate it when people do that. I have my book ready in my hand for fending off such people. Books are far more interesting than most people.

'We have several courses. We have programs for kids as well as for adults.'

'And when you say adults, do they do this as a one-off thing or do they pursue it further?'

'See, it all depends from person to person. We do corporate workshops, we host children's parties, and then we have full-length courses that typically run over eight weeks. And this is a basic course. Once you complete the basic course, you can go for an advanced course, if it interests you. We also have glazing, a potter's wheel foundation course, and something called "bring clay to life", which is free-hand sculpting. And yes, to answer your question, many start off with us as a one-off thing, but then they find that they enjoy it so much that they come back.'

'Wow! I didn't even know there were that many options. I haven't even seen a potter's wheel—except in movies—or ever touched clay. When you say potter's wheel, I always think of Demi Moore in *Ghost*,' he says.

'Haha—oh yes, it is very sensual. You must try it sometime! Working with clay is very therapeutic. Clay originates from the earth, which is the source of all things. Ancient civilizations—they all used clay for everything, right from their buildings to their vessels and jewellery. There's something very primal about giving it form. It's very soothing.'

It is unusual for me to talk so much but he has asked me a question about something I am passionate about. I feel like I have to explain how wonderful it is.

'I think you have convinced me. I will definitely give it a try sometime,' he says.

'We have a lovely sun-drenched rooftop studio with a lot of potted plants and terracotta stuff. Drop by anytime. We're closed on Mondays, but open on all other days including weekends,' I say.

He asks me for the name of the studio and asks me where it is located.

'It's called Mitti, and it's in HSR Layout.'

'Oh! That's next door to where I live,' he says and adds that he lives in Bellandur.

'Then the studio is only a five- to six-minute drive for you. Twenty if the traffic is bad,' I say, and he laughs.

When you live in a city like Bangalore, you measure

distance by the time taken to reach your destination, which depends on traffic conditions. Knowing the actual physical distance is a useless bit of information, best confined to Google maps.

His mobile rings. I recognize his ringtone. It is Avicii's W*aiting for Love.*

'Excuse me, I have to take this call, and this time I promise I won't be loud,' he says.

'Please go ahead,' I tell him and he smiles, almost embarrassed to take that call.

'Bro, I can't talk right now,' I hear him say. There's a pause, then, 'I'll tell you later. I am with someone.'

And again a pause.

'I'll call you back,' he practically hisses and turns back to me apologetically.

Five-and-a-half hours later, when we finally arrive at Chennai, it occurs to me that this is the first time I haven't even opened my book on a train journey.

It's all in the planets—your daily forecast: Darshita Sen

Leo (July 23 to August 22)

Beware of being forced into doing things you do not want to do. Bonding with your loved ones takes a front seat. A good time for new beginnings, new ventures. The possibilities in your life are immense. The world is your canvas. Go paint!

3

ANIKET

Subbu calls back when we are about two hours into the journey. By then Nidhi and I have been chatting away like old pals. This woman is so easy to talk to. She is neither as intimidating nor as pretty as Trish. Even though I have known Trish for two years, I still think twice before I say anything to her. I can never tell when an innocuous comment of mine will make her grimace and look away. I hate it when she does that. She makes a face and dismisses me almost instantly. I don't think she means to or is conscious of it. But I notice it. I notice everything about her.

In contrast, Nidhi has instantly put me at ease. She is definitely smart. I can tell by the way she speaks that she probably reads a lot. And she has a book open in her lap, facing down.

'Excuse me, I have to take this call, and this time I promise I won't be loud,' I tell her when the phone rings and I see Subbu's name flashing. She smiles and asks me to go ahead.

'Bro, I can't talk right now,' I tell Subbu.

'What happened? You seemed okay talking a little while back. Have you calmed down?'

'I'll tell you later, I am with someone.'

'Already? Don't tell me you have changed the browser now? Moved from IE to Firefox, is it? Got over Trish so quick? Have a heart—she hasn't dropped you yet,' he says and I smile.

'I'll call you back,' I hiss and then hang up. I notice that Nidhi is smiling.

'It's okay. I can listen to my music if you want to talk to him,' she says.

'Wait a minute. How did you know it was a he?'

'It was the friend you were talking to earlier, right?'

'Yes. But how in the world did you know that?' I am surprised at how correctly she has guessed this, when I didn't say anything to Subbu that could have given me away.

'It isn't hard to guess. I look around me, I observe things.' She smiles again. Her eyes crinkle when she smiles and she looks sweet. She is the kind of girl my parents would fall in love with. Not someone like Trish. They would be put off by Trish, for sure. She is too unconventional for their tastes. But I will have to convince them. Before that, though, I have to wait for her to get back from her shoot.

I check my phone to see if there are any more messages or mails from her and I find none. So I spend the rest of the journey chatting with Nidhi. She is very enthusiastic about what she does and I make a mental note to suggest the pottery course as a team-building activity to our HR head. The team outings are all so similar; they're usually at an adventure or nature resort where we do things like rock climbing and tightrope walking. I am bored of that stuff. It would be interesting to see what this pottery is all about.

The hours fly on this train journey, and we reach Chennai in what seems like no time. I ask her how she will get home and she says that her father will be picking her up.

'Okay, bye then! See you around,' I say. Funny how I have just met her but it already feels like she is an old friend.

'Bye! And don't worry about your girlfriend. It will all be fine,' she says.

'After you,' I say as I help her take her suitcase from the overhead rack.

'Thanks,' she smiles.

I notice that she has forgotten her book on the seat and I pick it up. It is Dale Carnegie's *How to Win Friends and Influence People*. Interesting. I would have never thought she would need tips in that. She seemed like a natural to me.

I follow her out, and as we alight, she spots her father and runs to hug him.

For a few seconds I stand still and look at them. I can see her hugging another woman now, who I presume is her step-mother. She turns to me and waves, and then she is on her way out with them.

The heat and humidity of Chennai assaults my senses as I sling my bag over my shoulder and make my way to the auto-rickshaw stand. Anisha is at home and when I ring the bell, it is she who opens the door.

'Hiiiiiii,' she greets me in that effusive way that only little sisters can.

'Hi. No college?' I ask.

'We have exams happening for some entrance test for which our college is the centre. So we all got an off,' she says.

'Oh, nice,' I say.

'Ani! When did you reach? I thought you were coming only tomorrow,' says my mom as she emerges from the kitchen, wiping her hands on an apron.

'What kind of a mother are you? You don't even know when your only son is coming home?' I fake-admonish her even as her face lights up with the joy of seeing me.

'I told her you were coming today, but she never pays attention,' pipes in Anisha.

'Good you are here, *kanna*. I am making your favourite veg pulav today,' she says.

'Mmmm, yummy, Mom, you are the best,' I say as I lug my bag upstairs to the room which used to be mine, but which has now been converted to a guest bedroom.

I love this house. My mom has managed to make a lovely garden. She even grows vegetables. Also, this suburb of Chennai, Besant Nagar, is close to Elliot's Beach, with which some of my favourite memories are associated. Dad bought this place a few years before he retired, and the family has lived here ever since.

Dad is in his bedroom and calls out to me. He asks for how long I am visiting.

'Three days, Dad. I need to get back to work on Monday,' I say. It feels good to be home, even though I technically don't even have a room any more and am a guest in my own house. I have my own place at Bellandur—rented I must add—but when I say 'home' it is always this place in Chennai that comes to my mind.

It is over lunch that they broach the subject of my marriage. We have been through this so many times and I wish they would leave this topic alone. But they don't.

'You know, *kanna*, Kasturiakka was talking about her cousin's daughter. Her name is Priyanka,' says my mother. I inwardly groan. Actually scream. But I manage to convert it into a sigh. I know what is coming next only too well.

'*Maaa*, I am not interested in marriage at this point,' I say.

'I am not telling you to get married straight away. I am only telling you to meet her,' says my mother.

'What wine pairs with a get-married-now mom-luncheon?' I say in a British accent.

Anisha giggles. 'That would be the don't-bother-me wine,' she says, adopting my tone and accent.

'What?' asks my mom.

'Nothing, Ma, you won't get it,' says Anisha, and I smile.

My dad says, 'There is a time and place for everything, Ani. Start looking for matches now, when you're twenty-seven. It may take a few years before anything clicks. By thirty, you should be settled.'

What is it about Indian parents? All they want is to see their children 'settled'. Like we are some grains of a chemical that have been shaken in a test-tube as part of an experiment, and we now have to wait to settle at the bottom.

'Dad, I am already "settled". Thank you very much.'

'Do you have someone in mind? If so, tell us, and your mother and I will start the process formally,' he says.

'He does, Dad,' chimes in Anisha. I dart a glare her way, but she doesn't get it. I want to sort this thing out with Trisha before I bring her up with my parents. But now Anisha has blurted it out. There is only one thing I can do now. Deny Trisha's existence. My parents won't get it.

'No, I don't,' I say, as I kick my sister under the table.

'Look, we are pretty broadminded. You can tell us freely if you do have someone,' says my mom.

Yeah right. So broadminded that you can't let your son decide when he wants to get married.

'No, Mom, I do not have anyone,' I say.

'Then why did Anisha say that?' My mom doesn't let it go.

'Anisha speaks any nonsense that comes to her mind,' I say, and I can see the outrage creeping up on her face. She is about to say something but I glare at her again and she keeps quiet.

'See, you won't know it now, but we all need someone as we get older,' says my dad.

'For what?' I ask.

'What kind of a question is that?'

'You said we all need someone as we get older. I don't see it that way. I have my friends, my family, my career. I want to travel, explore the world. A marriage ties you down.'

'How does it tie you down? If your dad and I had thought that way, you and Anisha wouldn't have been born.' My mom's tone is grim.

I laugh. And Anisha smiles.

'I didn't ask to be born, did I? I was born as you wanted to have me. Unless we were accidents,' I say.

My mom stretches out a hand and hits me on my head. 'Shameless fellow. Is this how I have raised you? What rubbish are you talking? Is this any way to talk to your parents?' She has launched into full mother mode now.

I know from years of experience that it's best to let her go on. She will run out of steam in a bit.

She does and then, finally, she is quiet.

'Aniket, all we are asking of you is to meet this girl. You don't have to say anything right now, you know. And you can meet her outside home, take her out for a cup of coffee and chat with her,' says my dad.

Finally, out of sheer exasperation and because I have no excuses any more, I end up saying yes to a 'date with Priyanka', a woman whose existence I did not even know of fifteen minutes back.

As soon as we are done with lunch and are out of earshot of our parents, Anisha corners me in my room. 'So what's with Trish, eh? Any trouble?' she asks. She zooms in, bang on target, in that way only a sibling can.

'Nothing at all,' I say and try to fob her off. But she doesn't back off.

'Come on, I can tell from your face. Are you guys breaking up or something?' she asks.

'Definitely not.' My reply is a bit quick, and the tone, defensive.

'Then? Has she said she needs time apart?' Anisha is relentless in her quest for details about her older brother's love life. She is also astute. A combination that can be deadly.

'Yes,' I am finally forced to admit it.

'Aaaah—see, that's what they all say. Then will come an email saying "Sorry baby this isn't working out, it's me not you, blah blah". An email, if you are lucky. A text if you aren't.'

'What? What are you talking about? Trish and I are not breaking up!'

'Oh well—that's the way the cookie crumbles,' she says.

I tug her hair and she pretends to yelp.

'What's happening with *your* love life?' I ask her.

'Tell me if there are any hot twenty-seven-year-olds in your office. I am done with younger guys. Immature, imbeciles, idiots,' she says.

'What? Get out of here. You aren't dating any of my friends,' I immediately retort.

'Hahaha, relax, I was only joking. Well, sort of,' she says.

I prod her a little more, and I get to know that she has broken up with Sanjay, whom she has had a crush on since Class Eleven. They had studied in the same school, and while she had joined a women's college for her degree in visual communications, he had gone off to Manipal to do his engineering. I knew that they had kept in touch for a while, as she used to rave about him. Now she looks crushed.

'What kind of a dumb-ass posts pictures on Facebook of himself kissing a girl on the mouth, and then decides to tell me when I confront him?' Anisha asks.

'Only a sicko. A jerk. You deserve better. That guy

was an idiot anyway,' I say, and I reach out and give her a hug. I am angry with Sanjay—but I had always had a bad feeling about him. I'd tried to warn Anisha, but she had paid no heed.

'Yeah, I should have listened to you,' she says as she hugs me back.

We chat for a bit about my work, her college and her future plans. And then my father's voice booms up the staircase.

'Ani, I have spoken to Priyanka's parents. I have told them that you will meet her tomorrow at the Taj at Nungambakkam. Take the car if you like,' he says.

'Wow—that was quick,' I tell Anisha.

'Go meet her. She is very pretty. And smart,' replies Anisha.

'How do you know?' I ask.

'I met her last week with Mom at the GSB Sabha,' she grins.

That's when I know this is all a conspiracy by my family. They are all in this together. There is no escape. And as much as I hate to unnecessarily inflict this on a girl, this whole process of meeting only to reject her, I can see that there is no way out.

It's all in the planets—your daily forecast: Darshita Sen

Sagittarius (November 22 to December 21)

You find yourself drawn into situations you seem to have no control over. The stars are aligning in a position which will propel you to act. An old relationship seems strained. A new friendship blossoms and you enjoy it.

4

NIDHI

Tara is chatty on the way back home from the station. But then, Tara always is. Dad occupies the passenger seat in the front, and Tara and I are seated at the back. Mani, our chauffeur, is driving as Dad hates to drive. Mani has been a part of our lives ever since I was a child. Mani was the one who fetched me from school when Mom died. I remember how he had broken down when we reached home, while I had sat shell-shocked in the back seat.

'So what's the latest with you and Manoj—decided on wedding dates yet?' asks Tara.

My dad turns around and says, 'Yes, what have you guys decided on that?'

'He wants to get married soon. But somehow I am not ready,' I reply.

'Why, what's the issue with getting married soon?' asks Tara.

Tara is one of those people who is certain about what she wants. When she met my dad, she knew immediately that he was the man for her. She had been a mid-level manager in his company then, and it never bothered her that he was a widower with a grown-up daughter. It had already been seven years since my mom had died, and by then loneliness was beginning to creep up on my dad as I was living away from home, for college. She pursued my dad and ultimately he had fallen in love with her. At least that's the way I saw it. I didn't mind at all, as I got along well with her. And I could see how happy she made my dad. I was excited at the wedding, which was a low-key affair. She was so young—I was twenty-two at the time and she was only thirty-six—I ended up calling her by her first name. She liked it that I called her by name.

Tara and I had quietly forged a bond, over the years. My dad had sold our home, the one he had shared with my mom, and bought another flat for him and Tara to set up. Initially, it had made me feel a little sad. But then, it was not fair on my part to hold on to that. Tara had been very sensitive about the whole thing. She kept emphasizing that it had been my dad's idea and also asserted that the flat would always be my home as well. And even though I was in college and not living with them, she had insisted on my involvement in the whole decorating process. Tara was sweet like that, and it had endeared her to me even more.

Over the years, my connection with Tara had only become stronger. More than a step-mom, I think of her as a confidante and a friend. So I am comfortable telling her what has been on my mind over the last few weeks. In fact, I *want* to discuss this with her.

'I am not sure if Manoj is the guy for me, Tara.'

'What?' say my dad and Tara in chorus.

I nod. 'I'm not sure. I think you are the only person in the world, Tara, who was certain about whom she wanted to marry and was so sure of it all.'

'That's not right. I was certain that I wanted to marry her too,' says my dad.

'Yeah—you both are the only couple still in love after so many years of marriage,' I say.

'Life is beautiful when you share it with a supportive spouse; otherwise it can be hell. So if you are having second thoughts about marriage, entertain them, examine them and keep rethinking. Don't take any rash decisions and, above all, don't get pressurized by *anyone*,' says my dad.

God—how I love my father. He is the most supportive parent anyone can ask for.

'I agree with him. But we will definitely talk about this over a nice glass of wine,' says Tara, and I smile. Tara knows exactly the right thing to say.

Once we reach home, I tell them that I want to rest for a while. I love the fresh aroma of pine that hits us as soon as I enter the flat. Tara is house-proud and keeps the apartment remarkably well. She has an eye for details, and I love how she has an entire wall painted yellow, with a lot of black-and-white framed enlarged photos of my mom and me, my dad and mom, and many other memories that she was not a part of. A long time back, when she had been setting it up, I had asked her why she would want these pictures on the wall—this was his and her home; wouldn't our memories encroach on her new life, the one she was starting with my dad? Her answer had taken me by surprise. 'No, Nidhi—this is a part of who he is, and I want to honour that,' she had said. I had to turn away quickly as my eyes had filled up with that reply of hers.

Tara is one of those rare women who has an endless capacity to love, and my dad is indeed a fortunate man to have found her.

At dinner time I find that Tara has set up a gourmet meal fit for royalty with a stunningly decorated table. The tablecloth is black with a rich floral embossing. The centrepiece is an eye-catching flower arrangement comprising clematis and orchids. She has used white plates with gold borders, and brass cutlery. The napkins are folded neatly and placed on the plates, and over them are tiny crystal vases with single roses. There are tall brass candlesticks, and Swarovski hand-cut crystal wine glasses twinkle, reflecting the light from the chandelier above.

'Wow, Tara—you are amazing. This looks straight out of a magazine!' I cannot hide my delight.

'Last month we had thrown an official dinner for visitors from Chicago, and they were full of praise for it,' says my dad, as he squeezes her shoulders with both his arms. She reaches out with her right hand, touches his arm, and looks at him tenderly. The exchange of that glance lasts only a moment, but it conveys so much. There is no mistaking the unbreakable bond of affection and tenderness in that look.

And I know that this is what I am seeking in my relationship with Manoj. This depth, this certainty. I fail to find it.

Once we sit down for dinner and are all about half a glass of wine down, I decide to open up to both of them about Manoj.

'Dad, Tara—I have a question to ask. Did you guys ever feel the spark between you die or dim or at least flicker a bit? Ever?' As soon as I ask the question, I already know the answer, as they both look at each other and smile.

'No, not even once. I am fortunate to have this woman in my life. I loved your mom too, but it was different,' says my dad.

I knew it was. My father had never been this effusive

with my mom. It had been an arranged marriage. And while there were no great disagreements or fights, they never brought out the best in each other. They compromised, adjusted and stayed in the marriage like most other couples who never have too much to complain about. But with Tara, my dad is such a different man. I could see the transformation between how my dad used to be and what he had turned into these last few years with Tara. I had never seen him this ebullient with my mom.

'I feel blessed to have this. I know, as I'd been in a couple of bad relationships before I met your dad,' says Tara.

'I think that's exactly what I am missing with Manoj. See, he's a great guy. He loves me a lot. But somehow it is as though he never *gets* me. Do you know what I mean?' I ask.

'Gets you in what way, Nidhi? Do you mean to say he doesn't understand you?' asks my dad.

'He says all the right things, Dad. But you know, he isn't passionate about things in the same way that I am.'

'He doesn't have to be passionate about the same things, Nidhi,' says Tara gently.

'I know—but it's like when I talk about a new sculpture I made or something exciting that happened at my centre—a student making a great piece, for example—he doesn't get how happy I am and, more importantly, how much it matters to me.'

'That's because he doesn't have the same passion for

his job. He is a number-cruncher who deals with figures and facts on a daily basis. You are in a creative field. You deal with ideas. Yours is a very different kind of work. You are very free-spirited, Nidhi. He is quite practical.'

'Come on, Dad—you are supposed to be in my corner. Not defend him and find fault with me.'

'I am not defending him, Nidhi. I am merely pointing out facts. Just because someone doesn't match your interests exactly, it doesn't mean you cannot have a great relationship with them. Take Tara and me for instance. She loves different TV shows from me. She hates to watch sports. She reads different books. And that's what makes our relationship so dynamic. We learn from each other, and we both help each other grow. With your mom, though we did things together, it was never like this,' says my dad.

He is a practical man. And honest, to the point of bluntness. But I am glad he is telling me exactly what he thinks.

'It is not uncommon to have doubts, Nidhi. Besides, you are now thirty-two. It is only natural to feel apprehensive about giving up your freedom. I guess, when you are in your twenties, you are a little more flexible in your approach. I know I was impulsive in my twenties but I am glad I did not act on them. And when I finally met your dad, there was only certainty. If you are not completely sure about Manoj, I think you should wait,' says Tara.

Both Tara and my dad have given me sage advice. I decide that I should sleep over it. I bid them both goodnight after we finish our dinner and head back to my room.

My phone buzzes and I see a message pop up in my inbox on Facebook. To my surprise, it's Aniket.

'Hey, it's Ani. The guy on the train with the girlfriend trouble. You know what—I have your book. I meant to give it to you when we got down from the train, but by then you had already met your parents.'

How did he track me down so easily?

'Hey, how did you find me?' I type.

A minute later his reply pops up:

'I have a magic wand. I pointed it and it led me to your page. It is called Google search with the name of the place you mentioned you worked in.'

'Ha ha—clever or creepy? I am not sure which category to place you in.'

'I leave it to you! How about creepily clever or cleverly creepy?'

And even before I can reply, he adds:

'Clearly clever or clearly creepy, could be either one. Well, we will find out, won't we?'

'Oh, we will. Heard from your girlfriend yet? My prediction is she will forgive you.'

He stops replying then, and I wonder if I have overstepped the limit. Have I touched a raw nerve? I should have been a bit more sensitive and not brought it up. Besides, I don't even know the guy and it isn't really my business.

But his reply comes after a few minutes.

'Sorry—my sis was talking to me. And—it's not like that at all. There is nothing to "forgive" here. Just that we seem to be going through a rough patch right now.'

My reply is instantaneous:

'Hope things get sorted for you.'

Fifteen minutes later, I hear from him again.

'I hope so too.'

A few seconds later:

'But I am "seeing" this girl tomorrow. Parents insisting. Feel like such a fraud.'

Four seconds later:

'Oh—but can't you tell your parents about your girlfriend?'

Three seconds later:

'Can't. They won't get it. I myself don't get it. I don't even know where I stand in her life currently.'

I don't know what to say to that. I have the most understanding parents in the world. But I know I am lucky there. Most parents start subtly hinting to their adult children that they would like them to get married, and then start match-making. Even before they realize it, the children are hitched. That's what happened with a couple of my friends; they're happily married now, well into the third or fourth year of marriage, and one of them has a baby too. I guess Aniket's parents are like that.

So I type:

'*Oh no.*'

A second later:

'*Oh yes. FML.*' And he adds a sad smiley.

I type a sad smiley back.

It is funny how much these emoticons can convey. I can actually feel this guy's quandary. Strangely, I want to comfort this guy and tell him to hang in there. I want to help him sort out his girlfriend troubles. I want to make everything all right for him.

And it is so odd that even though I have met him only a few hours earlier, it feels as though I have known him all my life.

It's all in the planets—your daily forecast: Darshita Sen

Leo (July 23 to August 22)

The stars are aligned for an adventure today! You are in the mood to be impulsive. Beware of promising more than you can deliver. A loved one hurts you in some way.

5

ANIKET

Whoever invented this process of 'arranged marriage' and 'seeing the girl' should be shot dead. Why is a twenty-six-year-old woman a 'girl' anyway? And why am I 'the boy'? Somebody kill me. I don't want to do this. But my father and mother are both so hopeful of me changing my mind.

I decide not to drive and instead take a cab to Taj Coromandel at Nungambakkam, which is where we have agreed to meet at half past three.

Don't be late—I hate to wait, she had texted. Our only exchanges have been on text so far. I had checked out her Facebook profile, and added her. She had accepted the friend request. She looked all right—maybe a seven on ten. Undoubtedly my Trish was a perfect ten if I was judging purely on looks. I wondered if women had such rating scales between their friends. Did they rate guys like we rated women? What did they look for? Definitely not penis size—that much I was sure of.

The ride from Besant Nagar to Nungambakkam is long and I decide to call Subbu. To my surprise, he answers even before it completes one ring.

'Dude! What are you doing? Sitting with the phone in your hand and waiting for it to ring, is it?'

'Ha ha. No, I'm at the dentist's and was about to check my mail when it rang. What's up?'

'Why are you at the dentist's?'

'Wisdom tooth giving me some trouble. Having it checked. You tell me, how is it going with Trish.'

'Haven't heard from her and now, bloody hell, I am on my way to meet Priyanka.'

'She is the one you hit it off well with on the train, right? Hook up with her, buddy. Dump Trish. Trish is a bug that can't be fixed.'

'No, no—that's not Priyanka. That's Nidhi. This one is some girl my parents want me to meet.'

'Whoa—you are a stud, man. Here I am struggling to hook up with one girl and you are juggling three? What are you? A Fastrack watch? I bow to you, master.'

'Hold on, hold on. I am not juggling anything. I am

just waiting for Trish to get back to me. Tell me, do you think women have a rating system for guys?'

'Rating system? Sure they do!'

'Really? How do you know?'

'They must be rating, right? I think they would probably look at our tummies. You lose big time there, bro. I am fitter than you, man. You need to lose the flab.'

'Nah, I don't think they look at tummies. Definitely they check out the butt. Either that or the pay package.'

'Ha, ha, yeah. That they do for sure. Anyway, good luck. Impress this girl. Get her to say yes to you. Make her fall in love with you. Then hold it over Trish. She will come running back to you. It's a good way to debug and fix the system errors.'

Subbu is as solution-oriented as ever and he doesn't hesitate to tell me how to fix my love life.

For a minute I actually consider this suggestion. I am that desperate to patch things up with Trish. It's been twenty-four hours since I last heard from her.

'I haven't even heard from her, bro,' I sigh.

'Chill, bro, you will. And relax. Have a good time with this Priyanka. Tell me later how it went,' he says and hangs up.

The traffic on Nungambakkam High Road is bad and I text her saying I will be a good twenty minutes late.

'No problem. Am waiting,' she texts back, and I curse this set-up 'date' some more. I hate to make women wait and the fact that she had texted earlier asking me not to be late isn't helping.

Priyanka is sipping a cold coffee and is busy with her phone when I arrive. She seems to be a lot plumper than her Facebook profile picture. Her face too looks different. She isn't bad-looking. She is wearing some kind of a long, light-grey dress that sweeps the floor.

'Hi, so sorry, the traffic was a killer. I'm Aniket,' I greet her.

'Yeah, I know,' she smiles and gestures to the chair opposite her. The waiter takes my order and I tell him to get me a cold coffee as well, with less sugar and no cream.

'This is so awkward for me,' I blurt out.

'Why?' She is staring at me now and refusing to break eye-contact. She is making me nervous and uncomfortable.

'Well—you know … because … I don't do this for a living,' I say. I expect her to laugh, but she doesn't even smile.

'I know you don't. You're a software engineer,' she says.

'Ha ha. That is what I have told my parents. They don't know my real job,' I say. Somehow I am irked by her serious world's-burden-is-on-my-shoulders attitude.

'Oh, and what is that?' she asks, sitting up a little straighter, her interest now piqued.

The waiter serves the coffee and I wait till he is out of earshot. Then I lower my voice and say, 'I work as a stripper at bachelorette parties.'

'Ummm, interesting. Do you have a business card?' she asks.

What? I can't believe she bought that. I nowhere have the physique of a male model. Is she blind? Or is she trying to be funny?

'In businesses like these, you don't carry cards. It's all word-of-mouth,' I say.

'And what do you do? The full monty?' She is so academic about it.

I quickly think about what to reply to that one.

'It depends on the money, the crowd. I prefer older women,' I say, surprising myself. Where is all this nonsense coming from? I have no idea, but I just can't stop.

'Wow, that is quite something,' she says and I am pleased to finally get a reaction out of her.

'What kind of older women hire male strippers?' she asks.

'The very rich kind. They hire them for their kitty parties. They have all this money but are so neglected by their husbands that they are grateful for any form of male attention. Even if they have to pay for it. It's very easy to please them,' I say. And then I start laughing uproariously at the absurdity of the stories I have made up.

She joins in the laughter and then the ice is broken.

'I too have a secret to share,' she says.

'What?' I ask. I bet she cannot match my story.

'I don't want to get married to you. I am doing this just to please my parents. I have a boyfriend. He is Bengali, and my parents do not know about us. We plan to tell them sometime soon.'

'Oh. What a relief,' I say.

'Why?' she asks

'It's the same with me. I have a girlfriend and I intend telling my parents soon. I too was forced into meeting you.'

'Well—that's sorted then. We can spend an hour here, and then you can tell your parents that you didn't like me. And I too will do the same,' she says.

'That sounds great,' I say, and the relief in my voice is evident.

'Do you believe in astrology?' she asks suddenly.

'I don't know. I haven't given it much thought. But it seems weird that some planets somewhere in the universe can control our lives, don't you think?'

'No, I think we all have our destinies. Especially when it comes to choosing our life-partners. My boyfriend's aunt—she is a well-known astrologer. She has a few celebrity clients. In fact, she writes the astrological prediction for a few newspapers.'

'Oh, does she? What is her name?'

'You might have seen it—Darshita Sen.'

'Ooooh, yes. Interesting! Trish—my girlfriend— always reads her predictions. She is big time into zodiac signs and all that. I am a bit of a sceptic. How can there be only twelve personality types?'

'Oh, you will be surprised. There are actually three hundred and sixty-five personality types based on the day you were born. You see, astrology is based on a) astronomy, which is pure science, b) mathematics, which is pure science, and c) prediction, which is not at all "scientific", as predictions can only be observed.' She holds up a finger for each point, like a professor giving a lecture. 'There are many, many astrologers taking advantage of the lack of knowledge, and many of them are crooks who are out there for a quick buck. But when a person who knows the subject makes predictions, you will be blown away by the accuracy. You know my boyfriend's aunt—his name is Shomo, by the way—predicted that he will marry a girl from south India, and that her name would start with P. This was way before Shomo and I even knew each other,' she adds.

'Wow—that is precise. And impressive. I want her to look at my natal charts. I am curious about what she will predict for me. You think you can get that done?' I ask.

'Well—I don't know. She does do readings for friends, free of charge.'

'You mean I am not a friend? Come on!'

'Ha ha, will you throw in a strip-show for us? Just me and my friends. Then I will arrange it.'

I had painted myself right into a corner there. How could I now refuse? So I find myself agreeing, mentally kicking myself. Then I call for the bill and she insists on splitting it, and then we bid goodbye.

She drives her own car and she waves to me as she drives away.

As soon as I get back into the cab to head home, I call Subbu.

'Get ready for a strip-show man, you and I are performing. You can show off your flat tummy,' I tell him.

'What? Did you drink in the middle of the day? Or have you been smoking up?' he asks.

Then I narrate the whole Priyanka story in detail, and by the end of it we are both laughing so hard we are unable to talk.

'Trust you to turn an arranged marriage meeting into this—a strip-show.'

'Uh-uh—correction. It is only the promise of a strip-show!' I say.

And we laugh at the wickedness of the thought.

When I hang up, I immediately check my phone and see a mail from Trish.

Yes! Finally. She seems to have got Internet access. Why didn't she ping me on WhatsApp then? I check WhatsApp and her last-seen-at status shows five minutes ago. If she has time to mail, then I wonder why she hasn't pinged.

Then I begin to read her mail and my heart starts sinking.

Dear Ani,

Hope you are having fun!

Have been giving all this some thought and I thought it best to come clean. I know we have been having some disconnect lately. I have been thinking about it. And even if it hurts you to hear it, I am going to say whatever is on my mind. That's the only way to have a genuine relationship.

A few things bother me. Your weight—it bothers me big time. I like guys who are fit. You don't seem to be concerned about your beer-belly. You are twenty-seven, Ani. If you have a paunch at twenty-seven, I can't imagine what you would be like in your forties.

Also, I hate it that I have to be the one initiating every single conversation. The links that you send are NOT conversation-starters in my book. I want to hear about you—what you did, how your day went. I want to share my day with you.

I don't want you to sit up and worry about me, or wonder if I will get home safe. I value my friends and I genuinely like having fun with them. And yes, they will drop me home. So quit playing the overprotective boyfriend.

If we are to go forward with our relationship, then there are a few things I would like you to change. Here is the list:

1. *Lose weight.*
2. *Talk a bit more, make conversation that is not nerdy.*
3. *Stop hounding me when I go out without you.*
4. *Stop sending me links to subjects that interest you. I find them boring! (Sorry!)*
5. *Get me gifts! Other boyfriends do this, you know.*
6. *Surprise me.*
7. *Develop a hobby. What do you do apart from coding?*
8. *Let us do some fun stuff over the weekends instead of me coming over to your place, ordering pizza and having sex. I am done with that.*

9. *Please stop over-analyzing things. Don't think so much. Loosen up, will you?*

10. *Love me and accept me as I am. Please.*

Ani—I hope you do not mind my being completely candid. Let's take a call after six months. What do you say? And if you have a list of things that you want me to change, do shoot me a mail. I promise I will try.

Leh is beautiful. I am attaching a couple of photos. I am having loads of fun.

Take care, eat healthy and think about what I said.

Signing off,

Trish

I read the email one more time. I can't believe she is so unhappy with me. She was the one who said she couldn't have enough of me and wanted to stay at home and order pizza. Okay, I admit, I was only too happy to do that. But still.

And I never even knew that the links I was sending her were boring for her. How can anyone not be interested in discovering something new? It wasn't like I had sent her links about programming in Angular JS. I had only sent her the fun stuff.

Then it occurs to me. Her idea and my idea of fun is not the same. How could I be such a dumb idiot to not have figured that out before? I look at the pictures she has sent me. They are all with Vishwa and a couple of other friends. It looks like she is having a blast.

By the time I reach home I am morose. My mood has

plummeted and landed in a pile of garbage. My parents are waiting eagerly to hear what happened with Priyanka.

'It won't work out, Dad,' I say.

'Why? What do you mean it won't work out?' asks my mom.

'What is wrong with her? What are you looking for? Kareena Kaif?' asks my dad.

'Katrina Kaif, Dad. And it is Kareena Kapoor,' corrects Anisha.

'Okay, okay. That's not the point here. What exactly are you looking for, Ani?' my dad asks.

'I don't know, Dad. I think these things are destined. We marry the people we are destined to be with,' I say.

I am tired now. I trudge up to my room. I lie on the bed for a long time, thinking about the day's events.

Then I pick up my phone, open Facebook messenger, and text Nidhi.

It's all in the planets—your daily forecast: Darshita Sen

Sagittarius (November 22 to December 21)

A new job opportunity will come your way. Say yes. It is likely to lead you to a place close to your heart. A misunderstanding with a loved one is on the cards. Stay clear and do not let things escalate. Lucky colours: yellow and orange.

6

NIDHI

One of the nicest things about being back in the place that you grew up in is catching up with your friends. I have many friends here in Chennai who go back a long way, way back to my childhood. Studying together in one of Chennai's best convents, an all-girls' school, we have been through some wacky adventures which would have sent the nuns into a tizzy had they known about it. Fortunately for us, we never got caught. We now have a strong alumni network, and whenever someone who lives outside Chennai comes back to visit, the whole machinery swings into action and a quick lunch or a coffee is arranged.

Today, it is lunch with Priya, Sujata, Mary and me. Mary got married at twenty-one to a Hindu guy, much against her parents' wishes. She is now divorced and a single mom to an eight-year-old. Priya is divorced too, and in a relationship with a guy; they hope to get married soon. Sujata is the only one who is 'happily married'. She has two children, a girl and a boy.

'So, tell me Suj, what is the secret of your "success", considering that among the four of us, you are the one who has the picture-perfect family?' says Mary, making quote marks in the air. I think I can sense a tone of bitterness there.

'Come on, girls. It's not like staying married and producing two kids is a great achievement or can be called "success". I won an award from the Ministry of Urban Affairs for a commercial building complex I designed last year. Now, *that* is "success"', replies Sujata.

Touché. Mary was asking for that, I think, but I do not voice it.

'Proud of you, girl! Way to go,' says Mary. And in the same breath she continues, 'We Agnites have a thing for break-ups, I think. Look at us four,' she says. Then she points to me. 'This one here took ages to even get engaged to someone. The other two have already broken the ultimate sacred vow—marriage. Only one is married and has even has produced the mandatory two children which everyone thinks should be the goal of a woman's life.'

'Yes—somehow society seems to think that if you get married and have kids, all problems magically vanish. What a load of bull,' says Sujata.

'Oh, what's the problem? Aren't you happy?' asks Priya.

'Yeah, I guess. For a while, I am. Then I remember my family,' says Sujata, and we all laugh.

They all want to know when I am getting married. Somehow I do not feel like sharing my concerns about Manoj with them. I have Tara for that. So I tell them that nothing is decided yet and the moment it is, I will let them know. We talk about our work and what a long way we have come since our schooldays. We rehash the madness and the memories and then it's a laughter riot all over again. After that, on an impulse, we decide to go for a movie, a Hindi one which we sit through, only because:

a) It's the only movie for which we get tickets at such short notice, and

b) The male lead has a superb physique.

As usual there are witty comments and we all giggle. It is like being back at school.

When I get back home, I find that Tara and my father have both gone out to attend a dinner. I see a text from Tara asking me to join them if I get bored. I consider it, but then dismiss it as it is a high-profile page-three kind of event for which I would have to dress up. After a day out, I am in no mood to do that. So I decide to update my blog instead.

I have never revealed my real name on my blog. I love writing my thoughts and sending them out into the cyber-world. I have a set of bloggers who are regulars on my blog now, and these virtual connections that I have built up over the last two years are strangely comforting. I call them my 'nameless friends'. They go to blogger meets and have been coaxing me to attend one as they all want to know who the person behind *A pot of clay that holds gold* is.

I had started the blog with the intention of posting my pottery projects. Then I discovered that there was more I wanted to say. They were mostly musings and thoughts, and so three months after I started it, I changed the name to 'A pot of clay that holds gold'. Somehow that seemed to appeal to a lot of people rather than 'The pot of clay', which had been the original name. Over the months, the number of readers steadily rose and I have a loyal readership base now.

It has been almost a month since I last updated my blog. I don't want to write the usual apologies, and so I decide to be creative.

A Pot of Clay That Holds Gold

Hi there. You haven't heard from me for a while. That is only because I was abducted by a cyber-biber. Now I will save you the trouble of googling who cyber-bibers are. They are these tall, handsome, charismatic guys who watch out for women who blog. If you blog too regularly, they abduct you and remind you that you must have goals in life. They tell you that your blog will take you nowhere. Then they deliberately *slow down* your Internet connection so you are terribly frustrated each time you try to post something. Then, for fun, they add some complications to your life, especially to your relationship sphere, and watch you as you go through agony, trying to sort out your mess.

(Okay, I admit I made that whole thing up. But I think it is better than saying I was busy. Which I was. But not so busy as to not blog. Now, that is inexcusable. But you are sweet and you will excuse me, won't you? I promise not to fall prey to cyber-bibers from now on. I now have a cyber-biber protection plan, guaranteed to protect against abduction, distractions and damage caused by neglect.)

Just then a ping pops up on my Facebook Messenger.

It is Aniket.

'*Hey. What are you up to?*' his message says.

'*Completing my blog post.*'

'*Wow, you blog?*'

'*Yes—am in the middle of a post.*'

'*Cool! Give me a link to your blog?*'

So I give him the link. Then I go back to writing my post.

I had a lovely lunch with my gal-pals today; we had such fun. Later, we watched a Hindi movie that was about a married woman who wanted to find herself. It made me think.

When it comes to relationships, how many of us are certain? How can we be sure of the person we are marrying? So many things can change. The person we marry might change, we might change. There are no guarantees in life, more so in relationships. They are always carpeted with uncertainty.

And yet, we all (okay, most of us) *want* to get married. We want a happily-ever-after. We see relationships around us breaking up all the time. And we say, 'No, but we are different. That won't happen to us.'

Isn't it strange?

We hope to find that thing called true love. And it seems elusive. But, we keep searching, keep hoping. If this isn't insanity, what is?

When I am happy with what I wrote, I hit publish. Then I remember Aniket's message and I ping him again.

'*You still there?*' I type.

He replies after about ten minutes.

'*Yes! I was reading all your back-entries. You write so well! I love what you have written,*' he gushes.

'*Ha, ha. Ummm … I am okay, I am not that good.*'

I still cannot accept a compliment graciously. Tara keeps telling me that a simple thank you will suffice. And that if I do not believe in my writing, then no one else will. Tara is the only one who knows that I want to write my own novel some day. This is a dream that I haven't shared even with my father. He thinks I am perfectly happy teaching pottery as my main job, and working as a freelance content writer on the side.

My freelance work is mostly technical writing, where I am writing, editing and proofing boring user manuals and guides for customers. Sometimes I also do content writing for websites. With Tara, too, it was one night of too much wine that made me admit to her my dream of being a published author. She had nodded and given me some sensible advice. She had told me to persist. That she would back me up and would be happy to read what I had written. I had shown her my blog then, and she was now one of my regular readers. She left comments too, under the pseudonym 'Starry Nights', which was a spin-off from her name, Tara. We had been sitting on the terrace, under a starry moonlit night, when I had shown her my blog. She had immediately grabbed the iPad and read it with great interest. She had promptly made a blogger id and commented on many of my posts with her pseudonym, and now I look forward to her clever, incisive, witty comments each time I post.

'Are you kidding? You are not just "okay". You are superb!' Aniket types.

And this time I manage to say a thank you.

'You know, I can so relate to your thoughts on relationships.'

'Can you?'

'Oh yes! Completely. I couldn't have said it better myself. But then I am no writer like you.'

'Ha ha ... Thanks again! And how was your day today? Did you meet that girl—the one you said your parents wanted you to meet?'

'Oh yes—and it was a fiasco. I promised her a strip-show in exchange for her boyfriend's aunt's predictions for my future. On top of that, I have got an ultimatum-list from my girlfriend. If I don't fulfil all the conditions on that list, I think she will dump me.'

'What?! A strip-show! Are you joking?'

'No! I am dead serious! My friend and I laughed about it.'

'Good lord. No wonder your girlfriend has a list of things she wants you to change.'

'Oh no, no. The two aren't connected. It's a long story.'

'I want to hear it.'

'It will take too long to narrate over chat. Which part of Chennai do you live in?'

'Boat Club Road.'

'I live in Besant Nagar. Fancy a trip to Elliot's Beach? We could grab lunch at By the Beach. It has a nice view of the sea and their menu is supposedly excellent.'

It takes me only a moment to decide to say yes. It has been ages since I visited Elliot's Beach. It was where my first-ever crush had taken me. It would be fun. Besides, I want to hear his story.

'Sure. At 12.30 p.m. tomorrow?' I type.

'Give me your number—so it will be easier to coordinate,' he says.

'That was smooth,' I type and then delete it. I don't think Aniket is trying to flirt with me. He seems like he is at his wits' end and he wants me to tell him what to do. He seems a little lost.

So I give him my number.

No sooner do I give him my number than the phone rings. I almost jump out of my skin. I expect it to be Aniket, but it is Manoj.

'Hey babe—just callin' to say I'm checkin' on you,' he says in a sing-song voice.

'Oh hi,' I say.

'Were you ... um ... working or something?'

'I was ... er ... yes. I was finishing a writing assignment, the deadline is tomorrow.'

'Ha, deadline. I love how you take this so seriously.'

'What do you mean by that, Manoj?'

'I mean, it's not like this is for *Time* magazine or *India Today* or anything like that, right? It's only content for a website. And it's not like your main job or anything. That's what I meant.'

'How does that have anything to do with deadlines? Deadlines mean you deliver on a promised date. I think it is professionalism. Which would be true whether I wrote for *Time* or whatever you think is elite enough to write for.'

'Oh-oh-oh. Calm down, babe, I didn't mean to rub you the wrong way. Just called to say I love you, okay?'

'Okay.'

I don't feel like talking to him anymore. This is one of the things about him that has begun irking me of late. The fact that he seems to disregard things that are important to me. I can feel the chemistry that used to be there between us in the early years kind of waning. But probably this is how it is when you have been engaged for more than a year? I have no idea. Perhaps I should talk about it a bit more with Tara. It's an issue that is nagging me, but I decide to put it out of my head for now.

The next morning, there is a WhatsApp message from Aniket.

'Hey—we're on for today, right?' he asks.

'Yes! See you at 12.30. At By the Beach.'

'Yes, sure! See you soon.'

Then I add him to my contact list and look closely at his WhatsApp display picture. It is a selfie—a snap of him and a girl. She is stunning! She looks like a model. No wonder he is this besotted and so keen to mend their relationship. She has her arms around him and is leaning on his shoulder as she smiles sultrily into the camera. I stare at her face more than I look at his. Compared to her, he seems very average. But then, I am being superficial here. When did relationships ever work out based on looks? I make a mental note to write about this in my blog.

When I reach By the Beach, Aniket is already waiting. It has been many years since I have been to this part of town, but the restaurant isn't hard to find at all. The moment I walk in, I draw in a sharp breath. The place is remarkable! It has an entire floor-to-ceiling glass wall with magnificent views of the ocean. It is extremely spacious and done up in a fresh, energetic kind of way, with splashes of orange and yellow against a predominantly white theme. I quickly scan the large restaurant and then I spot Aniket.

'Hi, there! Thanks for coming,' says Aniket as he stands up to shake my hand.

'Hi,' I say, as a waiter pulls back my chair and helps
me to be seated.

We order our drinks first—both of us decide to stick
to non-alcoholic beverages and, although I am tempted
to order a Margarita, I settle for a ginger-lemon cooler,
while he asks for an iced tea.

When the waiter leaves, Aniket looks at me and says,
'You look lovely, Nidhi.'

'Thanks,' I say. It isn't even like I have made an effort
to dress up. I have worn one of my old T-shirts, a grey
one that fits well, and my jeans. I am not wearing heels or
make-up. But whatever. Maybe he is being polite.

'So, I saw the picture of you and your girlfriend, and
oh my god, she looks like a model,' I say.

'She is! In fact, she is on a shoot now, in Leh. She has
done many print ads and also shot for commercials. She
does these fashions shows too.'

'Wow. That's interesting. Is that her main job?'

'No—she works in my company. That's where we met.
Let me begin at the very beginning,' he says.

Then he proceeds to tell me their story. He tells me that
they met at his company when she joined as a management
trainee, straight after college. This was her first job.

'And did she work under you?'

'No, she didn't. She is in Sales. Almost all the guys in
office were hitting on her, asking her out constantly, trying
to get to know her.'

'I can imagine! She is gorgeous. How did you manage
to get close to her?'

'That's the thing. I did nothing! I used to admire her but never thought I stood a chance. I mean—look at me and look at her.'

The guy is a realist. He knows exactly where he stands and has no illusions about himself. I like this about him.

'And then what happened?'

'You know my friend, Subbu? The one I was talking to in the train?'

I nod.

'Well, he set me up. He asked her out and she agreed as that was the very day she had split up with her previous boyfriend.'

'Oh—and then what happened?'

'So Subbu asks her out to this fancy place. He tells me he is meeting a girl there but with her friend, so it's not a date. And they want another guy there, so would I please accompany him. And I completely believed Subbu; I didn't suspect a thing. You see, he was in love with a woman for four years and he did nothing and finally she got married and went away, still unaware about how Subbu felt. So I thought I was doing him a favour by agreeing to go with him. But turned out it was all part of his well thought-out plan. When I reached the place, he texted me saying he wanted me to have dinner with her, and he texted her saying the same. That was how we went on our first "date".'

'Wow! What a story! This sounds so like something that would happen in the movies.'

'Ha—Subbu is a big movie nerd. I think he probably ripped this off from some movie. I wouldn't know.'

'Nice!'

'Anyway, we have been together a year-and-a-half now. And somehow I sense this unease in her. I mean—I haven't changed that much. I am exactly like how I was. She is the one who wants more.' There is a twinge of sadness in his voice now.

'My newly-found, innocent, lost, bewildered friend. That is exactly what the problem might be. That you are stuck in a rut and she wants to move forward. You are not able to keep up with her.'

'You know, I think you might be right. I have been reading your blog. You have such an insightful mind. I love what you have said there. Can I hire you? You can be my relationship coach.' His eyes are shining in earnest as he leans forward and looks at me expectantly.

'Whoa! Hire me? What do you mean? I am no professional!'

'No—but you are exactly what I need. I think you will be able to help me out here.'

I think for a minute. Then I say, 'Sure, I will be your relationship coach. But on one condition. I should be allowed to write whatever I want about this whole thing on my blog. I won't give away your name, or any other details. But the freedom to write about it should be mine. And yes, you can pay me by buying me dinner and coffee every now and then.'

'Yes! Thank you!' he says and I feel he is going to lean over and hug me. He seems so happy.

Then he takes out his phone and shows me the email she has written.

It's all in the planets—your daily forecast: Darshita Sen

Leo (July 23 to August 22)

New beginnings are indicated. You will push a boundary to-day. You are likely to venture into something that you have never done before. A new relation forged will give your life a different turn. Choose your path wisely.

7

ANIKET

By the time Nidhi reaches By the Beach, I have been waiting for about ten minutes. I am glad she isn't too late. I have read Trish's list about ten times now and I have almost memorized it. She has been specific here, so I guess it at least it gives me something to work with. I had no idea that she hated all those links I sent her. What a jackass I was being.

And my fitness—that is something I have been meaning to do something about for a while now. I know it is too many beers and unhealthy eating. It's nothing I can't fix.

The moment Nidhi walks in I spot her, and I catch her eye. She looks attractive. I love her confident stride.

'Hi, there! Thanks for coming,' I say as I stand up to shake her hand.

I love the perfume she is wearing, too. So different from Trish. Trish's hands are always soft, perfectly manicured. Nidhi, I notice, keeps her nails short and there is no polish. She wears a single ring with some kind of a shiny stone, probably a diamond.

'Hi,' she says as a waiter pulls up a chair and she sits down.

We both order non-alcoholic beverages, even though I am dying for a glass of beer. But Trish's ultimatum to lose the belly flab makes me change my order to iced tea.

There Trish—are you happy? I am making an effort— cutting down on my beer for you.

The waiter asks us what we will have to eat. She orders a garden green salad and I order nachos.

Then I see that Nidhi is waiting for me to say something.

'You look lovely, Nidhi,' I say.

'Thanks,' she says. 'So, I saw the picture of you and your girlfriend, and oh my god, she looks like a model,' she says.

'She is! In fact, she is on a shoot now, in Leh. She has done many print ads and also shot for commercials. She does these fashions shows too,' I reply.

'Wow. That's interesting. Is that her main job?'

'No—she works in my company. That's where we met. Let me begin at the very beginning,' I say.

Then I tell her the whole story. How she joined my company straight after college, how almost all the guys wanted a date with her, including me, but I was too shy to do anything about it till Subbu set us up. She listens intently and asks many questions. I answer her in detail. The more I speak, the more comfortable I get with telling Nidhi my story. She is open-minded and so easy to talk to. With Trish, it's like treading on eggshells these days.

'Anyway, we have been together a year-and-a-half now. And somehow I sense this unease in her. I mean—I haven't changed that much. I am exactly like how I was. She is the one who wants more.'

'My newly-found, innocent, lost, bewildered friend. That is exactly what the problem might be. That you are stuck in a rut and she wants to move forward. You are not able to keep up with her.'

I think for a minute. How has that not occurred to me? She is right! And then it strikes me. Nidhi can help me. She is very insightful. I love what she has written about relationships in her blog. And I think she will be able to offer me a woman's perspective. So I ask her if I can hire her as my relationship coach.

'Whoa! Hire me? What do you mean? I am no professional!' The surprise on her face is evident.

'No—but you are exactly what I need. I think you will

be able to help me out here,' I reply. I don't see what she will get out of it though. I would be more than willing to pay her for her trouble but I doubt she would accept.

Then she tells me that she will help me but she wants to blog about it. What a strange request. But if this is what floats her boat, so be it. She can blog away, as long as she gets me my Trish. Nidhi assures me that she will change the personal details when she's writing about it.

'Yes! Thank you!' I say. I am happy.

Then I take out my phone and show her Trish's email.

Nidhi is silent as she reads it.

Then she looks up at me and says, 'You know, this feels so weird to me. It's like you both are actors in a play and I am the director or something, instructing you on what to do. And I feel like an eavesdropper or a spy. I do not think I should get involved here. This is between you and her.'

'Come on, Nidhi. You agreed! This is what relationship coaches do! This is common in the US. You know, I stayed in that country for three months on work. One of my colleagues had major issues with his wife. He hired a relationship coach who helped them get back on track. I could easily talk to the same person my colleague hired. But you see, they won't get the Indian scenario. Our culture and our world-views are quite unique. They won't even understand why I met Priyanka even though I am in a relationship with Trish. You have to help me here. Don't back out, please.'

She is silent for a moment and then she tucks a strand

of hair behind her ear. She takes a sip of her drink and says, 'Okay, I'm in. I guess it's just that this is possibly the strangest thing I have done. Getting involved in someone else's love life.'

'What do you mean "someone else"? I thought we were friends.'

'We are! Which is why I am meeting you here. Otherwise I would have blocked you on Facebook as soon as you messaged.'

'Well, I thought I was being a good citizen by returning your book. Which reminds me, I brought it along,' I say and I hand it over to her.

'Thank you,' she smiles. Then she says, 'Don't worry, Aniket, we will see this through together. Let's see what we can start with.'

Phew. It *is* a relief to have someone take over this problem. Subbu is good to talk things over with, but considering that he loved the links I sent him, the same ones that Trish found boring, I don't think he will get it. I think a woman's perspective would help here.

'See, Aniket, I am going to be candid. You have to be willing to accept that. I will call a spade a spade. I won't sugar-coat anything and tell you only what you want to hear. Is that fine with you?' she asks.

'Yes, yes. That is what I want. The whole exercise will be a failure if you are not candid and only try and placate me. Bring it on. I can handle it,' I assure her.

She nods and then takes a deep breath.

'Here is what I think,' she begins. 'What is point number one on her list of the things she wants you to do?'

'Lose weight.'

'From what I understand, Trish is a person to whom physical appearances matter a lot. She is probably surrounded by super-fit people all the time. In comparison to them—just look at you. What is your height? Around five foot eleven, I am guessing. The ideal weight for you is seventy to eighty kilos. You must be around ninety-five kilos? Am I right?'

Wow. She has guessed not only my height but my weight as well almost accurately. I am impressed. And I love how she dissects the problem on hand with the precision of a surgeon.

'You are good at this! How did you guess my weight and height correctly?' I ask.

'I should know. I was overweight at one point of time.'

'What? You? I can't believe it.' The revelation comes as a complete surprise to me.

She smiles and nods. 'Yes, I was. This was a few years back. Almost seems like a different lifetime now. Then I got tired of being so unfit and I went on a major diet, exercised every single day, and managed to shed sixteen kilos, can you believe it? This was over a period of two-and-a-half years. I have managed to keep it off ever since. And you know, apart from the health aspect, losing weight knocks so many years off you. You look younger if you are fit. Can you guess how old I am? Or rather, how old I look?' she asks.

I take a good look at her. She looks about twenty-five. Anyone looking at her would think she was around that age.

'You look like you're in your mid-twenties, but I am sure that's not your age; otherwise you wouldn't ask me to guess. How old *are* you?' I ask.

'I'm thirty-two,' she smiles.

'What?! No way! You are older than me by five years! You definitely do NOT look your age,' I say.

'I know, I hear that all the time,' she says. 'Let me show you something,' she adds as she whips out her phone. She scrolls through the photos and shows me a 'before and after' picture of herself.

'That was me before I lost weight. And you know, there's a site online which has featured my story. I have another blog, where I have documented my journey. They came across it, were impressed and featured me.'

I look at her 'before' picture. Boy—she really was overweight. The transformation is so dramatic that the photograph looks like it is of a different person. Her hair is short in the 'fat picture'. Her face itself looks different— much plumper. She has worn a nice dress but you can clearly see she is overweight. In the 'after' photo, she is stunning. Her hair is much longer. She is smiling in both photographs, but the pride in her smile is evident in the second picture.

'This is amazing, Nidhi. You have motivated me. Tell me, where should I begin?' I ask her.

'The first thing is the diet, Aniket. Eighty per cent of weight loss can happen through diet alone. Then you need to put in the exercise. You know, I never went to the gym or anything. All that helped me was walking. You can start with twenty minutes of slow walking. You think you can manage that?'

'Sure, I can. I can easily spare twenty minutes.'

'That's good then. That's where we start. Mind if I call you Ani?'

'Of course not! All my friends call me Ani. Tell me more. What should I do with my diet?'

'We start by cutting out the alcohol. Completely. No more binge nights. No more booze.'

'NO!'

'Yes! Hell, yes. You want to lose eight kilos don't you?'

'Yes, I do.'

'Say it again. I didn't hear it.'

'Yes.'

'Louder.'

'YES, ma'am!' I shout and give her a smart salute, military-style, and she laughs.

The others in the restaurant turn to look at us and I bend down and play with my food.

'Good, good. I like cadets who obey. So we revise this every week, okay? Today is week one. We start with no booze and add a twenty-minute walk. We also start clicking pictures.'

'What? What pictures?'

'Pictures of your body? So you see the progress?'

'Why? Isn't a weighing scale enough?'

'Trust me—there is no greater motivation than seeing your own pictures. No weighing scale does that for you. You will be super-motivated. And this will be a slow process. Unless you click pictures, it is easy to forget how you used to look. Don't worry. I will click them,' she says.

I have no choice but to agree.

By the time the meal gets over, we have been chatting away like old friends who have known each other all our lives. I learn that Nidhi finished her MBA from a reputed college in Bangalore. Then she held a corporate job for six-and-a-half years, out of which she was posted in Sri Lanka for two years.

'That is so cool! Did you like living there?' I ask.

'Yes, I did. I fell in love with Buddhism there. That was also where I discovered pottery. There was this pottery place near where I lived. I was bored on the weekends and I joined up for a lark. Then I discovered how therapeutic it is. I had just been through a bad break-up. I had been with him since my MBA days.'

'Oh, I see. No wonder you understand relationships so well. You have never mentioned that once in your blog though. I read many of the posts.'

'Well, I don't like to divulge my private stuff there. I focus more on philosophy. If you notice, my blog posts are mostly musings, and true stories with details changed.'

'Yes, yes, I did notice.'

'So, it was only after the break-up happened that I decided to lose weight. It was like something in me was affected. I asked myself what I truly wanted. Then I quit my job and came to Bangalore. I had a huge amount of savings, as my corporate job was a well-paying one. And now, here I am, doing all those things in life that make me happy,' she smiles, and it is a look of pure contentment.

The waiter brings the bill and Nidhi insists on splitting it. She forces me to accept half the amount, as I have already taken out my credit card and paid.

As we head out of the restaurant, it dawns on me that I want to spend some more time with Nidhi. She seems to be having a calming effect on me.

'Want to walk on the beach?' I ask.

'In this afternoon sun?'

'Why not?'

'I don't want to get burnt in this Chennai heat!'

'Come on. It isn't that hot. Let me take you to this sugar cane juice vendor. My friends and I used to be regulars at his cart. He is around the corner,' I say as I lead her out.

'Another time, Ani? Let's meet up in Bangalore. Come to my studio. Also, we need to track your progress, so remove your shirt and let me click a picture. Then I will be off,' she says.

'What? Here?'

We are standing facing the beach. The sun beating down on us is fierce. In the distance I can hear the roar of the waves. In the background there is the Karl Schmidt memorial.

'Yeah! Here. We are on a beach anyway. Don't tell me you are shy.'

I was. How could I strip in front of her?

'Actually, I am kind of shy,' I confess.

'Nothing to be shy about! You better get used to it. Remove your shirt, and I will take quick pictures from the front and side. Wear these same jeans every time we click a picture,' she says.

I take a quick look around. There is hardly anyone on the beach at this time. I reluctantly take off my shirt. I feel extremely conscious and can feel the blood rushing to my face as I turn towards her and she clicks a picture with my phone. I have never been this acutely aware of my body, especially my tummy. It is ugly. Then she makes me turn around, and clicks a picture from the side.

'Okay, wear your shirt. That wasn't so bad, was it?' she says as she hands my phone back.

The whole thing is over in a matter of a few seconds. It takes a few moments for my heartbeat to return to normal. I don't even want to look at those pictures.

'So when are you getting back to Bangalore?' she asks.

'On Sunday evening. I need to get back to work on Monday. What about you?'

'I am here till Wednesday. So do you promise to walk every day for twenty minutes starting today?'

'Tomorrow? Today is already half over.'

'No, today. Go after dinner. I'll check on you, okay?'

'Okay, I will. For a relationship coach, you sure are bossy. But I will take it,' I smile, and she smiles too.

I asked her how she will get back home and she says she has a car.

Once I get back home, I ping Trish.

'Hey, got your mail. You will see some changes. In fact, you will see a lot of changes. I promise. I can't wait for you to get back. Will definitely do something about the weight. In fact, I have already begun.'

I wait for a while to see if she has read it. She doesn't reply for ages, which means she must be busy.

She finally replies after six hours.

'Good. Not too mad are you? xo.'

I hear the ping and immediately grab my phone.

'No. When are you back?' I type.

But she has gone offline and there is no reply to that.

Later that evening, I go for a walk on Elliot's Beach. There is something soothing about walking in the moonlight on the beach, barefoot, right on the edge of the water. I walk for a long time. When I finally look at the time, I realize that I have been walking for about forty minutes.

'Guess what—I exceeded the target by double,' I ping Nidhi.

Her reply is immediate.

'Well done! Send me your email address.'

So I text her my email id.

I return to Bangalore on Sunday evening. Each time I leave home, Mom gets a little emotional. Dad can't be bothered to budge from a television show he is watching, and Anisha is off for a movie with a friend. Hence it is only Mom who sees me off at the door.

'Take care *kanna*, eat well. Take enough rest. And be careful when you drive back from work, okay?' She is teary when we part. Every time. I find it cute, and I smile.

'Ma, don't worry. Your son is a grown man now. I will be fine,' I say.

'Yes, yes. But you're all alone.'

The thing being implied here is that, had I been married, she wouldn't have worried so much.

Though visiting my home in Chennai is nice, it's always a great feeling to come back to my own flat. I plop down on my bed, too tired to even change, and drop off to sleep.

Monday mornings are always a drag, but when I log in to my email, I am cheered up instantly. There's a mail from Trish, and she is coming back by the weekend. She has written a short email describing the beauty of Leh. She says she dropped her phone while trying to click a picture, and it's no longer working.

My eyes quickly scan the inbox, and there is a second surprise in store. It's a mail from Nidhi.

But my joy is short-lived; when I open it, I see a diet plan and instructions from her to follow it strictly.

Most days, she has given me oats for breakfast. She

wants me to drink at least four glasses of water as soon as I wake up. At eleven o'clock, there's a cup of tea and a handful of nuts. At one o'clock there are two rotis and a bowl of salad for lunch. Evening, a cup of green tea and two whole-wheat biscuits. Dinner is before eight o'clock. Then a bowl of fruits if I feel hungry.

This is the craziest thing ever. What a strict diet.

I call her up and she answers on the very first ring.

'Nidhi! You are killing me with this diet. I can't do this,' I say.

'See Ani—this is what I did. It's hard in the first few days. Then your body gets used to it. You do want to lose that gut, right?'

I do. And so I agree to follow her diet strictly.

'No cheating. I want you to maintain a food diary,' she says.

'What's that?'

'Write down everything you eat and report back to me, okay?'

'Yes, ma'am.'

'That's a good boy!'

I hate the diet, but now that I have got into this, I don't think there is any way I can back out.

It's all in the planets—your daily forecast: Darshita Sen

Sagittarius (November 22 to December 21)

You find yourself drawn into situations you seem to have no control over. The stars are aligning in a position which will propel you to act. A close relationship seems strained. Unless you take concrete steps to resolve it, chances are it will deteriorate further. Think about where you want to head with this one.

7

NIDHI

A Pot of Clay That Holds Gold

As you can see, the cyber-biber protection plan is obviously working. Here I am, a second blog post within a span of a week. Great, isn't it? (Please tell me it is, even if it isn't!)

I have just got back to Bangalore from the scorching Chennai heat, and while I miss home, I can't say I miss the heat. I am starting a new pottery course, and this is for complete beginners. If you are interested in pottery, or always wanted to try your hand at it but did not know where to begin, do show up. The first session is free, and if it interests you, you can sign up for the rest.

Many of you who have followed my journey here know about my other blog where I documented my weight-loss journey. (Links on the right side of this page for those of you have begun reading this only recently.)

I am helping a friend get back in shape, and it made me think about weight and relationships.

Would you stop loving someone if he/she gained a few pounds (or kilos, if you happen to be Indian)? When we sign up for a long-term relationship, we are signing up on the basis of the current reality and current circumstances. These may change over a period of time. We 'adjust' our love and our lives accordingly and the relationship train chugs along. The allowances that we are willing to make for 'transgressions' from what we originally signed up for is directly proportional to the love you feel.

If you feel deep love, you are willing to overlook many things. If you feel a disconnect, then the flaws begin to irk you. It is also important for both people in the relationship to feel the same way about core things that define them.

If fitness is a priority for one and the other doesn't care about it, then sooner or later there is bound to be a discord. A weighty issue begins pressing down on you. Whether you manage to carry it or shake it off is entirely dependent on you. And there is always the danger of getting squashed when the weight becomes too much to bear!

Just as I finish publishing my blog post, Manoj calls and asks if I want to go to a new Thai restaurant that he has discovered in Koramangala.

'But you know I don't like Thai! I've told you so many times now,' I say.

'Well, there are other cuisines available there, too. I thought it would be nice to try it out. Will you be able to get there by eight-thirty or so? I would have picked you up, but I am coming straight from work.'

'That's fine. I will make my way,' I say.

No sooner do I hang up than I regret agreeing to go to this Thai place. We have been to two Thai places in the last thirty days. I hated both. Manoj enjoyed it, though. This is another thing that strikes me. We always seem to be doing things that he wants.

I reach the restaurant and he has already made a reservation in his name. The hostess escorts me to the table as Manoj texts me saying he will be a little late. He finally turns up a full forty-five minutes later. I have finished reading almost half my book and half the glass of wine I ordered.

'Sorry, babe,' he says as he plants a kiss on my cheek and pulls up a chair.

'What happened?' I ask.

'The meeting went on and on. I couldn't even text you. How was your day?'

'It was good—quite nice in fact.'

'Is it? What did you do?'

'I submitted two of my writing pieces.'

'Nice. For the online magazine?'

'No, this is for a web portal. A real estate one.'

As soon as I say that I can see the slight frown creasing his forehead.

'You know, I do feel it's a waste of your talent, Nidhi. Don't you think it's better if you write for magazines and newspapers?'

I don't like his tone. It is that what-you-are-doing-now-is-a-waste-of-time tone.

'Why is it a waste of my talent? Also, I need to ask you this—do I routinely ask you what you did at work and then proceed to tell you what you should be doing?'

I know I am being snappy. But I hate his remark and this isn't the first time he has made such a comment.

According to Manoj, only writing for a newspaper or a magazine counts. The rest of it is not 'real' writing.

'Hey—no need to get aggressive. I was merely making a suggestion,' he quickly back-pedals, knowing he has annoyed me. But I am not ready to forgive him so easily.

'Thank you, Manoj, for the *mere* suggestion.'

It is hard to keep the sarcasm out of my voice.

The thing about my sarcasm is that it pops up unexpectedly, without warning. And then it completely takes over, changing the direction of what is being said, giving a sharp jab to a conversation that was otherwise merrily drifting along.

Manoj doesn't say anything for a few minutes. The

silence is uncomfortable. The waiter appears and asks if we're ready to order.

I tell Manoj to go ahead and order whatever he likes, and that I will have the house salad.

Food is the last thing on my mind as I am angry now. There was no need for that remark. If there is one thing I am sensitive about, it is my writing. I hate people commenting on it. Manoj knows that, and yet he chooses to ignore it.

He is also judgmental about the kind of books I read. People like Manoj think that the only books that count are literary books. They would probably enjoy a Sophie Kinsella or a James Patterson, but would never admit to it. When I once asked Manoj what his favourite books were, he said *In Search of Lost Time* by Marcel Proust and *Odyssey* by Homer.

I catch him looking at my book now, a Sophie Kinsella, and I quickly hide it in my bag before he has a chance to comment on it.

Manoj now tries to break the silence. He goes on and on about a documentary series that he has been watching. He thinks that I should watch it too.

'These are things that completely educate you on the history and politics of that era. It is important,' he says.

'Why is it important?' I gently prod.

'Well—you know ... uh... it is good to have a complete knowledge of these things. It makes for interesting discussions.'

I don't say anything. Manoj had once recommended another documentary series to me, and we had tried watching it together. He was horrified when I fell asleep during the very first episode. In my defence, I had got in from an outstation trip and had been up since four-thirty that morning. But, for Manoj, to fall asleep while watching a documentary that he considered 'intellectual' was an unimaginable, unforgivable sin that I had committed.

'What do you like watching?' he had asked.

'*Desperate Housewives* is good,' I had said, and giggled when I saw him getting annoyed at that. I had been joking—I hadn't watched even one episode of that series—but it was amusing to see how important all this was to him and how he hated that I was flippant about it.

The waiter brings our order and Manoj is quite pleased to see his dish. He has asked for a king's roll, which is a sheet of rice paper wrapped around mixed vegetables, tofu and sweet basil, served with homemade sauce.

'I think this is the Thai version of our masala dosa,' I remark.

'Please, it is nothing like that,' he says as he digs in. He asks if I want to try the dish, and I decline. I am quite buzzed now with the wine.

Between bites, Manoj pauses and says that he has been saving the best for last, and that he has big news to break to me.

'What? Tell me now,' I demand. I don't like to be kept in suspense like this.

'Wait,' he says as he proceeds to finish his roll. Each second that he chews and slowly swallows his food feels like an eternity to me.

He finally sits back, wipes his mouth with a napkin and looks at me.

'Guess what,' he says and smiles.

'I don't know. New job?' I ask. It must be something work-related for him to get this excited.

'Not a new job, but a new project. I am going to be based in Houston, Texas for the next one year. I need to leave in two months. It is a pretty big project and I will be heading it. And once it is set up, my role will probably expand and change. It is likely that I will get a chance to head the division. If that happens, I will be the youngest in the company to achieve it. So get ready to move, baby—we are going to explore the US of A!'

I am stunned. One part of me is very happy for him. This is indeed terrific news. But how can he presume that I will move with him? He hasn't even asked me what I want. He has assumed that I will be as eager as him about this.

'That is wonderful, Manoj. I am so happy for you,' I say.

'Yes!' he says as he reaches across the table and holds my hand. 'You know, they will give us an apartment and everything. You will love it.' His eyes shine as he speaks.

I don't know how to break this to him right now. I need time to think about this. I can't move that easily. What about my pottery? How can he think I will give it up and shift? One of the reasons I quit my corporate job was for this. To be able to do the things that I enjoy. Now my life is good. I quite like my little one-bedroom apartment with the large terrace. I like my life here. I love my pottery. To give up all this and move to the US with him?

He reads my silence as acquiescence.

'See, we could get married in the next one month. Before I move. Anyway we only want a small wedding. We are both on the same page as far as that goes. We will invite a select few guests,' he says.

This is moving too fast for my liking. Wedding? In the next one month? No way. I am not ready for this. Not now. Not this fast.

'Manoj,' I say.

He looks at me with love and tenderness, 'Yes, baby?' he says.

'I don't want to get married so fast. And I don't want to move,' I say quietly.

It takes a few seconds for that to sink in.

He stops talking. There is complete silence. I can hear the clink of forks and the low chatter of diners from the other tables.

'But ... but I thought you would be happy. After all, you can write from there too,' he says.

'And my pottery?'

'Aah—there are a lot of hobby things there too. I am sure you will find something to do with your time,' he says.

'Manoj, pottery isn't something I "do with my time". It is something that means a lot to me. I don't think you will ever get it. This is something that nourishes my soul. I need time to think about this. You cannot decide to run my life for me.'

'Yes, yes, baby. Please take your time,' he says.

I say nothing.

And I am quiet for the rest of the meal and in the car when he drops me home. He plays some classical music, but I am not listening.

When we finally reach, I say a clipped thanks to him and walk upstairs to my apartment without turning to look back.

It's all in the planets—your daily forecast: Darshita Sen

Leo (July 23 to August 22)

*Good things are in store today. Romance is rekindled.
A friend is helpful. Beware of over-committing and making
promises that you find hard to keep.*

9

ANIKET

We are in the office cafeteria when Subbu peeps over my shoulder to see what I am writing in the little brown notebook that I now carry with me. I shut it quickly. I don't like him creeping up and peering like that.

'Bro, what is that you are writing down? Some new project idea?' he asks.

'No, poetry,' I say.

'What? Since when did you become a poet? I mean, I know you miss Trish and all that, but poetry? Bro, what's with you?' he starts to chuckle as though it is the funniest thing in the world.

'Why? Do you think I can't write poems?'

That sends him into fresh guffaws, and he says, 'Okay, my Shakespeare, let's hear it.'

'Ummm…. Here is what I have written,' I say. Then I pretend to read from the book:

'Roses are red,

Violets are blue

Subbu is an idiot

And you are one too.'

'That I must say is absolutely fantastic poetry, bro. Send this to Trish, and she will hop on the next flight from Leh and rush straight into your arms. She will throw in a blow job too,' he laughs again.

I am in no mood to join in.

'Have you inhaled nitrous oxide this morning? Or are you high on something else?'

'High on life, bro, high on life. I've been looking at this super spot for a vacation at Koh-Samui. Want to come?'

'When?'

'Whenever! Let's plan and go.'

The idea of a vacation is tempting. Hours of lying on the beach with a beer in hand, doing nothing, the entire day stretching ahead in front of you. Then the next instant the vision is replaced by a disapproving Nidhi who is frowning at the beer glass, saying, 'Calories, calories. No beer, Ani, if you want to get fit.'

That jolts me back to the book and my present reality of being overweight at twenty-seven.

I sigh and I open the little book I have been carrying around and show Subbu the food diary.

7 a.m.: Mint tea and three glasses of water

8.30 a.m.: Oats porridge, bowl of watermelon, tea with no sugar

11 a.m.: Half an orange and green tea

12.30 p.m.: Rice, half a bowl of thin dal, one vegetable with no oil, raita (with low fat curd)

That's all I have had. In between, I was very tempted to have a cup of coffee and a packet of Lays to go with it. But the moment it occurred to me that I would have to write it down, I refrained. This food diary was sure helping me stay off food, because the thought of Nidhi getting annoyed at me for not following her diet strictly is very effective in sending waves of unease through me.

'A food diary! That's what this is. I am impressed!' says Subbu.

Then his eyes narrow and he asks suspiciously, 'You cheated, right? Is this all you ate since morning?'

'Yes! This is all I've eaten. No, I did not cheat. What's the point of cheating in this anyway?!'

'Who is the dietician? Have you joined that online weight loss thing?'

'No, no. Remember the girl I told you I met on the train? Nidhi? Turns out she has had some major success with weight loss. So I told her to help me out. I am following what she has asked me to.'

'Not bad! You changed the core processor? Trish

out, Nidhi in? I am pretty impressed at what a smooth transition you've made, I must say.'

'Bro! This entire thing is to get Trish back to liking me. She gave me a list of things she wanted me to change about myself.'

'And keeping a food diary is her top priority, I suppose?'

'No! Losing weight is one of the things she mentioned.'

'So are you doing it for her or for yourself?'

'For her. She wants me to lose weight, I want her to be happy.'

Subbu shakes his head. 'Look, bro, it will work only if you do it for yourself. If you are doing it for her, you are going to be unhappy.'

'Wow. Deep. Where did that come from?'

'I have been reading Seneca,' he grins.

For a guy with a track record of zero relationships, Subbu can be pretty insightful.

'You know what, you are right. I should do it for myself,' I say, and he nods.

But I know, deep down, that if Trish hadn't written that mail, there's no way I would have done anything like this. A little nagging voice in my head had told me sometimes to exercise, but I would shut it down with excuses. So I am glad Trish brought this up and that it is making me do something about my weight. It is in black-and-white now, and Nidhi is involved too, so there's no going back.

'When is Trish coming back?' asks Subbu.

'Tonight! She reaches Delhi this afternoon and is taking a late evening flight to Bangalore.'

'So are you going to meet her at the airport like you usually do?'

'Don't you know the unwritten rule of relationships?'

'What?'

'Good boyfriends always greet their girlfriends at airports.'

'Ten points for Aniket in the good-boyfriend department. Notch it up, collect your reward points and add it to your loyalty card,' says Subbu as he shakes his head.

He can say whatever he wants, I am definitely picking up Trish. I always have.

That evening, I reach Kempegowda Airport way before time. I sip a cup of Hatti kaapi and glance at the arrival board for the umpteenth time. It is so boring to wait and it looks like I have at least thirty minutes. The thing about Bangalore is you can never predict the traffic or the weather. It might be rush hour when you don't expect it to be. It might be blistering hot in the morning and suddenly, by evening, it may cool off enough to rain. Living in Bangalore has taught me quiet acceptance of the things I have no control over.

I decide to take a few pictures of my food diary, which I have been meticulously maintaining, and I send it to Nidhi.

She calls me instantly.

'Hey! That is super!' she says.

I smile at the enthusiasm in her voice.

'Thank you. It was hard but I have done it, as instructed. I have been a good boy.'

It is a little difficult to hear over the din of some construction work that is going on at the airport.

'I want to add one more thing to what you are doing currently. I want you to step up the exercise. You think you can walk twenty minutes more?'

'What? In addition to the twenty I am already doing?'

'Yes.'

'I find walking so boring, Nidhi. Have a heart, please. I somehow manage these twenty minutes,' I say.

'Then we need another activity for you. Cycling? Do you like cycling?'

'Yes! In fact, I have a cycle. I bought one from Decathlon and it's now lying unused on the balcony in my flat. I used it a couple of times to travel to work, then lost interest as it was simply too much hassle. Bad roads, dust, traffic. I would look like a mess even before I reached office. So I stopped that.'

'Okay, then. I want you to start off with cycling five kilometres. Do you think you can manage that?' she says.

'Okay. Done. I'll start,' I say.

'What is all that noise in the background? Out at a pub somewhere?' asks Nidhi.

'No no, waiting for Trish. She arrives today, I am at the airport,' I say.

'Oooh, let me not keep you then. Bye! Have fun,' she says and hangs up even before I can get in a word.

I wanted to talk to her a bit more. I thought we could discuss my diet in detail. Now I will have to wait till I speak to her next. Or perhaps I can message her.

But out of the corner of my eye, I can see passengers streaming out.

My eyes scan the crowd quickly. I try and look at the baggage tags of the passengers who are emerging. There are so many chauffeurs holding up placards on either side of me. I should have made a placard for Trish. Telling her that I love her. She would have been delighted for sure. I wished I had planned it a bit better.

Then I spot her. My Trish. I stand mesmerized as I watch her. She is wearing tight black leather pants, a shimmery dark brown halter top, and she has a leather sling bag carelessly tossed over one shoulder. She is laughing and she pushes her hair back as she looks at the guy she is with. A stab of jealousy runs through me as he laughs and pats her on the shoulder. I know who he is—Vishwa. *Asshole*. He has spent enough time with her, it is my turn now. He kisses her lightly on the cheek, a goodbye peck. Then she half-hugs him and he goes his way. *That's right, asshole—get out.*

I wait for her to scan the line of people and she does just that and then she spots me and waves. My heart bursts into a million melodies. I feel like I have frozen and have been glued to the spot as she walks towards me.

How stunning my Trish looks. As though in a daze, I walk towards the end of the barricade where I can meet her.

'Ani!' she says as she leaps into my arms and I hug her and half-carry her.

She smells wonderful, that familiar Trish smell. Autograph by M&S, I would recognize that perfume anywhere.

'Trish—how I missed you, baby! Did you miss me?' I say.

'Hmmm—there was no time, Ani, to miss anyone.'

'Lie a little, woman. At least you can tell me you thought about me. No need to be that honest.'

'Does it have to be said? I missed you, Ani. I am so tired, I can't wait to get home.'

'Your place or mine?' I smile.

'Yours! I haven't told my parents that my flight lands today. They think I am arriving tomorrow morning. So we get some time together.' She has a wicked grin on her face. I am elated to hear that.

I know then that every single thing I do to make Trish happy is worth the effort. I will fulfil everything on her list. I will make her proud of me. She is quite something, my Trish.

I want to talk to her on the way home, but she falls asleep in the car. It's a drive of about an hour to Bellandur. I am thankful that, at this time of the night, there is no traffic.

I watch her as she sleeps, her mouth slightly open, her

hair thrown back. It is so hard to keep my eyes on the road. I feel like the luckiest guy on earth to have her beside me.

I listen to a whole lot of new love songs, including Avicii, that I have on my iPod. I had planned to play these for her on our drive back, but now that she is sleeping, I play them for myself and hum along. Once we reach, I park in my parking spot and I gently nudge her awake.

She wakes up and stretches her body. She is so graceful, I can't help staring again.

'What?' she smiles. And I smile back. My heart is full.

Once we go upstairs, she says she wants to shower. She has a couple of her T-shirts and shorts at my place, and a toothbrush too. I like seeing her stuff in my cupboard.

She has a quick shower, and I pour out two glasses of white wine. *(Am I making an effort in the 'surprise me' department, Trish? Am I?)* I have chosen a 2012 Sauvignon Blanc, which the guy at the wine store assured me is a great choice. 'Many customers repeat buying sir, very good wine,' he had said. I hope he is right.

When she emerges, she sees the two glasses of wine and the candle that I have lit.

'Oh, Ani,' she says as she hugs me. I inhale deeply, already semi-erect. She has that effect on me.

She feels it and she grins. 'Ready for some action, already, are we?' she says, and I blush.

She sips her wine as she relaxes, leaning back against the large oversized cushions that occupy my futon.

I play John Legend's *All of Me.*

I have set up all the slow love songs. The music fills the cosy room and Trish's face glows in the mood lighting. This is heaven. If I can spend the rest of my life sitting beside Trish, watching her sip wine, glowing with contentment like this, I will not ask for anything more.

'Trish—I love you,' I say, as I gaze at her.

'Uh?' she seems lost in thought as though she is in a faraway place and has been jolted awake.

'You are so beautiful,' I say and she smiles and gestures for me to join her on the futon.

That's all the invitation I need. In a jiffy I have left my wine glass on the table and have leapt towards her.

I begin kissing her and she responds in that Trish-way that drives me wild.

I gently ease the wine glass out of her hand as I slip my hand under her T-shirt. She isn't wearing a bra and I find her nipples and tweak them exactly the way she likes it. She sighs and kisses me harder as she cradles my head in her hand and draws me closer.

Then she runs her hands down my back and squeezes my butt. I inhale sharply, and nibble her ear gently.

She arches her back and removes her T-shirt.

Then we make slow, languid love, and I pause only to put on a condom. Trish moans and tells me that it feels so good and that she loves me.

'Say it again,' I tell her.

'Love you, Ani,' she says.

The playlist is now playing *Counting Stars* by One Republic. We lie side by side on the futon and stare at the night sky through the large floor-to-ceiling French windows.

There are a million stars glittering, and as the moonlight trickles in, I swear to myself that I will do anything it takes to make this woman happy.

It's all in the planets—your daily forecast: Darshita Sen

Sagittarius (November 22 to December 21)

Someone you love might be drifting away from you. Or it is possible that you are confused about what your heart wants. Meditate, indulge your inner child. Go for a walk. Listen to the voice of your heart. The answers will come to you with clarity.

10

NIDHI

When I reach home, I kick off my heels. This is such relief. I walk barefoot to the fridge and grab a bottle of cold water and plonk down on my sofa.

How can Manoj drop a bombshell like that? I am happy for him. I genuinely am. But he can't make decisions for both of us. He doesn't even get what my pottery means to me. Manoj announcing his move to the US has dredged back every single memory of Vir. Things with him had fallen apart after he moved to the US too.

Six years with Vir—and all I had left of it was memories. Where do memories go when a relationship ends? Sometimes they stay buried in countless hours of chats, archived neatly. Sometimes they are trapped in photos, stored in an external hard-drive. They are scattered in gifts bought, perfumes used and songs you have dedicated to each other. And sometimes they stay deep, deep down within your heart, popping up inconveniently when you least expect them, taking over your very soul, and you live through the destruction yet another time.

It seems like another lifetime now. Vir had been my classmate at the MBA institute, and things had been so good between us. Then he had gone and accepted that posting to the US, while I had moved to Sri Lanka. When he visited me, he hated everything that I had organized to make his trip fun—the Buddhist temples, the beaches, the turtle-farms, our visit to Hikkaduwa, our boat-ride through the mangroves, none of it made him happy. Looking back, all he had done was complain and complain and compare it to the great US of A. How childish was that? He was so much in love with the US, and he too, like Manoj, had wanted me to move there with him.

While I had enjoyed my visit to New York, I hated his tiny, cramped apartment. My place in Sri Lanka—bright, airy and spacious—seemed like heaven to me. It is funny how much your attitude to living spaces matter in a relationship.

He had liked the city lights, the brightness, the night clubs, the pubs; while I craved for the organic farms, beaches, temples and nature. He liked to go pubbing. I wanted to curl up on the couch with him and watch Netflix. He asked me what was the point of coming to New York if all I wanted to do was that. Then I had dragged him to the Museum of Modern Art, one of the few places in New York I liked, and he had hated it. I remember a particularly nasty argument about Salvadore Dali's work. I had stared in amazement and wonder at the painting of clocks draped on a tree, and he had scoffed at Surrealist art and said that anyone could do it. I had pointed out that Surrealist art was different from Modern art like Pollock's. And he had said 'Pollock-bollock' and laughed. I had turned away angrily, refusing to talk to him for the rest of the museum visit. Funny how, years later, you remember stuff that is so silly in retrospect.

After I returned to Sri Lanka, we got busy with our respective careers. We were both completely immersed in work. Our Skype calls, instant messages and emails became more and more infrequent. Gradually we admitted that the relationship was practically dead. But it took us one year to make that final cut. I think we were both relieved.

One evening in Bangalore, many months after the break-up, I was so overcome by grief that I had called Tara and sobbed. I don't even know why I was crying. It was a strange sense of loss. I was mourning something that didn't exist. I was mourning a phantom relationship.

I told Tara I was missing my mother a lot (I was), and I had broken down. Tara said she would be with me in five hours. She had immediately called up Mani, our ever-dependent ever-obliging Mani, and by twelve-thirty that night she had reached my place in Bangalore from Chennai. My dad was away, travelling on business. By the time Tara reached my place, I had calmed down a little bit. I had been so overwhelmed by what she did—dropping everything and landing up to be with me, only because I was a little upset. I had told her the real reason I was this distraught was because of a sudden attack of nostalgia. I had sobbed, telling her how much I missed those early days with Vir, and she had held me, comforted me.

And now Manoj breaking this news has brought a stream of memories right to the forefront. I feel like talking to Tara now. And even though I have had wine at the restaurant, I go to the wooden cabinet in the living room and pour myself a neat shot of Canadian Cask. I rarely do this, but today I feel like I need a drink.

I sink into my leather recliner chair, fold my legs, take a sip of the whiskey, and dial Tara's number.

'Hey there, sunshine. How goes everything?' Her voice itself has the power to soothe me.

'Hey, Tara. Not so good.'

'Why? What happened?'

'It seems like a repeat of the Vir saga all over again,' I sigh.

'Oh no. Why?'

'Manoj says he is shifting to the US and expects me to join him. He wants us to get married within a month.'

'And?'

'And what? I am not ready, Tara. How can you get married when you aren't ready?'

There is a small pause from her side as she processes the information.

Then she says, 'Yeah, you can't. You have to be completely willing. You have to be eager to get married. You have to want it more than anything else you have ever wanted in your life. I know, because that's what I felt when I was marrying your dad. I was a little older than you then, and never had I been more certain about anything in my life. I was on fire. It was like I had been sleeping all my life, and the relationship with your dad had brought me alive. You have to feel that for a person, Nidhi. Or else things will collapse after a few years. I have seen far too many marriages breaking up. I know what I am talking about.'

'Yes, I knew you would understand, Tara.'

'So, what are you going to do about it?'

'I don't know. I told him I need time.'

'And what did he say?'

'He said yes, but I know he is hoping I will change my mind. You know how keen he is to get married. His love for me is true and deep.'

'I know, my darling Nidhi. But the question that you have to ask yourself is whether you love him the same way.'

I am silent for a few minutes. Tara's question has thrown me completely off-guard.

I had presumed until now that my love for him was a given, an unquestionable factor. Now I wasn't so sure. If I loved him so much, why wasn't my heart singing at the prospect of marriage? Was I commitment-phobic? Or had Vir scarred me too much?

'Hello, are you there, Nidhi?' asks Tara.

'Yes. I was thinking about what you said. You're right, I need to ask myself that question. I do love him. Or at least I think I do. But this marriage thing scares me.'

'Then wait. Do not jump into it. If he genuinely loves you, he will wait. Give it time.'

'What if we grow apart, like it happened with Vir?'

'So what? At least you know you weren't making a mistake by marrying him. And yes, you must remember that Vir happened at a different time in your life. You were much younger, busy building a career. You don't have that pressure now. You are certain about what you want to do. You have time for yourself now. And when two people love each other, they will always make time. Let this be the acid test of your relationship. Tell him to move and that you will stay here till you are ready to join him.'

I tell her I will, and after I hang up I rock back and forth in my recliner chair, thinking about it.

Talking to Tara always helps put things in perspective. I think that my dad struck the jackpot by getting this woman in his life. And the strange thing is that she feels that way about my dad too. They both feel they're so lucky to have found each other.

Later, I see a message from Aniket.

'Starting cycling tomorrow. Will do five kms.'

I reply, *'Great. Good going. And remember the diet too.'*

He is online as soon as he sees my message.

'Yes, ma'am. And you know what I have been thinking about?'

'What?'

'I want to come and see your pottery studio, and try my hand at it.'

'You should! It can be your new hobby. One more thing on the list you showed me.'

'Yeah! That's exactly what I was thinking too. I will surprise Trish.'

'Okay. Come by and take the demo class. Once you do that, see if you want to join in.'

'I will! Got to go. Trish is calling me.'

'Oh! Is she with you?'

'Yep! Right here. Bye!'

Over the next few days, I am surprised to find that Aniket is diligent about his diet. I hadn't expected him to follow it so religiously. He fills in his food diary every single day, clicks photos, and sends them to me. He also lets me know that he has been regular with his daily five-kilometre cycling. I am happy that he is sticking to this plan. If he keeps this up, I know that he will lose at least two kilos in a month. That will motivate him. From my own experience, I know that the challenge is when he hits the plateau. Once his body gets used to this exercise, I will have to tweak his routine a bit. But for now, we are good.

On Wednesday Aniket surprises me by calling me up at seven-fifteen in the morning.

'Hey! Guess what. I cycled all the way to Koramangala.'

'That's cool! You know I live in Koramangala, right?'

'Is that so?'

'Yeah.'

'Where in Koramangala are you?'

'Raheja Residency.'

'Oh! I know where that is. In fact, I am calling you from a lane near it. I decided to take a different route today and was resting before I cycled back home.'

I don't even hesitate before inviting him over. 'Nice! Come over then and have a cup of coffee with me,' I say and give him my apartment and block number.

He is over in less than five minutes, and the security personnel from my main gate call me up to tell me that someone called Aniket is here. I tell them to send him inside. Living in a gated community like this one has added advantages like security checks at the main gate, as well as at the apartment block itself. I know there will be a second phone call from my building security, and I tell them to let him in.

Aniket rings the bell, and I open the door to see him in a blue round-necked T-shirt drenched in sweat and a pair of shorts. His bicycling helmet is in his hands. And he is wearing knee-pads.

'Hi,' he says, almost shyly. He looks like a little boy.

'Come in, welcome,' I say as I lead him in.

'Wow—what a place! You have done it up so well, Nidhi!' he looks around.

The first thing that hits your eye when you enter my apartment is the beautiful bright red wall on which I've hung striking black-and-white paintings. Like everyone else who comes here, I can see that Aniket too is impressed with it. I have done up this place with great care and love, and it shows. There's a very comfortable white leather pull-out sofa on which are red cushions that match the wall. There are little knick-knacks that I gathered during my stint in Sri Lanka. Then there are a couple of sheesham wood chairs upholstered with a pale cream fabric. My entire living room colour scheme is cream with splashes of red and yellow. With the red wall as the focal point, the whole effect is dramatic, bold and makes a great visual. Aniket is now curiously examining each and every thing, while I ask him if I can make coffee for him.

'I make some very good south Indian filter coffee,' I say.

'Sure, I love it,' he says and asks about a singing bowl that I have placed in the living room.

'I picked that up from McLeod Ganj,' I say as he takes the little wooden mallet and strikes the rim. I hand him his coffee and take the bowl from his hands.

'That's not how it should be done, let me show you,' I say. We both sit down, he on the sofa, and me on the wooden chair. Then I twirl the mallet around the bowl. A soothing, calming, mellifluous sound starts, and I build up the harmony by taking the mallet around in slow circles, without once striking the bowl. The frequency increases in pitch and fills the entire apartment as I build up the crescendo, higher and higher. The effect is magical.

We sit in silence as we listen to the sound, and finally, when I stop, we are both too stunned to speak. It is as though we both understand that saying anything would spoil the experience we just had.

After about three minutes or so of silence, he says 'wow'. And he almost whispers it, as if afraid to speak.

'Your coffee, Aniket,' I remind him, and he smiles.

'Delicious!' he says as he sips it and looks at me.

I show him the view from my apartment, and he admires my place and praises my taste.

Then he looks at the time and says that he will have to cycle back to Bellandur and then get to office, so he better leave.

'Yes, you better go. And remember to follow your diet. And you know what, I can see some changes already in your body,' I say.

'Come on, Nidhi, you are just saying that. It's been what—a little less than two weeks?'

'It's true, I can. I'm not saying that to pep you up. Don't you feel it yourself?'

'No! I feel the same!'

'Well, wait for another two weeks. And meanwhile, drink lots of water.'

'I will, ma'am,' he says and does a smart military salute and I laugh.

Once he leaves, I think about how much effort he is making for Trish. He is such a great boyfriend. It is evident that he is mad about her. I hope that she appreciates his efforts or at least notices how much he is trying.

Later, when I sit down to write my article for the day, which is a commissioned piece for a tech company's newsletter, my mind is in a bit of a turmoil. Relationships. They are such strange things. Just when you think you have a grip on them, something surprises you. You are never in control. And it is always a power shift. Everything you do in a relationship so depends on how much you love that person.

It's all in the planets—your daily forecast: Darshita Sen

Leo (July 23 to August 22)

You will benefit by doing things that you have never done before. An unexpected train of events can send you on a downward spiral. Be guarded in your emotions. Do not do anything hasty that can cause regrets later. Decisions taken in haste will prove to be harmful.

11

ANIKET

Trish and I lie next to each other, spent, satiated, satisfied. She looks so beautiful, I swear she glows. After we have recovered our breath, Trish asks me if I would like a mug of hot chocolate.

'Thanks, baby, I would love that,' I say and she gets out of bed, gracefully, wearing only her T-shirt that barely covers her butt.

I inhale sharply, admiring my Trish.

Such a perfect body. Not an ounce of flab. God—she is like a porcelain doll.

Involuntarily, almost like a reflex reaction, my eyes go down to my own body—and the flab around my belly disgusts me now. She definitely deserves a fit guy.

I pick up my phone and text Nidhi. I tell her that I plan to start cycling the next day and that I would love to try my hand at pottery. She asks me to come by her studio.

Trish comes back with two mugs of steaming hot chocolate.

'Here you go,' she says as she hands over the mug.

I remember my food diary. This hot chocolate must be loaded with calories and Nidhi will definitely not approve. But Trish has made the effort to make it, and I don't want to annoy her by refusing to have it.

'Hey, thanks babe,' I say as I take it and put away my phone.

Then I place my mug on the side table and cradle Trish's face with my hands. I look into her eyes and say, 'Look, I will do everything on your list, my darling Trish. I will make you happy, I promise.'

She disengages from me and says, 'We will see, won't we?'

What? What does she mean by that?

'Don't you believe me?' I ask her.

'Time will tell, Ani,' she says and turns away.

Ouch. It hurts when she dismisses me like that. I decide then that I *will* prove it to her. I want to make this woman happy. Very happy. And I will do everything that it takes.

Early the next morning I drop Trish to her place. Whenever we have done this in the past, the routine is the same. I have to quickly drop her at the gate of her residential apartment complex and get away as fast as possible as she is afraid of her parents spotting me. She always calls to check where they are, under the guise of telling them that she is on the way back from the airport. She also invariably picks a time when she knows her dad will be away on his walk, and her mom will be busy cooking. Up until now we have never been caught. It is a risk that we take, but like she says—a calculated risk.

Once I drop her off and get back home, I decide to take out my cycle. The early morning coolness hits my face and it feels good. Over the next few days, I go further and further, and one morning I cycle past Agara Lake. Before I know it I have made it all the way to Koramangala. Nidhi would definitely be proud that I have cycled more than five kilometres.

I am tired now. My legs are beginning to feel like lead. I help myself to water that I am carrying in my backpack and remove my helmet. Then I wipe the sweat that I have worked up.

I whip out my phone, deciding to call Nidhi and tell her about my cycling achievement for the day. I need some motivation here, especially if I have to cycle all the way back to Bellandur.

Nidhi has a nice song on her phone as her ring tone. I recognize it instantly. It is Taylor Swift's *Blank Space*.

Nidhi answers. I tell her that I have cycled to Koramangala; we discover that she lives very close to where I'm calling her from, and she invites me over for coffee.

I had called her for a pat on the back; I hadn't expected her to invite me over. But now that I have an invitation from her, the thought of a cup of coffee is tempting. I tell her that I will be there soon, and in less than five minutes, I am at her place.

Her apartment is magic! She has done it up in red and white. She shows me a singing bowl—I love the way she manages to make it sing. A feeling of momentary peace and silence washes over us and, for those few minutes, I forget where I am.

Then I remember that I have to cycle all the way back to Bellandur, and so I excuse myself and make my way back home. I need to hurry and shower quickly if I want to get to work on time. My legs are hurting badly now and my chest burns from the effort of cycling what, I am guessing, is about ten or maybe even twelve kilometres. My face is red from the effort. Even after I shower and get dressed for work, the redness stays.

When I reach office, Subbu remarks on how I look. 'I can see the effects of last night, bro. You are getting old. You still haven't recovered. Just look at you,' he cackles.

I tell him that it is because I cycled at least ten kilometres, but I don't think he believes me.

My entire morning vanishes as I am immersed in my work and when I look up it is noon already. I head to the coffee machine and catch a glimpse of Trish. Dressed in a smart, fitted white shirt and black trousers, she looks strikingly sexy. It always takes a little adjustment from my side when I see Trish at office. Sometimes I still cannot believe that this is the same woman who was moaning under me last night, and telling me that she loves me. I don't usually run into her at work, as her department is on the fourth floor and mine is on the seventh. But today she has a meeting and the board room is on my floor. She catches my eye, smiles, and looks away. We've agreed that, while we are at work, we pretend to be nothing more than colleagues.

'It's not anybody's business but ours, Ani. And I want to be professional at work. As it is people think I am dumb just because I am into modelling. I don't want allegations that I don't focus on my work as I am busy romancing you,' she had said. I said I was okay with whatever made her happy.

Trish leaves early that day. Her boss is on leave and she says she isn't going to miss that opportunity to take some time off for herself. I ask her if she wants to catch a movie over the weekend.

'Which one?' she asks.

Trish is very picky about the movies she watches. She dislikes Hindi movies, and if it's a Hollywood one, she always looks at the IMDB ratings before she decides.

'We can pick a nice one, baby. You choose,' I tell her.

'So you haven't made any concrete plans?'

'Well, no—but I want to hang out with you.'

She sighs.

'I have a modelling gig,' she says after a pause.

'Oh! I thought you didn't want to work this weekend because you were tired after your trip to Leh?'

'Well, this is a great brand. It's two days' work and the money is good. It's easy work and it is ramp. I can't possibly refuse.'

'I guess not,' I say, even though I am disappointed. I was looking forward to spending the weekend with her. But I guess if I was in her place, I would do the same. Also, it's not like there won't be any more weekends.

Now that there are no plans with Trish, I text Nidhi and tell her to put my name down for the pottery class that is starting that weekend. I might as well try out the demo class.

'*Do I have to bring anything?*' I ask.

'*Just yourself and a willingness to learn,*' she replies.

The pottery class is on the terrace of a residential building in HSR Layout. There is no lift to the third floor where the terrace is; instead, there is an old-fashioned staircase leading upstairs. I take the stairs two at a time. There's a dog lying on the first floor but he looks friendly and doesn't even raise his head as I gingerly tiptoe past him. When I reach the third floor, I am pleasantly surprised by how well this place is done up. There is an outdoor and an indoor area. The outdoor area is full of plants in earthen holders. The seating is in the form of low wooden chairs, and the tables are unpolished wood. Everywhere you turn, every nook and cranny, is a beautiful little piece of pottery. The studio itself is large and has terracotta flooring. There are individual stations with mini potter's wheels that run on electric power. There are shelves along the wall on which various projects neatly rest.

There are five people there already, and as soon as Nidhi sees me, she greets me with a half hug.

'Hey! So glad you made it. Come on and sit down,' she says.

I feel a little awkward now with the others there. There is only one other guy, who looks like he is in his forties; the others are all women. Two of them are in their fifties or perhaps sixties, there is a girl in her twenties, and another woman who looks like she is her late thirties. Nidhi tells us all to introduce ourselves and we do. Nidhi asks each person what they hope to learn from the class and why they are taking the workshop. She has a way with people, and makes everyone feel comfortable. At the end of the introductions, we don't feel like strangers any more. I learn that the woman in her thirties joined as her children had taken the summer workshop last year and she loved what they had made. The guy in his forties has been laid off, is in between jobs, and is also recovering from a heart attack for which he had been hospitalized.

The two women are retired and wanted to do something 'fun and creative'. The girl in her twenties is an art student at Karnataka Chitrakala Parishat, and she hopes to get some extra credits with this stuff; plus she is interested in sculpture and pottery. Then there is me. I do not tell them the real reason—that I am here as my stunningly gorgeous model girlfriend thinks I am boring and wants me to get a hobby. Instead I tell them that I met Nidhi on a train and was curious to try my hand at pottery.

'As good a reason as any,' says Nidhi, and there is a twinkle in her eyes as she smiles at me.

'So now that you have got to know each other, let's start by acquainting you all with how clay feels,' says Nidhi as she places a large lump of clay in the centre of the table around which we are all seated. 'Your hands need to be moist to work with clay, and so you will have to moisturize them from time to time,' she says as she hands over a moisturizing cream, which she instructs us to apply liberally. We are also given a mat which is our 'work area'. We are asked to cut off a chunk of clay from the big block placed in the centre using a twine tied to two small wooden blocks. It is a very sharp string and she shows us how to stretch it and cut the clay with it.

Then she asks us to knead the clay and make it soft.

It feels squishy. The moisturizing cream itself makes my hands feel funny and handling the clay is a strange sensation. It takes me a couple of minutes to get used to it, and once I do, I begin to actually enjoy it. Nidhi was right when she said that working with clay has a kind of therapeutic magic to it. It indeed feels soothing, calming, comforting.

Then she tells us that she will teach us a few basic beginner techniques—very easy, she assures us—and using those we could make something to take home.

She suggests that we each make an animal. I am not sure what animal to make and the others can't make up their minds either. So she asks us to walk around the studio and have a look at the things there for ideas. I like a cute little whale that seems to be winking, which is placed on one of the shelves. These are all works of students which have been fired and are waiting to be taken home, or works-in-progress, waiting to dry. I come back to our table and tell Nidhi that I will make a whale. One of the two retired women chooses a whale too. The others have chosen turtles, a rhino and an elephant. The girl asks if she can make a plant holder, and Nidhi says that since it's the first class and we are yet to learn the basic techniques, it is best to start with a small project.

Nidhi is a wonderful teacher. She explains and demonstrates all the techniques well—pinching, flattening, joining, the coil method, slab method, what to do, what to avoid. She helps us, gently correcting us, and at the end of two hours, none of us can believe what we have created. Each one's finished piece looks splendid! She tells us that we have to wait a day, as it has to dry. Once it does, she will fire it in the kiln and then we can take it home.

'Why can't we fire it straight away?' asks the man.

'Because clay shrinks a bit when it dries. The water evaporates. In the process of firing, further shrinkage happens. If it has dried unevenly and then you fire it, it is likely to crack or warp.'

'So how will we know when it is time to fire it?' asks one of the two retired women.

'You learn from experience,' says Nidhi.

Then she tells us that this was a demo class. She goes on to outline what the rest of the course will entail, the projects we will do and what we can expect. She says that if any of us wish to sign up for the full course, we could pay up now and register. Without an exception, all of us want to learn more, and we all sign up.

I have new respect for Nidhi now. She is simply amazing—an incredibly good teacher and very passionate about her work. She clearly loves clay and creating stuff. Now she has managed to spread that magic to us too. Nidhi tells us that our projects will be ready in two days, and if we are eager, we could collect them then. Otherwise, we could wait till the next class.

When the others leave, she smiles at me. 'You did well, Ani! You are a great learner. I love what you made.'

'Thanks. I've always had a fascination for sea-creatures.'

'It's very nice. You could do a whole sea-theme, you know.'

'That's an idea! I will give it some thought. Want to grab a quick cup of coffee?'

'I wish I could, Ani, but my next batch starts in fifteen minutes. Weekends are the busiest days for me.'

'Oh, right! I had forgotten that. Another time then?'

'Sure,' she says and goes back to preparing for her next class.

I get home and spend the rest of the evening binge-watching *Breaking Bad*, even though I have seen the entire series.

The whole of Sunday too I spend by myself. I don't hear from Trish at all till eleven o'clock at night, and then there are only monosyllabic replies to my messages. When I ask if we can meet before we go to office, she says she has client meetings at the other end of town and won't be getting into office till three o'clock.

'Fine, be like that. We aren't getting any time together at all,' I want to type. But I don't. I don't want to come across as the clingy, demanding, possessive boyfriend.

My mother calls and wants to know in detail what I have been up to and how work is and whether I have been eating food on time. She tells me that Anisha is going on a ten-day college trip, and so she and my dad have booked a pilgrimage tour to Udupi, Mukambika and the temples around that area at the same time.

'Good, good. You and Dad hardly go anywhere. You should travel more,' I encourage her.

'You know how your father is. Only if it's a pilgrimage will he be interested,' she says.

'Plan a trip to Vaishno Devi temple, Ma. I have friends

who have gone there. It is supposed to be breathtakingly beautiful. And if you do plan it, Anisha and I can come along too,' I say.

The thought of that cheers her up considerably. 'That's a great idea, Ani. It has been so long since the four of us went anywhere. I will talk to your father,' she says.

On Tuesday afternoon, Nidhi calls and tells me that my whale is ready and that I can pick it up from the studio if I want.

'I have instructed them, and they have kept it packed and ready for you to pick up,' she says.

'Won't you be there?' I ask her.

'No, Tuesdays are my weekly off from Mitti,' she says.

I am eager to see the finished product and so, during lunch break, I drive quickly to HSR Layout. Without peak-hour traffic, it is a mere six minutes from work. The attendant hands it over to me, and I am mighty pleased with it. I can't believe that I created this whole thing myself. They have packed it well too, in a beautiful, handmade paper cover.

This is going to be a real surprise for Trish. I show it to Subbu and even he is impressed. 'Wow—that is quite something! And, bro—cycling, pottery—you are turning into a new man. System upgrade. I like it!' he says.

The next day, I message Trish and ask her to have lunch with me. There's a nice south Indian restaurant very close to office, and she says she will meet me there. Subbu teases me saying that he wants to come along. I tell him that I will hide under his bed on the first night that he spends with his wife and, as they are about to get into the act, I will scream and boo and scare the living daylights out of them. He laughs.

Trish is already at the restaurant by the time I reach.

'What took you so long, Ani?' she asks.

'I got something for you,' I say and I proudly hand her the packet.

'Ooh, a surprise! How exciting,' she says as she unwraps it. I have covered it in layers of newspaper before placing it in the final package, which is the handmade paper cover. She removes the newspaper layer by layer. It is such a joy to watch her excitement.

Then she removes the final layer.

'Oooh—what is this? A mud whale?' she looks at it, puzzled.

'Yes,' I smile, and before I can say anything, she bursts into laughter. 'You know what, Ani, this cute little whale—it looks like you! I will call it my Ani-whale,' she says and pats my belly.

I am silent. She hasn't even given me a chance to explain that I *made* it especially for her. Can't she appreciate the surprise, the effort, the thought, the emotion? Her laughter has come crashing down on me like a tonne of bricks. All she can say is that I look like the whale? Ani-whale? Granted I have indeed put on weight, but I am not anywhere in the whale category. And, okay, I am willing to let that go; but what hurts is the way she has not even bothered to ask what was special about the gift or why I chose it or whether there was a reason behind it.

She is laughing uproariously now at her own joke. Her laughter stings. Mocks me. Makes me feel like a prize idiot.

And all I can do is sit there stupidly with a fake grin plastered across my face. Immobile. Frozen. I open my mouth to say something. To tell her that I fucking made it just for her. Created it. And doesn't that count for something?

I want to say a lot of things. But no words come out.

It's all in the planets—your daily forecast: Darshita Sen

Sagittarius (November 22 to December 21)

You, the fiery Sagittarian, have a way of always being candid. Today, hold your tongue. If you speak your mind, there can be misunderstandings. It's not in your nature to hold back, but caution is advised. Sometimes you have to take a step back to move forward.

12

NIDHI

A Pot of Clay That Holds Gold

So, we started the new pottery classes. It is always fun when a new batch starts.

This one is for adults. There are people of all ages, and from all walks of life. It is a motley bunch. Almost none of them have ever handled clay before.

We start with the basics. Everyone in the class first handles clay and plays with it, kneading it, feeling it, getting used to it. You should see how they transform into children as they discover the joy of handling clay. There is something very therapeutic about pottery. Then I teach them basic techniques like roughing out, adding clay, removing clay. Once they get that, we move on to manoeuvring, repositioning and, finally, detailing.

Since this was a demo class, we started with something easy. Each of the students chose an animal to make out of clay, and I helped them create it. When they're satisfied with their work, we fire it in the kiln and they have their first piece to take home. Awesome, isn't it?

And, for me, it is double the fun when a friend joins in. Remember I told you about helping someone lose weight? Well, he has joined my class too.

At the end of this class, there were some extremely happy adults, a couple of turtles, a whale, a rhino and an elephant too. As for me—the joy on my students' faces and the pride at what they have made—it is priceless.

I finish the post and I am shocked when I see what time it is. Where does time vanish? I could have sworn that it had been only ten minutes since I sat at my laptop. Instead, the little clock on my laptop tells me two hours have gone by. And I have zero words to show for it. *Zero*. Other than my blog post, I have written nothing. I have two articles to write and submit. Granted my deadline is two days away. Yet all I have been doing is browsing the Internet, reading collective-evolution articles on chakra balancing and life-mates versus soul-mates—a topic I find fascinating.

The article I read said that, in our lives, we come across people who are destined to be soul-mates. We also come across people whom we choose as life-mates. We might get married to our life-mates, have children and even raise a family with them. But that deep, uplifting, spiritual connection would be missing. With soul-mates, every cell of your body comes alive. You know that person is your soul-mate as you instantly 'fit' together, have a strong sense of déjà vu and you think alike. You are a lot in sync.

This is something I have never considered before. I think about whether I can classify Manoj as a soul-mate or a life-mate. He definitely isn't a soul-mate. In the initial days of courting, when I had met Manoj, he was a lot of fun. We had got along well. But now, half the time he doesn't even get what I am saying. Despite this, I was certain till now that he was my life-partner; but his announcement that he is moving to the US has thrown me off-guard.

I have been thinking about it. Moving to the US is not something that I want to do. It's best I tell Manoj that I am not moving and that I am not ready for marriage. I text him, and he texts back saying he wants to meet that very evening. He asks me to come over to his apartment so we can talk things over.

The last time we had met at his apartment, we had ended up having a big fight. It was about such a silly thing too. We had fought over where to go out that evening. He had wanted to go to a Thai restaurant again, and I wanted to go to Zuri, as it was Bollywood night there.

'Who in the world listens to those songs, Nidhi? Are you trying to deliberately provoke me?' he had asked, his voice turning icy.

'Why would I do that, Manoj? And why is it that you always get to pick where we go?' I had countered.

Things had quickly escalated from there. That is the thing about fights. It starts with one thing and, before you can do anything about it, several unrelated issues are brought up so quickly that it gets out of hand. He brought up irrelevant things like me not having a focus in life and not being ambitious enough and quitting a great career.

'Do you mean to say that you are ambitious only if you stick to a career? What about personal happiness?'

'What about it?' he had asked.

'Look, Manoj, I am following my heart. I did work for a corporate organization. I ran the rat race. It doesn't make me happy. Now, I am doing things that make me happy.'

'Sitting at home and writing, and then teaching pottery to some dumb-ass people who have no other work in life?' he had said.

At that point I had stood up to leave.

He had tried to stop me by grabbing my arm. He had twisted it hard. I had told him to let go.

He had increased the pressure and twisted it and I had yelped in pain.

That was when he backed off.

It had taken me a week to recover from that incident. My arm had been bruised and there were blue marks on my skin.

Every single day he had apologized and sent flowers. He had said he was thoroughly ashamed and that he did not know what came over him. I had relented after a week.

It was over three months now since that incident had happened, and we had never met at his apartment since then. And today, his wanting me to come over is making me uneasy. I don't like the sound of 'talk things over'. Yet, his request is a perfectly rational one. He wants to try and sort things out and the only way to do that is by communicating. So how can I be irrational and say that I do not want to meet him there?

I call him up and he is at a meeting. He calls back later.

'Yeah, baby, did you call? Sorry, I was in a meeting,' he says.

'Manoj, why don't we meet at a restaurant, or my place?'

'Well, I want to cook for you. I have already got all the ingredients. I also have some incredible wine. And we can talk this out better at home rather than at a noisy restaurant. We anyway argue about Thai versus non-Thai, don't we?'

When he puts it like that there is nothing to do but agree. He then asks me whether he should pick me up and I say that I will get there myself.

A part of me dreads this visit. It must be the residual memories of my last time there. The other part asks me not to be silly. To simply go and have a good time.

I take a cab to his place because I know I will be

drinking. Manoj lives in a posh, exclusive residential community on Haralur Road that consists only of row-houses. It's a twenty-minute car ride to his place. I put on my headphones and listen to music as the taxi crawls through the traffic-infested streets of Bangalore. I get off at the entrance, make an entry in the security register and they wave me in. I walk to his house and ring the bell.

He opens the door and greets me with a bouquet of roses. My favourite flowers.

'Ha! Thanks. But I have come to your house. I'm the one who is supposed to bring something for you,' I say, surprised.

'How does it matter? Your place, my place. Flowers for a beautiful lady,' he says as he goes down on one knee and kisses my hand. A huge grin plasters itself across my face.

His apartment is always tidy, but today he has lit candles and laid the table. He has switched on dim lights. There's a bottle of wine chilling on the centre table, in a bucket of ice.

The whole place smells terrific.

'What is that smell?' I sniff.

He points to an infuser in the corner. It is a beautifully crafted ceramic one with an intricate pattern through which a tea-light candle glows. The shadows make a pretty pattern on the wall.

'Sacred sandalwood fragrance oil. It's a scent I discovered helps me relax,' he says.

'Umm, nice,' I say.

He has already switched on music and it's some kind of soft instrumental piano that is playing. I can see that Manoj has gone the whole hog. And as reluctant as I am to admit it, I am impressed and pleased that he has made this much of an effort. It is indeed different from our usual restaurant outings where he turns up late and is always distracted because of work.

I settle down on the sofa, slip off my sandals, and prop my legs up on the centre table. His sofas are the kind that you can sink into and completely disappear.

'You look beautiful, Nidhi,' he says as he hands me my wine.

'Thank you,' I smile back. I have worn a pretty, sleeveless, off-white chiffon dress that clings to my curves, and I've braided my hair into a fish-tail braid, which is a little bit more effort than I usually make. Most of the time I wear it loose, or if I am at the pottery studio, it is always tied back in a ponytail. I have also worn makeup today—mascara, eye-liner and a lipstick which makes my lips shine. I am pleased that he has noticed.

'It's a 1995 vintage Clos du Marquis wine,' he says as I take a sip.

'Aaah, this is good, Manoj,' I say.

'Told you it would be better meeting here. Just trust me sometimes at least, my lady,' he says.

'When have I ever not trusted you?'

'See, this moving to the US thing. Why don't you give it a try? Why be so adamant about it?'

He has come to the point straight away. I would have thought we would talk about other things first.

'You know why. My pottery does mean something to me.'

'I know it does. I am not asking you to give it up.'

'What do you mean you aren't asking me to give it up? How do I conduct my classes from the US? Through Skype? Also, what will I do there the whole day?' I can't comprehend what he means when he says that he isn't asking me to give it up.

'That's why I want to get married before we move. If we are married, then the spouse has some privileges.'

'Come on, Manoj. You aren't going on an H1 Visa, are you?'

'No, it's an L1.'

'Then it is impossible for me to work there. What are you even talking about?'

'Look, Nidhi, we can work all that out. I can probably get an H1 visa eventually. Then a Green Card.'

'Manoj—that will take years.'

'How will we know unless we try? Why are you being so pessimistic?'

'Because you don't even have an action plan. You are throwing stuff up in the air.'

'How is it throwing stuff up in the air? I want to marry you, damn it.'

His voice has increased a few notches in the decibel level now. It instantly puts me on high alert. This isn't going well. I can see a vein throbbing in his forehead. I sit up a bit straighter. I have removed my feet off the centre table now.

I am silent. I think he notices my discomfort.

'Look, Nidhi—do you have a better solution?'

'Manoj, I cannot give up my pottery studio. It means a lot to me.'

'But you would agree that you hardly make any money out of it, right? My assignment would be more lucrative. We could have a nice lifestyle there.'

'It was never about the money for me, Manoj. If it was, would I have quit my corporate job? How many times have we gone over this now?'

My phone buzzes at that moment; it is Aniket.

'Hey, what are you up to? Do you think a few beers are okay?'

'Actually, no. It will undo everything you have been doing. But if you find it hard to resist, well, then we will work harder!' I reply.

'Who is that?' Manoj asks.

'A friend,' I reply.

'Anyone I know?' he persists.

'No—this is someone I met recently. He has joined my pottery class. And I am now his fitness coach too.'

'New occupation, Nidhi?' he asks. He is pouring himself a second glass of wine now and he lifts his chin a little as he looks straight at me. I sense an edge in his tone which was not there before.

'Yes, a new occupation,' I meet his gaze.

The atmosphere has changed. There is an unexpressed tension between us now.

'And what makes you qualified to be a fitness coach, if I may ask?'

'The fact that I have managed to lose sixteen kilos. I wasn't always like this and you know that.'

'Oh yes, you have mentioned your weight-loss story. But a coach? What does the guy do? And why in the world is he hiring you? Doesn't he want a professional to help him out?' He shakes his head.

'Manoj, why do you always have to be so dismissive of anything I do?'

'How am I being dismissive? I asked you a logical question.'

'Everything doesn't have logic, Manoj. He is my friend. I am helping him, that's all there is to this. Don't make a big deal of it.'

'Me—making a big deal? Come on, Nidhi. Why are you getting defensive?'

'I am not.'

'You so are.'

'You are the one who brought this up.'

'I wasn't the one who got the text.'

'So what if I got the text? How is it your business?'

'Oh—so now that is wrong, is it? My asking you whose text it was. Are you saying that was what caused the problem?'

I am angry now.

'Look, let's come back to the issue at hand. I am not moving to the US. Period.'

'You are so stubborn, Nidhi. You only look at your own interests.'

'I could say the same about you, Manoj. That you do not understand what makes me tick. How hard it is for you to get that I *love* my work. Have you even once come to the studio and seen what we do there?'

'I am not gay.'

'What?'

'Gay men are usually interested in pottery and art and stuff.'

'Ridiculous. Look, I am leaving. I will talk to you when you are in a more reasonable frame of mind.'

I stand up.

In an instant he has jumped up and he holds my arm.

'Don't leave, Nidhi. Please. I have made pizza.'

I recoil slightly. The pressure on my arm is increasing now. His fingers dig into my flesh.

'Manoj. Please take your hands off me,' I say, and he grips me harder.

'Please stay, let's talk,' he says.

'That hurts. Remove your hand right now.' I don't recognize the high pitch or the slight panic that comes out in my voice.

He lets go. I breathe a sigh of relief.

I don't want this to turn into a fight. Yet I am angry

now. He has once again squeezed my arm hard. I don't like him doing this. It intimidates me.

'I'm sorry, okay? I never meant to squeeze your arm like that. It's just that … that … you infuriate me.' He looks helpless and hurt.

But I am too angry to comfort him. We finish the rest of the meal in silence.

I am too upset to enjoy his pizza.

He tries to make conversation, but my replies are monosyllabic now.

'Can you see this? Can you see the bruises?' I show him my arm.

'Nidhi, baby—I am so sorry. I told you, it is just that it is exasperating talking to you sometimes. You are unmoving. Logic doesn't work with you, reasoning doesn't work. You are hell-bent on doing exactly what you want. Marriage always means certain adjustments, you know.'

'Why the fuck don't *you* make those adjustments then?' I say, and before he can reply, I leap up from the dining area, grab my bag and am heading towards the door. He shakes his head and watches me leave.

He doesn't come to see me off. I am walking fast now, my head spinning at all that he has been saying. His only agenda seems to be to get married as quickly as possible, and for me to move to the US with him. It is impossible to make him understand the concept of doing something because you are passionate about it.

I have reached the main road now. I open an app on

my phone and check for a cab. Hell. There are none nearby. I check another taxi app. Again there are none. What is with these apps? I restart my phone and check again.

I know I would probably get an auto-rickshaw on Sarjapur Main Road, but it is a very long walk there from Haralur Road. If it was daytime, I could have easily walked the distance. But now it is pitch dark, and the road is not lit up at all. Definitely not safe for me to attempt the walk.

Stupid Manoj. I sure as hell am not going back to his house now. He hasn't even followed me out. Ass. I look at the time and it is now past midnight. Where are all the taxis when you need them? I refresh the app again and again. After about thirty minutes there are still no cabs around. I am growing desperate with each passing minute. I need to get home somehow. I am tired and the wine is beginning to have an effect on me. Fucking hell. I am stuck now. I don't know what to do.

It's all in the planets—your daily forecast: Darshita Sen

Leo (July 23 to August 22)

A friend needs your help. However, you need to carefully weigh the pros and cons of every decision that you take today, considering all the possible alternatives thoroughly.

13

ANIKET

Trish does not even notice that I am not laughing with her. When she recovers from her laughing fit, she asks me what I will have.

'Nothing,' I say.

I have lost my appetite.

'Aww, come on, don't sulk like a kid. I will order for you then,' she says and goes ahead and orders two masala dosas and filter coffee for both of us.

I am silent.

Trish looks at me. It's the kind of look that conveys half-exasperation and half-scrutiny.

I still do not say anything.

'Come on, Ani. You know I meant that as a joke. You do have a paunch, don't you? We have talked about it. I didn't know you would feel bad, I was only teasing.'

Ouch. She is making it worse. Can't she see it is not about her callous comment, but her whole attitude?

'Trish—do you know I *made* that thing for you?'

I can't bring myself to call it a whale any more. Like 'whale' is a bad word. It now feels like an insult she hurled.

'Made? What do you mean *made*?' she asks, a frown creeping in between her eyebrows.

'Created it, Trish. Made it with my bare hands. I joined a pottery class. That was my first project and I thought you would like it.'

'Oh,' she says as the frown clears. 'I didn't know that. You should have told me. Why didn't you say anything?' she asks.

'You never gave me a chance, you were busy laughing.'

'How could I know? You should have told me before you gave it to me. See—that's the thing with surprises. They can go either way.'

I can't believe this! She doesn't even think this warrants an apology.

I wait. I want her to say that she is sorry that she hurt my feelings. Is she so thick? Haven't I just told her how I feel?

No apology comes.

The waiter brings our dosas and she takes the whale from the table and places it beside her on the seat.

'I love the dosas here. Don't you think the chutney is awesome? You know, I really missed south Indian food when I was in Leh,' she says as she digs in.

'What did you eat there?' I force myself to ask.

'There's something called paba. It's their traditional food made using peas and wheat. Then I tried thukpa, which is a thick soup with vegetables. The flavours are all very mild. I got sick of it after two days. I was craving for this,' she chatters on.

'Yeah, I can imagine. When I travel I crave home food too.'

It is a gigantic effort to keep my tone normal. And neutral.

'I know, right? Mom made some great food for me on Saturday,' she says.

'Saturday? Didn't you say you had a ramp walk?'

'Oh, did I? It got … um … cancelled. Last-minute thing.'

'We could have met, Trish. You know I wanted to meet.'

'Ani—I was exhausted. Didn't I tell you? I needed to recover from my Leh trip.'

'I don't know, Trish. Sometimes I get this feeling that … that you don't care about us spending time together any more.'

'Come on, Ani. You know that's not true. You know what, let me make it up to you. Let's go to a pub today, after work? I know a nice one in Koramangala—Ab-Salut. It's new and they keep the place open past the eleven-thirty deadline. It'll be fun. I can call Ananya too. She was telling me she wants to go out. And you ask Subbu.'

'Who is Ananya?'

'Don't you remember Ananya? You met her once when you picked me up. She was with me on the Ladakh shoot. She is a crew member at the agency. She is the production co-ordinator.'

I remember now, though only vaguely. It was in passing that Trish had introduced me to her. It was a very brief meeting: she had waved and I hadn't even got out of the car.

'Okay, let me ask Subbu. He might have something planned already.'

'Call him. I'm sure he will say yes. It's not like he has a social life anyway,' says Trish.

That angers me again. What is with Trish today. Or am I being a tad oversensitive as she hasn't apologized for what she did earlier? But I don't want to create a scene over this now.

'You know what, you ask him,' I say.

She immediately whips out her phone and dials his number. She asks him straight away if he is free and whether he would like to come with us for a drink. She tells him about Ananya.

'Yeah, tonight. Great. See you at Ab-salut then, at eight o'clock,' she says and hangs up.

Then she turns towards me.

'Done,' she smiles.

Trish is pleased when she gets her way and she always manages to organize these jaunts even at short notice. Nobody says no to Trish. And she loves going to pubs. I don't like them much because of the smoke and noise. Also, it's not like you can have a conversation there. But she has made an effort now and there is no backing out. I didn't want a double date with Subbu and Ananya; I should have spoken up the minute she suggested it. Now I have no choice. Well, at least Subbu might have some fun with Ananya, who knows.

The waiter brings the bill and I reach for my wallet to pay, even though Trish says that she will take care of it. As we stand up to leave, I notice that Trish has forgotten the whale on the chair.

I look at it and then look at Trish, who is pushing back her hair now and is taking out her sunglasses from her handbag. I don't say a word as we head towards the door. I don't even want to remind her that she has forgotten it. I see the waiter push the chair forward, and I see the whale tumble down to the ground. It breaks into three pieces. I see that the waiter is taken aback and he looks around. But we have reached the door now, and before he can call us, I have ushered Trish out of the restaurant, and we walk towards my car parked in the basement.

Trish is talking now about going out with Vishwa and the gang and how it is a big party planned for the Ladakh crew to celebrate a successful photoshoot. But I am not really listening.

All I can think of is the broken pieces of the whale, which are probably being swept away even as we drive to the office.

Once I reach office, Subbu is all gung-ho and excited about Trish calling him.

'This came out of the blue, man. Have you seen this chick? What does she look like?'

'Which chick?'

'Your Trish's friend. The one who is joining us tonight. Please tell me she is smoking hot.'

'Why don't you ask Trish? She spoke to you directly, didn't she?'

'Whoa—I just asked. What's with you, bro?'

'Nothing, Subbu. I've got a tonne of work.'

'Come on, Ani. I have known you long enough. She didn't like the whale?'

'She laughed, and called it an "Ani-whale". And she didn't even know I made it till I told her. Then she forgot it in the restaurant. And as we were walking out the waiter moved the chair, and I saw it fall down and break.'

'Oh no, bro. BSoD error,' he says.

'Eh?'

'Blue screen of death. You need to go into reboot mode to fix it.'

'Done is done. Let's move on,' I say and head towards my cubicle even as Subbu makes a yeah-right face. Subbu can be incredibly perceptive at times.

Later that evening Subbu picks me up in a cab and

we both arrive at Ab-salut before the girls do. We wait for them outside. I wonder if Nidhi would approve of my drinking beer. I feel like I might be cheating here and it's best to tell her.

'Hey, what are you up to? Do you think a few beers are okay?' I type.

I know what she is going to reply and she says exactly what I expect.

'Actually, no. It will undo everything you have been doing. But if you find it hard to resist, well, then we will work harder!' it reads.

I smile. My willpower isn't that phenomenal that I can go to a micro-brewery and resist beer. Now that I have got 'clearance' from Nidhi, I feel better.

This place is quite peppy, and I see a string of girls dressed in figure-hugging, off-the-shoulder dresses and high heels. The guys are mostly in jeans and T-shirts or smart casual shirts. Such a stark contrast between how women and men dress up for these places.

Trish texts saying that they are almost there. When they emerge from the taxi, Subbu and I can't help but stare. Both are dressed to kill. Trish is wearing a one-shoulder white mini dress that emphasizes her boobs, tiny waist and long legs. The dress is short in a sexy way. Ananya is wearing a black, pleated, strapless, short cocktail dress and four-inch strappy stilettos. I think I hear Subbu gasp.

'Hi, this is Ananya,' Trish says as she introduces Subbu first, who immediately half hugs her like he has known her all his life, and then me. I shake her hand.

'Ananya, you are looking great,' says Subbu.

'Thanks, and that's a nice shirt you are wearing,' she tells Subbu, and he preens.

When we enter the pub, many people turn to look at us. Undoubtedly it is because of Trish and Ananya. There is no way anyone is checking Subbu and me out. The ambience is very rustic. It is an industrial theme with pipes, chutes and fans all over. There is a lot of noise. People are talking loudly over the music in order to be heard. There is seating on the first floor, near the brewery, and in the smoking area. The noise is too much to handle in the brewing area so we decide to sit in the smoking area, as Ananya says she would like to smoke.

She lights up almost as soon as we are seated and asks Subbu and me if we want a cigarette. Both of us are non-smokers and we shake our heads. She exhales, narrows her eyes, and looks at Subbu. 'So, tell me about your job,' she says.

I jump in before Subbu can answer. I know what will happen if he answers. He will go into such technical detail that both these gorgeous women will head for the nearest exit.

'We fix problems. We are the problem-fixers. You tell us a problem you have and we will fix it,' I say and she laughs. Then I sing the words to the tune of *Ghostbusters*. And both of them laugh.

Subbu shoots a look at me as if to say 'why are you stealing my thunder', and I give him a look that says 'let me handle it, bro; you will mess it up'. The good thing about being such close friends is you can communicate even when you do not say anything.

The waiter brings the menu and the place is so dimly lit that we have to use the torchlight on our phones to read it. Subbu and I order a set of beer samplers that contain six of their crafted beers. Trish asks for Tequila shots and Ananya orders a whiskey-based cocktail. We also order some starters.

The drinks arrive, and Ananya and Trish are clearly having a great time, as is Subbu. I dislike the smoke here but Subbu doesn't seem to mind it at all. I wish Ananya wouldn't smoke but I don't want to be a party-pooper and so I put up with it. Ananya narrates a funny story about the shoot in Ladakh where Trish had to wear a leather outfit in the freezing Pagong Tso Lake and how she found it so hard to balance and strike a perfect pose. Subbu is mesmerized.

When the food arrives, Subbu says, 'Bro, are you going to be writing this down in your food diary? Is she going to let you off the hook for this?'

'Who?' asks Trish.

'His fitness coach, Nidhi. She monitors him like a prison warden,' says Subbu.

'Oooh. Oooh. Sounds like she *likes* you,' teases Ananya.

'Whoa, hold on folks. She is a just a friend, okay? And she's engaged to someone,' I say.

'Oooh, we're *just friends*. That's what they all say,' says Ananya. Subbu and she laugh but Trish looks a bit annoyed.

'Look, that's what it is. She is helping me lose weight,' I say.

The conversation flows smoothly after that, and as the evening progresses the girls get more and more drunk.

I am buzzing from the beer, but only very slightly. I have had so much, I have already taken a leak twice. The beer is nothing like I have tasted before and, though I am enjoying it, and I can see that Subbu is having a great time, I still wish it was slightly less noisy and less crowded. This place is packed even on a weekday.

My phone buzzes then and I look to see who is messaging me this late. It is Nidhi. She asks where I am; she says she is stuck at Haralur without transport and asks whether I can pick her up. She says she has tried all the taxi apps for the last hour and there are no cabs in sight. She apologizes for any trouble caused.

I quickly switch on an app on my phone and I can see that there are at least six taxis very close by, within a distance of eight hundred metres. It is always easy to get taxis around pubs as most people don't want to risk driving after a drink.

'*No worries at all. I will be there in fifteen minutes, twenty tops. Lots of taxis here,*' I type back.

Then I tell the others, 'Hey guys, so sorry. A friend is stuck and this is an emergency. I have to go.'

A look of disbelief spreads over Trish's face. Her drunk mind struggles to comprehend what I am saying.

'What! You're going now? You can't be serious. You can't leave. This party is just getting started, right Subbu, Ananya? Tell him!' she says.

'Look, Trish. I wouldn't leave unless it was an emergency. I need to go,' I say.

'Why?' asks Trish.

'Because I promised Nidhi I would be on the way soon. She is relying on me. She's stuck at Haralur without transport.'

'And out of all the people in the world she calls you? Why?' asks Trish, her eyes flashing. 'Tell her to call someone else.'

'I can't, Trish. Subbu, please drop them home, bro. Here is my share of the bill,' I say and place two thousand rupees on the table.

'So sorry, and bye! I had a nice evening,' I tell them and walk out, leaving behind a visibly upset Trish.

I have promised Nidhi that I am on my way, and whether it angers Trish or not, I am bloody well going to keep my word. I whip out my phone and call for a taxi.

It's all in the planets—your daily forecast: Darshita Sen

Sagittarius (November 22 to December 21)

A close relationship gives pain. The candidness with which the fiery Sagittarius fires their arrows may end up singeing someone. A friend helps you out of a difficult situation and proves to be a balm....

14

NIDHI

Never in my life have I been this glad to see someone arriving. My head is throbbing now and I am beginning to feel dizzy. Aniket has arrived within twenty minutes of that text to him.

'Ani—thank you,' I say as he jumps out of the taxi and gives me a half hug.

'Don't be silly, what are friends for?' he says as he shuts the door after me and runs around and gets in from the other side.

'Are you okay?' he asks.

My throat is parched and I feel terrible. My arm hurts where Manoj held me.

'Do you mind if I close my eyes? I desperately need water,' I say.

'No worries, Nidhi. Want me to get you water? We can pick it up on the way,' says Aniket.

'At this time of the night, I doubt anything is open. Never mind. I'll drink water when we reach home.'

Then I lean back on the cab seat and shut my eyes. With Aniket beside me, I feel safe. Cared for. Comforted. I must have passed out because, the next thing I know, Aniket is gently tapping me on the shoulder.

'Nidhi, come, I will see you to the apartment,' he says.

I sit up with a start. 'Ani, it's fine. I can manage,' I say.

'No, I insist. I have come this far. Let me escort you and see that you are safely in.'

Ani walks beside me and I fish out the keys from my purse. I am wide awake now and the effect of the wine has worn off. My arm still hurts though.

I enter my home, flick on the lights, and ask him to come in.

'No, I better be going,' he says.

'What? Then why did you come till the door? Come in now, and I will make you a cup of coffee.'

'All right, then,' he grins as he walks in after me. He looks so boyish when he smiles like that. Like an overgrown kid. I walk towards my kitchen and thirstily glug down half a bottle of water.

Then I exhale.

Ani has made himself comfortable on the bar stool in my open kitchen and swirls around, watching me make filter coffee with the intense, south Indian decoction that is always available in my house.

'So, how did you get stuck at Haralur Road without a ride?' he asks.

'Yeah, I didn't expect that there would not be any cabs. I was visiting a … friend,' I say.

Somehow, I do not want to tell Ani that Manoj did not even see me to a cab and did not offer to drop me, and I was too pissed off to go back to him and ask for his help.

I make the coffee and it is perfect. I am pleased. I pour it into a steel tumbler and rest it in a little circular steel bowl, just the way they serve it in restaurants. Then I hand it over to him.

'This smells good! You are a pro at it,' he says as the aroma of coffee wafts through the kitchen. He inhales and he takes the tumbler from my hand.

That is when he notices the blue marks on my arm where Manoj had gripped me. They are very obvious now, standing out against my pale skin. Like a tattoo that calls attention to itself. I am hoping he doesn't say anything, but he does.

'Gosh—that is nasty. What happened?' he asks.

'Nothing, I banged my hand.' I try to be casual about it.

'What did you bang against? And how in the world did you manage to bang your arm?!'

'I wasn't watching. It happened in the gym,' I say, but I am unable to look at him.

'No, it didn't.' He is looking directly into my eyes now. Maybe it is my tone that has given me away.

Hell. My lie has been caught out. I know he knows. He knows I know he knows.

'Nidhi, are you aware that this is physical abuse? What were you doing alone at Haralur Road at this time in the night? Are you okay? What is going on?' The questions come flooding out of him.

'Whoa, Ani. Slow down. Physical abuse is such a strong term. It was a little fight with Manoj. I didn't want to go back into the house and ask him for a ride, which is why I texted you. I hope I didn't disrupt your plans?'

'I was with Trish and some friends. But hey, that's fine. My friend Subbu is taking care of them. And while you may try to defend your Manoj, what he did is not on,' Ani purses his lips and shakes his head.

I look away.

'He isn't evil or anything.'

'Never said he was. But this I still do not condone. This is not how couples fight. I have had a fair share of fights with Trish myself, but I can't imagine laying my hands on her ever....'

'Look, Ani, leave it. He has never hit me or slapped me. Just holding my arm tightly can't be abuse, can it? He gets me flowers, wines and dines me, goes the whole hog. He does love me a lot. Yes, maybe you have a point. It does make me uncomfortable when he squeezes my arm. But to term it physical abuse would be going to the extreme.'

I'm trying to be rational about this. Manoj is indeed caring in many ways, even if he doesn't get my love for pottery or why I gave up my corporate job. He is fun to talk to, we go out, watch movies together and we have got used to each other in the last two years that we have been together.

'What was the fight about? Or is that too personal? You don't have to answer if you don't want to.'

I find now that I actually *want* to talk about it. Somehow I feel a need to explain to Ani what happened. I want him to see my point of view. Also, I feel obliged to tell him. After all, he has come all the way to pick me up, abandoning his friends.

'I want to. But it's a long story. Are you sure you want to listen?'

'Well, we do have coffee now,' he says and smiles, raising his cup.

'All right then, let's go and make ourselves comfortable,' I tell him and we move to the couch in the living room.

'Gosh, Nidhi, you have done up this place so well, I can't help repeating myself. I think I told you this last time I was here too. My place looks like a dump in comparison. You should help me do up mine. This is so good,' he says as he settles down on the couch with his coffee.

I sit next to him and tuck in my legs, relaxed and at peace, now that I am home.

'So tell me your story. We have all night,' he says.

I glance at the clock on my wall. It is already past one o'clock.

'We don't have all night, my friend. We have only a few hours before sunrise,' I say.

'Have you seen the movie?'

'Which one?'

'*Before Sunrise*. Ethan Hawke, Julie Delpy. I thought it was beautiful. Such powerful dialogues. Such poignant thoughts, and so romantic too.'

'Oh yes, I have seen it. I loved it too. It was indeed beautiful. Imagine taking such a call. To leave things to fate. To part without even exchanging phone numbers and then agreeing to meet after a year to check if their love is true. Do you think it is possible in real life?'

'I don't know. Maybe it is, when you find a soul-mate.'

'You know, Ani, I was reading something the other day—about life-mates and soul mates. I found it very interesting.'

I tell him then about what I had read. He listens intently. Then I tell him about Manoj and me. I also tell him about my earlier relationship with Vir. How it seemed great at that time. But how we had both moved on with our lives once our careers got in the way. I tell him about how Manoj came into my life and how our relationship progressed.

'You know, today's fight with him was because he very badly wants me to move to the US with him, and he wants to get married before he leaves to the US.'

'And I presume you don't want to?'

I nod. 'I told him that to his face. That's what angered him.'

'I see. But still, anger is no excuse. He needs to control himself. I think such men … such men are pathetic. You can't hurt a woman like that. It angers me.'

Ani's phone rings then and both of us look at it startled.

'Trish,' he says as he answers the call.

It's all in the planets—your daily forecast: Darshita Sen

Leo (July 23 to August 22)

*Unexpected events throw you off guard. You must
re-evaluate your priorities. A new friend needs help
and you are forced to step in....*

15

ANIKET

Strangely, I don't even feel annoyed or upset to be dragged
out of Ab-salut. Normally I would be irritated if a fun
evening was interrupted this way. But today I am not. The
smoke was getting to me. Ananya might be hot but her
habit of chain-smoking was beginning to annoy me. All
that second-hand smoke that I was being forced to endure,
and the noise too had started grating on my nerves.

Nidhi kind of leaps into my arms when I pick her up at
Haralur, and almost immediately closes her eyes, even as I
instruct the driver to take us to Koramangala. She doesn't

seem drunk though. She seems worn out and exhausted. When we reach her place, she insists that I come in and makes coffee for me. It strikes me again how well she has done up her place. I love the details.

When I see the bruises on her arm, I am shocked, and then we get into a long conversation about her relationship with Manoj. She has a calm way of talking. And even though she is telling me about her previous relationship which ended in a break-up, I find that her voice is soft and mellifluous. There is a kind of quiet acceptance in her tone. I listen carefully. She definitely doesn't seem keen on getting married to this guy Manoj. He sounds like a scumbag, if you ask me. But I don't tell her that.

My phone rings and it jolts us both. I look at the screen and see that it is Trish. I pick up at once.

'Hey, babe,' I say.

But I can only hear some traffic noise at the other end. Then some male voices and a female voice saying, 'Get in the car, Trish. You are so drunk.'

'Ani, where are you when I need you.' Now, that is distinctly Trish's voice.

Then there is a sound like water being poured.

'God—you have thrown up … shit. Are you okay, Trish? Help her get in, guys. What the hell.'

That was clearly Subbu's voice.

I have no idea what is going on. Good lord. I cut the call and immediately dial Subbu, gesturing to Nidhi to excuse me.

Subbu picks up and I heave an enormous sigh of relief.

'Bro—bad scene. Trish is drunk beyond her senses. She threw up all over the place. I just put her in a cab.'

'What? What the hell, Subbu.… I told you to take care of them, didn't I? What the fuck. Why didn't you go with them? Who is with her?'

'Bro—she insisted she was fine. And Ananya seemed okay, though a little high. Ananya said she will take her to her house.'

'Subbu—are you nuts? Both those girls are drunk. How could you let them go? Why didn't you call me?'

'They threw us out of the pub, bro.… Trish made a scene there. She climbed on the table.'

'What?'

'Yeah, things got out of hand almost as soon as you left. Someone she knew joined us. The guy works with them or something. She said she wanted to dance. She said India was too conservative. And she was talking about loosening up and having fun. Then she started stripping.'

'God. Shit … fucking hell.'

'No, no—it wasn't so bad, bro. She unbuttoned her top and everyone got a good look at her in her bra and then Ananya and I managed to grab her and bring her down. But some people took out their phones and were taking pictures. That's when the bouncers came in and politely asked us to leave. Trish kept telling them that she was a model and that they could see her picture in next month's *GQ* or something. And she was posing and shouting, telling everyone to go ahead and click away.'

'Good lord, Subbu. I should have warned you.'

Trish does have a way of losing control when she is drunk. But when I'm with her, she always listens to me.

I hang up, angry with Subbu for sending the girls in a taxi, and dial Trish's number. There is no answer.

'What happened, Ani? Are they safe? Is Trish okay?' Nidhi asks.

For a moment I had forgotten that she was there.

'The girls are drunk and Subbu let them go on their own in a taxi. I am so worried, Nidhi. Give me a minute. Let me call her.'

I dial her number again but she doesn't answer.

I don't even have Ananya's number.

My mind works furiously. Then I call Subbu back.

'Who called a taxi for them?'

'I did.'

'Then you would have the track journey option right? Send it to me.'

'Yes, I do have that. Okay, let me send it to you. But you are worrying for nothing. Ananya was very much in control.'

'I don't fucking care. Send it to me right now.'

'Yes, yes. Chill. Sending,' he says and he cuts the call.

I get the link within a few seconds. I click on it and I can track her trip now.

The destination shows Indiranagar. That's probably where Ananya lives. Ab-salut to Indiranagar is not too bad a drive.

And yet, the recent rape cases in the country come to mind. I am worried sick. All I can think is that my Trish is drunk, in a taxi alone, and she needs me. I have to be there.

'Nidhi—can I borrow your car? Do you mind?' I ask her.

'Please do. I don't mind at all. Are you okay to drive though?'

'Yes, it's been a couple of hours now, and I've had coffee too. I'm fine. I am worried sick about Trish. I want to make sure she is safe. The link Subbu sent me shows that they are still on Outer Ring Road. I want to ensure that this cab driver takes no detours. I'd better hurry, Nidhi. Can I have the keys?'

'Ani, let me go with you.'

'Are you sure? Aren't you tired? I'm quite sure they'll be fine, but I want to check on them.'

'Yeah, I'm sure. And no, I am not tired,' she asserts.

She owns an i20 and we zoom out of her apartment complex. I hand over my phone to Nidhi and tell her to keep checking where their cab has reached and, more importantly, if it stops somewhere.

Nidhi does as instructed. She keeps checking their location and I drive like a maniac on Outer Ring Road. At this time of the night there is hardly any traffic and driving on this road is a breeze.

However, we still do not catch up with them till they are almost home. Nidhi keeps guiding me, tracking the route the taxi is taking. We are on 100 Feet Road in

Indiranagar, which is where I am finally able to pull up right behind the cab and keep him in sight. The cab takes two quick turns—a right and then a left and then slows down and finally stops. I am guessing this is Ananya's home. It's somewhere in the by-lanes of Defence Colony. I pull over and see Ananya scrambling out. Trish is trying to get out of the car on the other side. She can barely stand.

I park behind them and jump out. Nidhi follows close behind.

Ananya sees me only then.

'What are you doing here?' she asks.

I can see that Ananya is drunk too.

Then she turns towards Trish and says, 'Babe—Ani is here.'

Trish is very drunk. I hate to see her like this. I have told her so many times to control her drinking but she never listens. I am concerned, annoyed and angry, all at the same time.

She holds out her hand and says, 'Who? Ani-whale? You know I called him that to his face? He is a whale, he needs to lose weight.'

Even in her drunken state that's all she can say.

'Trish, you better get out, you are home now,' I say.

'What? Ani? Am I dreaming?'

'No, you are not. I followed you. Come, let me help you,' I say as I move towards her.

She struggles to stand up and I half-lift her. She puts her arm around my shoulder. Then she spots Nidhi.

'Who the fuck is she? Is she the one you rushed off to meet?' she points at Nidhi.

'Trish—this is Nidhi. She is my friend,' I say.

'Stupid cow. You are the one. You had to spoil my evening. Can't you text your own guy to pick you up if you are stuck? Bitch.'

Nidhi turns away. She doesn't say anything.

'Trish—stop it. Don't say anything,' I warn her.

But she laughs. 'Who told you to follow me, Ani? You just can't leave me alone can you? It's not like I couldn't have managed, you know? And then you bring ... this woman with you?'

I tell Nidhi to wait in the car, and she does that. My ears burn with what Trish said. I didn't expect her to be this nasty. But then, Trish has never seen me with another woman. Ever. This is the first time.

'Look, let's get her home,' I tell Ananya, who starts rummaging in her bag for her keys.

Trish starts swaying and I steady her.

Then we make our way inside the building and towards the elevator. The security guard looks at us. He doesn't bother to get up from his chair and Ananya merely nods at him. He nods back with disinterest as if to say, 'These youngsters. They are at it again.'

Ananya's flat is on the third floor. She struggles with the key and I help her open the door. Trish is still hanging onto my shoulder, and almost her entire body weight is on me.

I manage to open the flat door and Ananya points to the guest bedroom and asks me to take Trish there.

'You know what, Ani—we should have a threesome. You, me and Ananya. Not that stupid woman you brought along,' she says and starts nibbling my ear.

Ananya laughs. 'Girl, you are wild!' she says and she looks at me and raises her eyebrows.

'Ladies, you are both lovely. But you are also very drunk. Let's talk about this tomorrow,' I say.

Trish has plonked herself down on the bed now. Her dress has ridden up almost to her panties. I yank it down. I remove her heels and place it near her. She passes out almost as soon as her head hits the pillow.

My beautiful Trish. She looks so good even this drunk. I cover her with a blanket.

When I turn around and look for Ananya, I see that she is in her bedroom.

'Byeee Ani! Thanks for helping. Please close the door behind you when you leave,' she calls out.

I head back downstairs towards the car where Nidhi is waiting.

What a mad day it has been. My head has started pounding now. I can feel the stress of the last few hours beginning to take its toll. I have handled more than my fair share of drunk women for the day.

Now all I want to do is get back home and rest.

It's all in the planets—your daily forecast: Darshita Sen

Sagittarius (November 22 to December 21)

… You are likely to have unexpected visitors. Misunderstandings are expected. Mantra to remember: if you stand erect, why bother if your shadow is crooked.…

16

NIDHI

As I wait in the car for Ani, so many thoughts buzz around in my head. What a long day it has been. I have had a fight with my fiancé and here I am waiting in the middle of the night for someone I have barely known for two months, who has chased after his drunk girlfriend halfway across town to ensure she is fine. And, in comparison, there's Manoj who can't even be bothered to see if I made it home safe. The more I think about it, the angrier I get with Manoj. How could he abandon me like that and not come after me? So what if I had marched out—he could have easily followed me. If he had, I would probably not have called Aniket.

And good lord—what a girl Trish is. She is stunning. No doubt about that. I can see why Aniket is crazy about her. But boy—she has called me a bitch, and she hardly knows me. I don't even hold it against her. There is an element of truth in what she said—that I have indeed hijacked her evening with her boyfriend. Also, she is so darn young. I try and think back to my twenties. I was very different from Trish. There is no way I would have called anyone a bitch, ever. Not behind their back, not to their face. Not ever. I would rather shut them out and not think about them.

I glance at my watch now and wonder what Ani is doing. He has been gone more than fifteen minutes. It shouldn't have taken him this long. Poor Ani—first he had to pick me up, and then he has to handle his drunk girlfriend and her friend.

Ani emerges from the building then, and he looks tired.

'So sorry about that, Nidhi. I apologize for Trish. She has no control over what she does and says when she starts drinking. I am sorry.'

He looks so contrite that I want to give him a hug and tell him it's okay, but I hold back.

'Hey—it's not your fault. And I haven't taken it to heart. Don't even worry about it. After all, she does have a point. I did spoil your evening with her,' I reassure him, trying to make him feel better.

'Well, I hated all the noise and smoke in the pub anyway, and your call was the perfect excuse to get away. I did it for selfish reasons, not to pick you up,' he grins.

'But you did rescue me. Looks like your entire day has consisted of rescuing drunk women. In my defence, though, I wasn't drunk.'

'No you certainly weren't, and yes, you are right. No more drunk women for me, at least not today.'

'A pity! I was going to ask you if you wanted to go pub-hopping now,' I say and I laugh when I see his jaw drop and he gives me a 'are-you-serious' look.

'Phew! I thought for a moment you were actually serious.' He sounds relieved.

'What if I wasn't joking? What if I did actually want to?' I ask.

He thinks for a few seconds.

'Want to?' he smiles.

'Mmm, why not. But we have a small technical difficulty here. It's almost three in the morning now and all the pubs will be closed.'

'But I know a place that stays open long past midnight.'

'Wow. Not kidding, right?'

'No. I do know one.'

I am tempted. But then logic and sense prevails and I decide against it.

'You know what, Ani—this has been stressful for both of us. Let's call it a night. We will go another time.'

I think I spot a flicker of disappointment on his face,

but I can't be sure. It has indeed been an awfully long night for both of us.

By the time we finally get back home, it's three-thirty.

At my apartment lobby, Ani takes out his phone and checks for a cab.

'There are no cabs at all,' he sighs and looks away.

'There won't be. Look at the time, and it is Bangalore. What do you expect?'

'Oh no! How will I get home now?'

'Look, I have a suggestion. In fact, I think that's the only option now. Crash for the night at my place. It's fine. That couch of mine opens out to become a bed. You will be comfortable.'

'Are you sure?'

'Very. I wouldn't have offered if I wasn't. Come on, Ani, it is the least I can do.'

He accepts my offer and we make our way back to my apartment.

'Will you make coffee for me in the morning?' he smiles as we enter my apartment and the smell of the coffee we were having earlier hits us.

'Depends on whether you are a good boy or not,' I smile back as I push the centre table to one side and pull out the couch which slides out easily as it has wheels. This couch is one of the best investments I have made so far. It is large, luxurious and incredibly comfortable. It's the kind of couch / bed you can sink into and forget the worries of the world. I bring out a pillow, a bed-sheet and a thin comforter from my bedroom, and make the bed quickly.

Ani watches with interest and then says, 'Wow, Nidhi. You know how to pamper your guests. This is nice!'

I smile and then notice that he is still in his jeans.

'Are you going to sleep in your jeans?' I ask.

'No. I am waiting for you to leave, so I can strip down to my boxers. I don't want my shirt crumpled. And it will be very uncomfortable to sleep in my jeans.'

'I can lend you a night-dress if you like,' I grin.

'Yes, wearing a woman's nightie was always my secret fetish. Thank you, Nidhi, for helping that desire come true,' he says and I chuckle.

'Good night, Ani,' I say as I leave the room and retire to my bedroom.

'Good night, I look forward to my coffee tomorrow. I have been a good, good boy today,' he calls out, and I smile again.

Ani is such a kid sometimes. He sure deserves that coffee.

It has been such a long, hectic day and I fall into a deep sleep almost as soon as I hit the bed. The next thing I know it is seven-thirty and my phone alarm is buzzing. I am still groggy with sleep, and I shut it off and put it on snooze mode.

When it buzzes again, the happenings of the previous day slowly play in my mind and I sit up, remembering that Ani is in my living room.

I brush my teeth, comb my hair, change into a pair of shorts and a T-shirt and go out, something I never do, as I am always on my own. My usual routine is to lounge around in my nightie till it is time for my shower. But there is no way I am walking around the house with no bra and a sexy nightie with Ani here. I step out and look at him. He is sprawled out on his tummy, the sheet only half covering him so his back is exposed. He is in his boxers and his shirt and jeans are folded neatly and kept on a chair. I smile at how fastidious and proper he is. He sure has been a good boy!

I make him his coffee and gently wake him.

'Ani ... Ani. Rise and shine,' I say as I nudge him, placing the coffee on the centre table.

'What the...' he says and sits bolt upright, startled out of his sleep.

A wide grin spreads across my face.

'So sorry, you wanted coffee. I didn't mean to startle you,' I say.

It takes him a few seconds to remember he is shirtless.

'Nidhi.... What a fright you gave me. Mind if I put on my shirt?' he asks.

'It's nothing I haven't seen before and hey, there are small, small changes in your body. You sure are getting fitter. I am not kidding. Want me to click a pic and show you?'

'Get out of here and give me my coffee,' he says as draws the sheet right up to his chest.

I can't help laughing now.

'Ani, you are so shy!'

'Nidhi, you are so shameless!'

'Ani, you are a sweetheart.'

'Nidhi, you are a monster.'

'Ani, you are a good boy, you earned that coffee.'

He laughs in delight at that. 'I sure am. I was with two very hot drunk women who wanted a threesome but I didn't take advantage of that offer. I must be insane.'

'What?'

'Yeah—when I dropped them off in the flat. Trish suggested it.'

'You've got to be kidding!'

'I am not! Trish is like that; she can be *very* wild when she is drunk. And that friend of hers was game too.'

'Oh! Good lord. So why didn't you take them up on the offer then?'

'Because you were waiting downstairs in the car and the threesome would take a couple of hours at least. Otherwise I definitely would have. You spoiled my threesome opportunity,' he says, and when he sees my expression he laughs.

'Hahaha—got you there, didn't I? Look at your face!' he guffaws.

'Idiot,' I say as I chuck a cushion at him and he ducks.

'Come on, Nidhi. You know me better than that. Do I seem like the kind of guy who will take advantage of a drunk woman? Anyway, I better get going. Can you … er … I want to get dressed,' he says.

That's when I understand that he wants me to leave

the room so he can put on his clothes. And he is too polite to ask me. What a shy guy!

'Of course,' I say and I go to the bedroom.

'Thank you,' he calls out, and a minute later he says, 'Okay, you can come out now, I am dressed.'

Ani folds the sheet; he helps me push the couch back in, and we place the centre table back to where it was. I ask him if he wants breakfast, and he says that even though the offer is tempting, he better head home as he has a lot of work to finish. He is working on a presentation which is due, and he needs his laptop for that.

'Okay—don't forget your diet, exercise and your food diary, okay?'

'Yes, ma'am. I'll continue reporting everything to you.'

After Ani leaves, I sit on my balcony thinking about him and what a sweet chap he is. My phone rings and it is Tara.

'Hey Tara, how are you doing?' I say.

'Hey, sunshine. You sound happy. What's up?' she asks.

'Nothing.'

'Come on, Nidhi. I know something is up. Had a good time last night, didn't you? I can tell,' she says in a sing-song voice.

How far from the truth that is!

'Actually, I had a fight with Manoj last night.'

'Oh no, why?'

'Same old. He wants to get married, and I said no.'

'Oh no. Look—do you want me and your dad to speak to him?'

'And say what? If I can't make him understand, how will you guys?'

'We are coming to Bangalore for two days. I called to tell you that.'

'Oh! Nice. Stay with me.'

'You know how your dad is—he needs his comfort and luxury. We'll be staying at the Oberoi. Have dinner with us on Monday?'

'Okay, sure. I'll keep myself free.'

'Take care, sunshine. Love you, bye!'

'Bye Tara, take care.'

The intercom buzzes and the security guy says there is a deliveryman with a parcel for me. I wonder who is sending me a parcel this early in the morning. I tell them to let him in.

The doorbell rings and I open it. There is a guy with a gigantic bouquet of flowers along with a tiny note. It is always strange to see Manoj's words written by the florist.

'Forgive me, my darling. It is only because I love you. I am sorry,' it reads. I thank the guy and sign for it.

Then I place the flowers in the middle of my dining table.

I look at the bruise on my arm. It is beginning to turn purplish now.

Then I look at the flowers—they are exotic orchids. Rare. Expensive. Beautiful.

I stare at them for a while. Then I take out my phone and type, *'Thanks for the flowers. The colour matches my bruises.'*

I sit for a while staring at the text I have composed. One part of me wants to hurt him. Make him understand how it feels. The other part wants to let it go. He has apologized.

I am still angry though.

After a minute or so, I delete the second sentence.

And then I hit send.

It's all in the planets—your daily forecast: Darshita Sen

Leo (July 23 to August 22)

… If you do not plan your move carefully, you could get into a massive misunderstanding that causes a permanent fissure in a close relationship. Forewarned is forearmed. Play your cards carefully. A sudden vacation is on the cards.

17

ANIKET

Nidhi is a real sweetheart. It was indeed kind of her to let me crash at her place. All I wanted to do was rest after that encounter with Trish and Ananya. Nidhi suggesting that I spend the night there came as a blessing. I didn't want to worry about getting home after all that had happened. And, boy, is her coffee great!

I take a cab from her place to mine; I get one easily now that it is daytime. On the way back I text her. *'Hey, thanks for the coffee and the bed. It was so nice. You should go into the hospitality business, you sure know how to make your guests feel like a million dollars,'* I type.

Pat comes the reply: *'Not ALL guests. Only a few special ones make it past the screening. I have stringent norms.'*

'Glad to know I made the cut! Honoured. I take a bow, mademoiselle,' I reply, to which she sends a smiley.

I text Trish after that. *'Hey, babe—are you doing fine? Hope your hangover isn't too bad? Drink lots of water and eat some fried eggs. It will make you feel better.'*

A couple of minutes later I check and see that Trish hasn't seen the message yet. She is probably fast asleep. We do have to go to work today, and she is rarely late, so I presume she will see it soon.

I get her reply as I am entering my home.

'God, Ani—I feel like shit. And I don't have anything to wear to work. I don't know what to do. Was it too bad last night?'

Bad? Bad doesn't even begin to describe it. She does not even remember. I don't know what to tell her.

So I call her.

'Hey, baby,' she answers in her sultry, I-am-still-in-bed drawl. I find her voice bewitchingly sexy.

'Hey yourself, drunk panda,' I say tenderly.

'I am not a panda,' she protests sleepily.

'You so are,' I smile.

'You mean I am fat?'

'Ha! You and fat? You are lovable and cute and cuddly.'

'Why do you love me so much?'

'Why do you think?'

'How did I get here last night? Why didn't you take me home to your place? That's what we always do, right? Ooooh, wait. You upped and left me alone, Ani. You left me alone with Ananya and boring-bloody-Subbu. You got a phone call from your—ahem—friend. How could you leave me alone?'

She is fully awake now. I can tell from her voice. She is probably sitting up in bed. It's her indignant voice.

'Trish, I followed you home last night. Don't you remember? I wanted to make sure you were fine.'

She is silent for a few seconds.

Then she says, 'Yes. And your friend was with you. I remember now. And what did you do after that? You dropped her home?'

'Yes, I did.'

'And why was it important to you that you drop her home? She has a fiancé, doesn't she?'

'Yes, she does. But I didn't want her to drive back home alone. We were in her car.'

'You were in her car? Why?'

'Because I was in her home when you called me.'

'What were you doing in her home, Ani? I called you because I needed you. I thought I could depend on you.'

'My baby—I came as soon as you called. I chased your cab halfway across town. I wanted to make sure you were safe. What more could I have done?'

'Come on, Ani—you shouldn't have been at her house

in the first place. What the hell? You abandon me and go to her house? Then you drive her car? And wait, you dropped her back after that? Why do I find this story fishy?'

'What do you mean you find this story fishy? It is the truth! I chased after your car and she was with me. Then I went back to her place.'

'Then what happened?'

'What do you mean what happened?'

'You know what I am asking, Ani. What happened after you went back to her place?'

'Nothing! There were no cabs, so I crashed at her apartment. I have only got home now.'

'You spent the night at her apartment?' Her tone is clipped now. Terse. Controlled.

'Trish—yes. I slept in the drawing room. And she slept in the bedroom.'

'What the fuck, Ani? You vanish, leaving me alone to pick her up, and you spend the night at her place? And you expect me to believe there's nothing there?' she explodes.

'There *is* nothing Trish. You have to believe me. I am not hiding anything from you.'

'FUCK OFF, Ani,' she says and hangs up.

What the hell. I call her back. She cuts my call. I call again. She cuts it again.

'Don't be childish, pick up,' I message her.

'FUCK OFF … JUST FUCK OFF,' comes her reply.

How can she be so stupid? How can she be this childish and unreasonable? What a situation.

'Aaaaarggh,' I am so mad, no words come out. I kick my laundry basket in frustration and my leg hits a shirt that was lying half outside. It goes flying and lands on the fan.

I switch on the fan and watch it twirl faster and faster and then it gets thrown off and lands on the floor. It is dirty now.

Trish is being so goddamn stupid. And ridiculously jealous.

I pick up the phone and call Nidhi.

'Hey,' she says.

'Hey, you free? Got five minutes?'

'Sure.'

'Nidhi, you know what. Trish is mad at me. After all that I did last night. I mean, you were right there with me.'

'Why is she mad?'

'Because I spent the night at your place. She thinks there's something between us because I picked you up last night. How absurd is that?'

'Ummm...' she says and trails off.

'What? Aren't you going to say anything? Isn't she being stupid?'

'Ani, I guess jealousy in relationships is not all that uncommon. Love does come with an element of possessiveness, which you have to accept. You do love her, don't you?'

'Undoubtedly.'

'Then why not show it in a way that she gets it?'

'How?'

'Remember her list?'

'How can I forget?'

'Remember the point about surprising her? Why don't you plan a vacation with her? Some kind of a weekend getaway. I am certain she will love that.'

'Currently I am in no mood to plan anything for her. But yeah, I do see your point.'

'Cool down, Ani. Let it go. No woman will like it if her guy spends the night at some other woman's house where they are both alone. It does ruffle feathers. You need to smoothen them out.'

I pause for a moment. 'Yeah, you are right,' I say. Then I remember that she herself has had a fight with her fiancé and I am going on and on about my Trish-troubles.

'Heard from Manoj? Did he apologize?' I ask.

'Yes I did, and he sent me some nice flowers.'

'Oh good. Did you like them?'

'What's the point being nasty and then sending flowers? He didn't drop me back last night. Wasn't he concerned about my safety? If you hadn't come to pick me up, what would I have done?'

'I guess he was angry too.'

'Yes, I guess he was. It is going to take me a while to forgive him though. Sending flowers doesn't cut it for me. This is the second time this has happened now.'

'I can only imagine how upset you must be. What do you think would make you forgive him?'

'Why are you grilling me on this, Ani?'

'I am curious! The guy said sorry. He sent you flowers. I am trying to understand women.'

'I want him to stop putting pressure on me about this whole marriage thing. I guess that's what I am actually mad about.'

I see what Nidhi is saying there. She does have a right to be angry with him.

'Friendships are any day better than these blessed relationships. Why does everything have to be so complex?'

'They are complex for sure. But I guess that's love for you.'

There is something in the way she says it that suggests she is not happy. I cannot yet put a finger to it. Something about this whole thing doesn't quite fit. But I am not able to point out or articulate what it is. And so I decide to let it go.

She tells me to watch my diet and I tell her that I will. Then I hang up and leave for work.

When I reach office, Subbu greets me with an apologetic look and even before I can say anything he throws his hands up in the air and says, 'Run time error, bro. Sorry!'

'No, it's a logic error,' I retort.

'You should have told me that Trish and alcohol do not mix well. How was I to know?'

'Okay, so they got a little more drunk than expected.

Big deal. But then where was the sense in sending two drunk women home alone in a cab? Are you nuts?'

'Ananya seemed fine!'

'Anyway, I followed them to make sure they got home all right. So it's okay.'

'What? You drove all the way?'

'Yes.'

'God, I so don't want to be in a relationship. It sucks,' he says and then heads back to his cubicle.

I smile and shake my head in a you-walk-away-because-the-grapes-are-sour way. Then I go back to my cubicle and start looking for good weekend getaways around Bangalore. In less than ten minutes I have made up my mind. Pondicherry it is! I love the resort that I see. I quickly read the reviews and it more than meets my expectations. It is a quirky eco-resort right on the beach. It consists of forty-five uniquely-designed cottages that are made in different traditional styles, spread over thirty-five acres. Each of the cottages has a different theme. The resort promotes organic food and natural living. It even has an artists-in-residence programme where they host artists from around the world to promote culture and art. I call them up and my reservation is made.

I have chosen a beautiful Chettinad-style cottage. The staff informs me that a special activity is organized for guests every weekend. I ask them what they have planned that weekend, and they tell me that there is a glass-blower and an interactive session with a well-known astrologer.

They say that there are no extra charges for it, but if I am interested, I will have to register in advance so they can take care of the seating, snacks and other things. I tell them straight away that we are definitely interested.

Then I text Trish, asking her if she has reached office yet, and whether she can meet me for coffee at eleven-thirty or so when she takes her coffee break.

'What is this? Your idea of an apology?' she texts back.

'Is that a yes or a no?' I type. Then I add a heart and a kiss and I hit send.

'K,' she says.

My grumpy Trish. I know she is still mad at me. But this Pondicherry surprise is going to change that. She is going to be delighted. I know her well. I want to see her face light up when I tell her.

She meets me at the office canteen at eleven-thirty. She is dressed in a pale cream silk blouse, black fitted trousers and black heels. Each time I see her, I can't help thinking how gorgeous she is.

'Trish, you look stunning babe,' I say as we both sit down.

'I went home and changed, and came in a little late,' she says.

'I have a surprise for you,' I tell her.

'What?' she asks.

'If I tell you then it won't be a surprise any more, will it?'

'At least give me a hint,' she says, and there is a spark

in her eyes. Trish is like a little child when it comes to these things.

'A vacation! A weekend getaway. Just us.'

'No!!'

'Yes!'

'Where?'

'It involves a beach! So get ready, pack your beach wear.'

'Nice, Ani! Not bad at all. I didn't expect that big a surprise.' She is smiling now. What a killer smile she has.

I am happy to see that she is pleased. Nidhi was right. This vacation was a fabulous idea. Then I remember that I have signed up for the pottery class. Hell! I would be missing that. But I decide it is best not to bring that up with Trish. She is happy now and I don't want to say anything that might upset her. We have our coffee and she chats about her work and how she is getting to make a product pitch to an important client.

When I go back to my cubicle, I text Nidhi, telling her that her vacation idea was a great one.

'I know. Which is why I suggested it. I am not only your fitness coach remember? I'm your relationship coach too. Maybe you should pay me,' she texts.

'Wasn't picking you up in the middle of the night when you were stuck enough payment?' I text back.

'Touché,' she types, and then there is another text from her saying that she will schedule a pottery class for me to make up for the one I am missing.

I smile, humming a jingle I heard on the radio while driving to work, causing Subbu to peer over his cubicle and comment, 'Somebody is very happy this morning. What's the good news? Boss praised you?'

'Even better. I am going on a vacation with the super boss.'

'What?! Are you going on a vacation with Amit?' He makes a gagging action and I smile.

'Trish and I are heading to Pondicherry this weekend.'

'Oh nice! Can I tag along? We can even invite Ananya if you like,' he says, and we both laugh.

It's all in the planets—your daily forecast: Darshita Sen

Sagittarius (November 22 to December 21)

*… Sound advice is handed to you on a platter.
There are bitter truths you will have to face and they are
bound to cause unpleasantness. Accept things the way
they are or risk losing inner peace and harmony.*

18

NIDHI

Manoj calls me as soon as he gets my text. Maybe he senses the very matter-of-fact tone in it.

'Hey, I am sorry, okay? I genuinely am. What do you want me to do? Grovel more?'

I don't know what to say to that. There is anger even in his apology. But if I point that out, this is going to end up in a fight again.

'It's okay,' I say, though I know that we haven't quite settled this yet. I am merely pushing it under the carpet for now. I want to ask him why he didn't follow me. I am waiting for him to ask me how I got home at night. But he doesn't.

I tell him about Tara and Dad's visit and that they have invited me for dinner. I tell him that he can come along too. He asks me to give him a minute while he checks his schedule for the week. Then he comes back on the line and says, 'I am so sorry, baby, I would have loved to come but I have this important call at nine at night. It's with my boss in the US, the one I will be reporting to. This is one call that I can't get out of. I hope you have fun,' he says.

'No problem. I always have fun when they are around,' I say.

Manoj then says he wants to meet me for dinner. He says we won't go to a Thai place this time and I can pick the restaurant. But I have tonnes of work to do. I have to write and create an entire brochure for a real estate developer. I also have two other pieces to write. So I tell Manoj that I will not be able to make it. He says, 'Okay, how about tomorrow then?'

'Manoj, I will be eating out when my dad and Tara come. I do want to watch my diet.'

'So order something healthy.'

'No matter how "healthy" you order, you still end up eating more in a restaurant. Look, let's meet next weekend.'

'I know you are still mad at me, Nidhi. Please … I did apologize.'

Manoj is right. He has picked up on my reluctance to

meet straight away. I *am* still mad at him. I don't want to meet him so soon after the fight. I need some time.

'Manoj, let's leave it and meet on the weekend, okay?' I tell him.

He finally understands and asks me to have a good day and hangs up.

I need to clear my head now. So I turn to my blog.

A Pot of Clay That Holds Gold

Like I promised, I am back again with a new post and there's not too much of a gap between the last one and this. I have been busy with my content writing. I have also been pondering about relationships, especially about how a couple handles conflict. I mean, it's bound to happen. If you have been together for a while, at some point one of you is likely to want something different from what the other does.

How then do you compromise? How much are you willing to put the interests of the other person before your own?

These are questions to which there are no easy answers. It is up to each couple to decide how much they are willing to give up that which they most want in order to please the other.

Also, I have been thinking about fights and making up after a fight. Each couple definitely would have a ritual of making up. One of them is almost always the first one to apologize. But will an apology count if that very action which you apologized for is repeated again? Doesn't it mean that the person disrespects you?

Leave me your thoughts. I would love to know.

One of the things I love about blogging is the comments that I receive and the discussions that follow. I have a dedicated set of readers who diligently go through and comment on things that I write. I get so many different perspectives. But never have I waited as eagerly for someone to comment as I have today. I work on the content of my real estate brochure but keep checking to see if anyone has left their thoughts on what I posted.

When I check for the third time, there are two comments.

One of them says that an apology should be accepted for what it is. If the other person has apologized and is genuinely sorry, then you should bin it as the past and move on. The other comment is by 'Starry Nights', which makes me smile. Tara is a darling to read all I write and then respond. She says that if the action is repeated then it negates the apology. I tend to agree with that. There are no more comments by the end of the day.

On Sunday night, Tara calls me.

'Hey, sunshine! We are in your city! Your dad and I just checked in. So we will see you tomorrow right?'

'Yes Tara. I have kept myself free. And hey I loved your comment on my last post,' I say.

Then I ask her what she would be doing the whole day tomorrow. I am hoping that she and I can spend some time together. But she is busy as her presence is required at Dad's business meeting.

I haven't heard from Aniket after his Pondicherry

weekend. I want to know how it went, and how his diet is going but I don't want to intrude if he is with Trish. So I let it be and decide to wait for his text. He is probably driving back today, unless he has taken Monday off as well and they have extended their stay at the resort.

I find myself eagerly waiting for the dinner with Dad and Tara. I drive to the Oberoi and Dad and Tara meet me at the lobby.

'Hi, baby,' says my dad as he gives me a hug. Dad looks so dashing in his suit and tie. Tara is wearing a shimmery ankle-length designer dress. In comparison I am dressed extremely casually in jeans and a Fabindia top.

'Dad! You should have told me to dress up!' I exclaim.

'Aaah—we closed a great deal and we met for a quick celebratory drink. It got over a few minutes ago and that is why we're still in these clothes. Don't even bother about it,' says Tara.

'So where do you want to eat? We can go to the hotel's Thai restaurant. Or they have a Mediterranean and north Indian one. And then there's Chinese. Pick,' says my dad.

'Dad, anything but Thai! I am sick and tired of Thai,' I say.

Tara gives me a questioning look and I tell her that I have been having too much Thai of late. So we go to the multi-cuisine restaurant.

Dad orders a bottle of champagne, his favourite Krug. I ask Tara and Dad how their drive to Bangalore was.

'Oh, with Mani around, it is a breeze. There was a lot of traffic after Hosur, though,' says Dad.

The champagne arrives and Dad raises his glass. 'To happiness and inner peace, may we all find it,' he says.

'Dad, have you been watching *Kung Fu Panda* again?' I smile, and he smiles too.

The time when he sent me a clip from that movie and asked me to watch it is a special memory for both of us. Later we had talked about various paths to inner peace, whether it can be found through pain and suffering, or whether there was a better way.

'So what's the latest between you and Manoj? Got any clarity yet?' asks Dad.

'No, Dad, not really. I'm still not sure,' I say.

Dad nods and takes a sip of the champagne. 'Good stuff,' he says appreciatively.

I tell them that I won't drink too much as I am driving back.

'It's okay, we can ask Mani to drop you back. And we will organize for your car to be delivered back. I'll get someone to drive your car home,' says Dad.

He is such a sweetheart. 'Thanks, Dad. That would be awesome,' I say, and then I take a large sip of my champagne as well. He was right. This stuff is good.

We talk about Dad's business and how this deal that he has closed catapults the company to the next level. Dad asks me whether I would consider joining his business and take over as a business head. They will soon be starting a new division in Bangalore, and Dad says I can handle all of it.

'Dad, it is because I was fed up of the corporate life that I decided to give up my job and do what I am doing currently,' I point out.

'I thought it was a sabbatical you are taking. You have an MBA after all, from a premier institute,' Dad says. I can see that he is keen for me join the business. But I don't want to. I can't imagine myself dealing with crane automation and inventory management, which is what Dad's company does.

Tara gets my reluctance.

'Your dad wants someone reliable in charge, Nidhi. Which is why he was suggesting the option. You do have relevant business experience too. But, hey, if you don't want to, we completely understand,' says Tara.

'Yes. It was only a suggestion,' agrees Dad.

I do not want to refuse outright, so I tell them that I will think about it. I change the topic now and tell them how much I am enjoying teaching the new batch. I tell them how I have a new friend and how I am now coaching him to lose weight. Tara asks me what he is like, and I find myself going into a long description of Ani.

Tara nods and smiles in a knowing way.

'What?' I ask. 'Aniket is only a friend, Tara,' I say.

'I know, I know,' she says and smiles again. Then she adds, 'It is evident how much you love his company. You know what, you aren't this animated when you talk about Manoj.'

'It's just that he takes a lot more interest in my

work than Manoj does and he has even joined my pottery class.'

'Hmm...' says Tara. Then she says that it is important to have good friends. 'Friendship is one of life's greatest gifts, Nidhi, and we get to choose whom we are friends with. A friend is a gift you give yourself,' she says, and I nod.

Dad has finished his first glass of champagne now and is halfway through his second. He looks at me tenderly. I know that look. 'Nidhi, you look so much like your mother. You are a spitting image of her.'

I know then that Dad is buzzed. He always talks about my mother when he is.

'She was a good woman, your mother,' he says.

I have heard this a few times before. I try to gently steer the conversation to some other topic, but Dad goes on.

'Thing is, Nidhi, you live only once. And we all deserve happiness. Most of the time we are so afraid to break out of that rut, the routines, the sameness which we are used to. I did that with your mother. For seventeen years I led a mediocre life. I "adjusted" and "compromised" and I thought I was happy.'

'Dad, enough,' I say.

'No, it is not enough, Nidhi. You have to listen. Do you remember all those vacations we took when you were a child? I hated each and every one of them. I don't think your mother was happy either. But we were too polite to voice what we wanted. I wish she had once told me what she badly wanted. Anytime I asked her opinion on something, her reply was always, "Whatever makes you happy". Thing is, Nidhi, you have to *know* what makes you happy. Then you have to pursue it. I never did it with your mom. Do you remember the house we used to live in?'

I nod.

'It never felt like that house was mine. It was as though it was without a soul. It was like I didn't care much about it. In contrast, the one I have built with Tara—that one I look forward to coming home to. It is heaven, bliss. I feel at peace. And I am not even talking about the decor or comforts here.'

I totally get what he is saying. And I know what he is saying is true. I feel sad. There is no point talking about the past and when he talks about my mom like this, he is destroying that picture of the ideal happy family that I had built in my head. I do remember those vacations and I thought we were all quite happy. But obviously Dad was not. And the thing is, he feels so earnestly about all of this that I have no choice but to listen to him.

'Don't marry this Manoj chap. He has to make your heart sing. Does he do that, Nidhi?' asks my dad.

I think about my last exchange with him. I think about the flowers he sent. I think about how little he actually knows about my work. He hasn't even seen my pottery studio.

'I don't think so, Dad. I think at one point we *were* very

much in love. At that time we were happy. But somehow things changed. Now, there seems to be some kind of a distance. He definitely does not make my heart sing any more,' I answer.

'A good life partner should encourage you to be the best version of yourself. If you cannot find that rapport with each other, it isn't worth getting married. You will be ruining not only your life, but his too.'

I see Tara nodding in earnest. 'I completely agree. Marriage is pointless otherwise. And fortunately your dad and I are fine with you being unmarried at thirty-two rather than jumping in and marrying the wrong guy. Have you thought about having children?' she asks.

'I have thought about it, Tara. I do want kids, but not right away. Maybe in a couple of years. And only with the right guy. Otherwise, I have considered adoption. I have to be certain of my life first, before I take on the responsibility of another life,' I answer her honestly, and she understands.

Later that night, Mani drives me home in Dad's and Tara's car. I think about how fortunate they are to have found each other. I think about how much difference true love can make in your life. I think about what a burden a relationship becomes when love starts waning.

As I enter my home, there is a message from Manoj. He has forgotten that I am meeting my dad and Tara for dinner. Or he remembers but can't be bothered to ask about it. Instead it is a long, detailed message about his discussion with his boss and how well it went. I decide to reply the next day. I don't have the inclination to do so right now.

And it is only when I brush my teeth, change into my night clothes and get into bed that it strikes me that there is no message from Aniket at all. Which is puzzling. I wonder what is happening.

'How was your weekend? Did you have fun?' I type and hit send.

When there is no reply from him even after fifteen minutes, I finally curl up under my duvet and escape into the land of blissful sleep.

It's all in the planets—your daily forecast: Darshita Sen

Leo (July 23 to August 22)

A paradigm shift is about to occur, so slightly, that you will not even be aware of it. The new moon brings unexpected developments. Things have been brewing under the surface for a while. Now is the time to take a call. Choose your options wisely.

19

ANIKET

Trish tells her parents that she has a weekend shoot in Pondicherry. I pick her up outside her home at five-thirty in the morning. I want to leave early to beat the heat and traffic.

'You will click lots of pictures of me, won't you? So, technically, it *is* a shoot. Only a shoot of a different kind,' she smiles as she gives me a quick hug and I load her bag into the boot of the car.

'Anything for you, my lady,' I say.

She gets into the car and, as we zoom off, I feel like I am the luckiest guy on Planet Earth, to have this gorgeous girl by my side. I am certain that Trish will love the place.

I play a Tamil song with a racy beat, which is a popular road-song, and Trish scrunches up her face.

'What is that you are playing?' she asks.

I am too happy to care.

'It's a nice song! I had a Tamil roomie in hostel who used to play this. I love this song,' I say, and she makes a 'whatever' face.

As soon as the song gets over, she asks if she can play something and she chooses Major Lazer's *Powerful*. I like that song too and so I sit back, focus on the road and enjoy the music.

Trish falls asleep after a while and I keep stealing glances at her like a lovelorn teen. Her chiselled features, high cheekbones, flawless complexion—all of it makes her look like a porcelain doll. No matter how many times I steal glances at her, I don't tire of it.

We stop once for tea on the way. Trish doesn't get down from the car. I fetch her a cup of tea which she sips and then says that she can't drink the stuff as it's too thick and too sugary. I end up finishing her tea as well as mine.

'Won't you at least get down? Don't you want to stretch your legs a bit?' I ask.

Trish takes in her surroundings. It is a tiny shop by the highway that we have stopped off at. The person manning it is probably the farmer who owns the land behind. Vehicles zoom past on the highway.

'Nah—I am fine,' she says.

Just then a stray dog walks up to our car and starts wagging its tail. In an instant Trish is out of the car and she starts to pet it.

'Trish, aren't you scared? What if it bites you?'

She laughs and shakes her head.

She is so unafraid. I am terrified of strays. But I know how fond she is of dogs. She's even volunteered with an animal shelter. It's one of the things I love about her.

Trish once again dozes off the moment the car hits the road. We reach the resort in about six hours. The feel is very rustic. The person at the reception explains the concept. He says there are no air-conditioners, no phones and no TVs in the room. He says there is a private beach which we are free to use. Trish's eyes light up at that. Then he tells us that each of the cottages come with two bicycles which we can use to get around the resort. He says there is a painting class today by an artist-in-residence and we can join in if we want to. Each day we will get a schedule sheet in our room, outlining the day's activities. Then he hands over something that looks like a pager and tells us to press a button in case there is anything we need; it will connect us to the Reception. However there is no room service as the property is too vast. Also, he says, they like to encourage guests to come to the restaurant.

They then drive us in a battery-operated buggy

to our cottage. I fall in love with it instantly. It's got a high ceiling, carved pillars and a beautiful, wide sit-out outside the main door. The pillars are made out of teak wood with intricate carvings on the top and they have a smooth, polished finish. The guy who has driven us here points out the Athankudi tiles. Even though there is no air-conditioner, the interiors are very cool. There is a tall four-poster bed, and we have to use a little step to climb on to it—it is that high.

'So will you be joining us for the painting class today?' asks the guy and I tell him we will let him know as we haven't decided yet. I hand over a tip and he thanks us and vanishes.

'How did you find this place, Ani?' asks Trish.

'Research, baby. I am glad you like it,' I say.

'Well—not sure if I *like* it. It's … different.'

'Come on, Trish. It is better than your usual five-star properties, isn't it?'

'I still like the comfort of television and room service and a little luxury. This is a bit too rustic for my liking. There is not even a tea and coffee maker,' she scrunches her nose.

Can't she pretend even a little? Can't she see the effort I have made here?

I try to hug her but she pushes me away. 'I am tired, Ani, let me shower and freshen up a bit,' she says.

'Tired? I should be the one who is tired. I have been doing all the driving. You were asleep most of the journey.'

'Awww, I know. You have been a sweetheart. I'm sorry I am not appreciating all this a little more. I'm in a grumpy mood. It's just … well … not quite what I expected.'

Damn. And I had thought this would be a great idea. The holiday has already started on a not-so-nice note.

Once Trish showers, we walk on the beach and that puts her in a better mood. There are a lot of stray dogs around.

There is a shack on the beach that sells eggs, bread, fried fish and hot beverages. I ask Trish if she wants coffee or tea. She doesn't, but she buys some buns from the shack and she feeds them to the dogs. All of them surround her now. I click so many photos, but Trish is oblivious to me and the camera. She speaks to the dogs in a low voice, and that seems to calm them.

When we get back to the room I switch on some slow music.

'Come here, gorgeous,' I say, and this time she kisses me right back on my mouth. I grab her ass and pull her towards me and we climb onto the bed and we end up having half-clothed sex. God, I love kissing Trish. She lets me slide my hands under her shirt and I go mad with desire when I hold her breasts. She unbuttons her shorts and slips them off. I take off my shorts and my boxers. I am already hard and she is so ready.

'Forget the foreplay, Ani, fuck me,' she whispers.

It is music to my ears and I oblige.

We both collapse with the effort after that and she starts to laugh.

'What?' I ask.

'You can't wait, can you?' she smiles.

'No, with you, I can't. You are so irresistible, Trish,' I say as I cuddle her. It feels so good to hug her.

After a while we get dressed and decide to have a look at the painting class, which is in the area next to the restaurant. We cycle to the place and go inside. It is a large hall with red tiles and done up in the same rustic way. It reminds me of Nidhi's pottery studio, but I decide not to say that to Trish.

There are about eight guests there already. The artist-in-residence is a German guy by the name of Hans Kirchner. There are many paintings by him on display, most of which are abstracts.

'Eet does NOT matter how you paint, what eees most important eees the expression,' he says as he gesticulates with his hands to emphasize his point.

Most of the guests look eager to start, and they have their own canvases and paints. There is only one lady who isn't taking part. Her hair is more grey than black. She is wearing a white cotton saree and a large pendant. I notice she has rings on almost all her fingers. She keeps looking at me. After a while, it begins to make me uncomfortable.

'Let's get out of here,' I whisper to Trish and guide her by the arm towards the exit. I turn around and see that the woman is following me. I walk faster and Trish gives me a look as though to ask what the matter is.

We are outside the building now.

'Excuse me,' I hear a voice behind us. Trish and I turn to look, and it is the same lady hurrying towards us.

God. What does she want?

'Aniket? Are you Aniket from Bangalore?' she asks.

Good lord. Who is she? How does she know me?

'Yes ... but ... sorry, I don't recall meeting you,' I blurt out.

'Ha! I knew it! I have a distinct memory for faces. I have seen your picture. Priyanka? Do you remember? I am Darshita Sen. Her husband's aunt. Well, soon-to-be husband. The wedding is next month. You promised a strip-show in exchange for a reading. Ha ha ha,' she guffaws.

I am shocked. Trish is looking at me in disbelief.

Oh my good lord. What a crazy thing to happen. Whoever would have thought that I would run into her of all people, here. And then for her to actually recall my face. I am so embarrassed, I want the earth to swallow me right there.

'Err ... well, you know, I didn't mean it,' I say.

'I guessed that. But you wanted a reading, didn't you? Priyanka told me about it. She showed us your photo. Shomo, she and I laughed over your offer.'

'It was completely in jest,' I quickly try to redeem myself.

Trish looks at me for an explanation. I give her a look to tell her that I will explain it later.

'So what brings you to Pondicherry of all places?' I ask.

'I have a talk here tomorrow. Actually, I was visiting Chennai for Priyanka and Shomo's engagement. Whenever I come to Chennai I always visit the Aurobindo Ashram. I am a huge devotee of the Mother. Priyanka told me about this resort. She was raving about it, so I thought I'd try it. They are taking care of my stay here, in exchange for my talk on astrology. So far, I've really enjoyed myself.'

'That is nice. I must say, ma'am, that I am most impressed by your memory for faces and that you remembered my name too.'

'Well, I do face readings as well, in addition to astrology. I never forget names or faces.'

'Wow! Face readings? Is it, like, legit? I mean, can you actually tell a person's character based on their faces?' asks Trish.

'Like an open book. It is a science and it takes years of training. I trained under a teacher in Rishikesh for many years.'

'That's very interesting, I would love to know more,' says Trish.

Darshita Sen looks at her closely. And she doesn't say a word. She looks straight into Trish's eyes. Stares. Suddenly it is as though she is transformed into a different person. Her demeanour has changed. Trish can sense it too. I can also see that Trish is beginning to get unnerved now. Darshita Sen is beginning to give me the creeps too.

'What is your date of birth?' she asks Trish suddenly.

Trish tells her the date.

'Time?' she asks, still not taking her eyes away from Trish's face.

Trish is flustered now.

'Eight-thirty in the morning,' she says.

Darshita closes her eyes. Then she tells me, 'Can I talk to you for a moment?'

'Sure,' I say.

'I mean, I just want to have a word in private with you.'

I look at Trish. I don't know what to do. I can see that Trish is completely shaken by this lady.

Darshita doesn't wait for my response. She pulls me aside and says, 'Get out of this relationship. It is not good for you. It will only end in disaster. End it with her.' And then before I can ask anything, she walks away.

I walk back to where Trish is waiting.

'Goodness, that was strange. That woman is mad,' I murmur.

'What did she say, Ani?' asks Trish.

'Forget it, Trish. Just a bunch of nonsense. She is creepy,' I say.

'Tell me. Please,' insists Trish.

I can't bring myself to tell her the truth, so I tell her that the woman said I will soon go abroad. I add that this is what all these astrologers tell everyone who consults them, and it is all rubbish.

'So why did she want to say that to you in private?' asks Trish.

'I don't know, babe. She was ... weird,' I say. I hope Trish can't see that I am shaken.

Trish and I walk on the beach, and keep walking until we come to the same shack we had visited earlier. We end up having bread and egg-porimas, which is what they call scrambled eggs in this part of the country. I tell her all about my meeting with Priyanka—how my parents had forced me to meet her and what had happened. Trish nods every now and then.

This Darshita Sen seems to have cast a shadow on our evening and both of us are somewhat subdued. I try to joke about it but Trish doesn't laugh.

Even though our booking is till Sunday evening, we decide to leave in the morning itself.

Neither of us want to cross her path again.

It's all in the planets—your daily forecast: Darshita Sen

Sagittarius (November 22 to December 21)

There is a huge change that is happening as Mercury is in retrograde. Mercury rules communication and so there is room for misunderstanding. On the personal front there are some dark clouds that need to be cleared....

20

NIDHI

By the time I wake up, it is already eight-thirty. I sit up with a start. I never sleep this late usually. It must have been the champagne—it's something I rarely drink and therefore am not used to.

I check my phone and there is a message from Tara saying that they are halfway to Chennai and would be reaching soon. She hopes I have slept well, and says she will call me later in the day.

I feel a little sick. Queasy. My throat is parched and

there is a dull ache in my head. This blasted hangover is killing me. I fix myself breakfast. They say the best cure for a hangover is scrambled eggs, juice and plenty of fluids. Most advice includes avoiding caffeine, but I desperately need it today.

I feel like I have been run over by a truck or something. It takes all my willpower to drag myself to my computer. Two of my writing assignments are due today and, hangover or not, I cannot miss a deadline.

I am puzzled that there has been no call or message from Aniket. What has happened to him? Has Trish banned him from talking to me? For a minute I wonder if he is cutting off from me. I would have thought that he would at least explain if he was making that decision. I don't think he is. But this silence from his end is puzzling. I check his last-seen-at status and it is Sunday evening. Could he still be in Pondicherry? I debate whether to send him another message or not and then decide against it. I figure that he will get in touch when he wants to. I am surprised that I actually care whether or not he messages. I have a kind of connection with him now, and I feel responsible for his diet and to get him back into shape.

After I finish my breakfast, I fix myself a cup of strong filter coffee and I get the newspapers in. I love this ritual of reading my morning papers with my coffee. One of the things I hope to do is write for a newspaper. But I want to build a good portfolio of my writing online, so that when I approach them, I have a body of work to show.

Once I finish reading the newspapers, I check out news sites on my laptop, including one that has all the local city news. As soon as I open the site, a headline flashes. Big, fat letters which run across the screen. You can't miss it. I read it once and then read it again in sheer disbelief. With each word I read, my heart plummets further.

This cannot be. Yet it is.

How is this even possible?

I freeze.

It's all in the planets—your daily forecast: Darshita Sen

Leo (July 23 to August 22)

*Unexpected events throw you completely off track. There are many planets in retrograde and communication does not go as expected. It is not a good time to start anything new.
Hold back, lie low and gather your strength. Those in relationships will find more downs than ups in this period.
Be patient, this phase will pass.*

21

ANIKET

By the time we get back to Bangalore, Trish is in a completely low mood.

I drop her home and she gets out, barely even saying bye to me. Hell. I feel terrible about this trip now.

On Monday, Trish comes to work as usual. But we don't meet. I don't even see her.

'Coffee?' I text her.

'*Not in the mood, Ani. Focusing on my work at the moment,*' she types back.

I hate that she is upset. I wish I could do something to cheer her up. I ask her if she wants to go out that evening. Perhaps she will like that.

'*Can't. I am meeting Vishwa and friends. He is throwing a party to celebrate the Leh shoot,*' she types back.

One part of me wants her to have a good time with her friends. The other part is jealous that I am not invited to these bashes. I am sure Trish could take me along if she wanted. But she has never asked me and I haven't brought it up either. I know I will not fit into her modelling-world crowd. They are all very different from me.

I want to tell Nidhi what happened in Pondicherry, but I am so caught up in back-to-back meetings that I don't get a chance to call her. Explaining my bizarre experience with Darshita Sen definitely warrants a call. I won't be able to explain it in an instant message. I decide that I will call her tomorrow. Also, my diet has been going for a toss, and I don't have anything to report to her. I will resume my diet and my usual cycling routine the next day, I decide. And so I don't text her at all.

I open my phone and look at Trish's display picture. She has used one of her modelling shots and she is breathtakingly stunning. Why am I acting like an over-possessive, jealous boyfriend? She herself has told me many times that she hates it. Point number three on her list was to stop bothering her when she goes out without me. I guess after the encounter with that horrible woman, Trish needs her space and wants to forget all about it. I have to back off here. Allow her to be. Let her come back to me after she has had her fun.

'Have fun, babe. Don't drink too much and if you want me to pick you up, call me,' I say.

'Don't worry. Ananya and I will get back together. She said she will drop me back,' she replies.

I roll my eyes. It's not as though Ananya can hold her alcohol herself. Ananya is not getting any award for the most responsible drinking partner. I wish Trish would at least message me from these parties to let me know she is fine.

That night I lie awake in bed and I keep checking my phone to see if there are any messages from her. There are none. Even though deep down I know I am in for a disappointment, I can't resist checking. She never calls or messages me during any of these bashes. It is almost as though she switches off from me mentally. I can now hope to hear from her only the next day.

My darling Trish. If a party makes her happy, even if it is without me, so be it. I love her far too much to pick a fight with her about this. I only hope she doesn't stay up too late—I know she has a client presentation the next day. Finally, I am unable to resist messaging her. I pick up my phone and text her, reminding her about the client meeting.

But till I go to sleep, she hasn't even seen that message. She must be busy partying with her friends.

I sigh, read a book and then curl up in bed.

The persistent ring of the telephone wakes me up. I am in deep sleep and it takes me a few minutes to figure out that my phone is ringing. By the time I reach for my phone, which is on the bedside table, it stops ringing. It is an unknown number. I look at the time and it is four-thirty. What the hell?! Who is calling me at four-thirty in the morning? I am debating what to do when there is a second call from the same number.

'Hello?' I say.

'Aniket? Aniket Prabhu?' says a male voice.

'Yes,' I answer, trying to decipher who it is.

'Calling from Jayanagar Police Station. Do you know Trisha? Trisha Barot?'

I sit bolt upright. Oh no. My Trish is in trouble. I shouldn't have let her go to the party by herself last night.

'Yes, she is my friend. What happened?' I ask.

Nothing in the world prepares me for the words I hear next.

'There has been an accident. She is no more,' he says.

It's all in the planets—your daily forecast: Darshita Sen

Sagittarius (November 22 to December 21)

*… There is high drama, tension, stress and possibly bad news.
Lie low. Do not blurt out the first thing that comes
to your mind. Be tactful.…*

22

NIDHI

I read each word with a racing heart. Oh my god. I can't believe this. This is surreal. Unbelievable. This cannot be happening.

> **City model falls to death from tenth-floor flat**
> A young, upcoming city-based model, who is also an employee of Connect Technologies, fell to her death from the balcony of a tenth-floor flat in Jayanagar here in the early hours of Tuesday morning.

Trisha Barot, twenty-four, was allegedly under the influence of alcohol when she climbed over the railings of one of the two balconies in the flat. According to an eyewitness at the party, she was trying to cross from one balcony to the other. The two balconies are separated by a distance of three feet and have an interconnecting parapet. Barot climbed over the railing to get onto the parapet, but lost her balance and fell to her death, the eyewitness said. She died instantly.

Barot was at the apartment allegedly for a party and everyone present at the time of the death is being questioned. The police are also investigating whether it could have been a suicide and are questioning friends and family. Her phone records are being examined for any clues.

Trisha was an only child, and is survived by her parents. The post-mortem is being conducted at Vinaya Hospital. The funeral is expected to take place today.

For a moment I wonder if this is some other Trisha, but I dismiss it instantly. There is no mistaking that it is indeed Ani's Trisha. God—what a tragedy. And where was Ani when this happened? All these questions race through my mind.

I pick up the phone and immediately call Ani. He doesn't answer his phone.

Then I switch on the television. None of the national channels have anything about it, but a local channel has their TV van right outside the building where the party took place. The reporter is speaking Kannada, and he is pointing to the house and giving the details that were mentioned online, but with a lot more melodrama.

I want to reach Ani now. I am worried about whether he is okay or not. My brain works desperately. I google Connect Technologies, find the phone numbers, and call the board line. I give them my name and ask for Aniket. They put me on hold and say that they are transferring the call. After a while the receptionist comes back on the line and says he hasn't reported for work.

I have no idea what to do any more. This is shocking. I can't believe this is happening.

I ping Ani on instant messenger, asking him to call me as soon as he sees my message. Then I try his number once more. The phone keeps ringing, but there is no answer from him.

It's all in the planets—your daily forecast: Darshita Sen

Leo (July 23 to August 22)

There is a storm brewing. Play it safe. Losses of some kind are indicated. Old relationships, if in turmoil, will end. Hang in there and make 'this too shall pass' your mantra....

23

ANIKET

It takes me a few seconds to even understand what is being said.

'What?' I ask.

'Sir, Trisha Barot is dead. We have her phone and we are informing you, as yours was the last message. There will be an investigation later on.'

'What? What happened?'

He repeats what he said mechanically, clinically. And this time says it is standard procedure.

My hands are cold and clammy. My heart is racing. Yet

there is a part of me in total control. I am shell-shocked, yet calm. It's like a gale wind has hit me, but I am still miraculously standing. It seems like all of this is a dream.

I quickly wash my face, throw on a pair of jeans and a T-shirt and run towards my car. I am on auto-pilot.

I know where Vishwa's house is. I have picked up Trish from there twice before.

One part of me feels this is all a terrible mistake. When I reach, my Trish will be right there. Another part of me asks me to shut up. It is a surreal feeling. It is like there are two of me. One is dying and lying curled up on bed, willing all this to not be true, and the other is calmly doing everything that has to be done.

I reach the apartment complex and take a deep breath as I park the car outside. This seems too absurd to be real. There is a huge group of people standing there and some are pointing to the balcony and looking up. I walk to the gates of the apartment complex, identify myself and tell the policeman that I got a phone call and I am a friend of Trisha's. He takes me in. He points to a spot and says 'It is where she fell. We have taken the body inside now.'

I look at where he points. My heart almost stops beating at the sight. There is blood. A lot of blood.

That is when I throw up. I walk to the side, where there is some kind of a lawn, and I retch.

'Sir, are you okay?' asks the policeman, and he hands me a bottle of water.

I am unable to speak. I wipe the sweat off my forehead.

And then he takes me to the lobby.

I would know only a day later that I had been digging the nails of my right hand into my left hand when I see the blood I have drawn with my fingernails.

The first thing I see are her parents, standing together, deathly pale. I recognize them from the snaps she has shown me. This is the first time I am seeing them in the flesh. Her mom is leaning against her dad and crying. Her dad looks stoic. I still can't wrap my head around the fact that this is happening.

Then I see her. Correction. She is now a body. I want to throw up again. It seems like she has only half of her head. There are deep gashes on one side of her face, the eye is almost outside. I can tell it is her as the other side of her face is untouched. She is wrapped in a white sheet.

'Oh god,' I say.

'The last message in her phone is from you. We need to take a statement from you,' says the policeman.

I want to hit him.

What statement do you want from me, you fucking moron. She is dead. Her stupid friends could have prevented this. And I wasn't around.

I control myself and say, 'Yes, okay.'

Then I experience a sharp pain that shoots right through my heart and goes to my head. I have broken out into a sweat again. I feel suffocated now. I need air. I need to sit down.

I turn away.

'Are you okay?' asks the policeman again.

If he asks me that one more time, I swear I will fucking kill him.

I walk to the side of the lobby and lean against the security guard's table.

That's when I notice the others there. Vishwa and Ananya.

Vishwa walks up to me and says, 'I am so sorry, man, we tried to stop her. She wouldn't listen,' and he puts his hand on my shoulder.

I want to fucking kill him too.

Ananya walks up to me and takes my hand. I recoil at her touch and jump back.

'What kind of a friend are you, you dumb bitch?' I say, and I don't recognize my own voice. She looks at me in shock. My eyes are blazing now.

I want to scream.

I want to gun them all down.

I want to escape from here.

But mostly I want my Trish back.

But the worst isn't over yet.

They tell me that I will have to be available for the rest of the day as there are formalities to go through. I call Subbu and tell him what has happened. He can't believe it either.

'Oh fuck, no. Bro, I am coming right over,' he says.

I tell him not to. I want to be left alone. All of this is still sinking in.

He asks me if I am sure. And I tell him I am dead certain.

The policemen come to my home afterwards. They ask me all kinds of questions about Trish. They tell me this is standard procedure and that they are speaking to her other friends too. I answer them as patiently as I can. A couple of times I snap.

Do you also want to know how many times we fucked?

I know they are only doing their job, but it takes all my self-control to answer them. I want to be left alone. Then I tell myself that the faster I answer them, the sooner I can make this questioning stop. I tell them details about the Pondicherry trip as they ask me when it was that I last saw her. But I do not tell them about Darshita Sen or her prediction. It would make them think I am completely cuckoo. I myself find it all so strange to come to terms with.

Once the policemen leave, I sit with my head in my hands for a long time. I try and picture my Trish on the balcony. Why didn't those idiots stop her? Why did I listen to her? / Why wasn't I there for her? / Why did I let her go to that party alone? And that stupid Ananya—why in the world did she let my Trish drink? She knew what Trish was like when she got drunk. Why, why, why? The questions come down on me like hailstones. Each question hits me, attacks me, mocks me. Why didn't Trish call me? She had reached out to me the last time she was drunk. She could have done that this time too. Why didn't she? And were there any drugs there? Had Trish taken any? Was she stoned? As far as I knew she had never tried anything. But these morons might have forced her to.

I cry then. A piteous wail emanates. It is a sound I do not recognize. I sob. I weep. I muffle the sound with a pillow as I can't bear to hear myself. I punch the pillow, kick it. And then when I have exhausted the tears, I go and wash my face.

I see a message from Nidhi and a missed call. I wonder if she has heard the news. I am in no mood to call her now.

I want to reach out to Trish's parents. If there is anyone whose grief is as much as mine, it is them. I have her landline number which I had saved but never used. I call now and her father answers. When I tell him who I am, he is silent for a while. Then I can hear him cry. The sound of his sobs tears my heart. I ask him if I can do anything to help and what he asks of me almost kills me.

He asks if I can come to the hospital to collect the body.

I tell him I will be there.

When I reach the hospital, her dad walks up to me and grips my arm. I hug him.

It is strange how death unites people. Had Trish been alive, her dad would have probably been wanting to skin me alive. And yet here we are now, hugging each other like long-lost friends. I am surprised that I am able to think so clearly, calmly and coherently even in this situation. It feels like I am in some movie, playing a role.

Trish's parents have to now read the completed documentation and sign it. The discharge form has all the facts.

It is all so clinical now.

My Trish is now a body with a number.

'Have you read all this? Are the details correct?' asks an attendant.

Trish's dad's eyes have clouded over and he hands the paper to me. He is unable to read it.

I read the documentation.

Each line I read sends a fresh wave of pain searing through my body.

There are the following details, all of which have been filled in meticulously.

Name, sex, age of the deceased person:

Date and time of death:

Identification marks of the deceased:

Details of near relatives:

Name, relationship, address and phone number:

Date and time of autopsy:

Name of the autopsy surgeon:

Date and time when the body is placed in the cold storage:

Length of the body and breadth across the shoulder:

A list of valuables, if any, which have not been removed from the body such as rings, bangles and others:

Signature of the mortuary technician:

Date and time when the body is removed:

Name of the relatives or police collecting the body:

Signature of relative collecting the body:

'Have they given you her gold chain and ring?' I ask her father.

Her mother replies that she has them.

'All the details are correct,' I say as I hand the paper back to the technician.

Then we transport the body to the crematorium in an ambulance. A group of people have already gathered there to pay their last respects. I have never been to a crematorium before. It is a huge hall with white walls and small gaps to let in light and air. Trish's father says that the pandits have already been arranged. I had no idea that there would be ceremonies as well. There are a whole lot of Hindu rituals, and there is chanting.

I spot all her friends there. Then I see Subbu too. I don't know how they know. I don't know who told all these people the details of the cremation.

I have no idea how long I stand there. The air is dry. My head hurts. I am unable to talk. After a while the ceremonies and the chanting ends. They then place Trish's body on some kind of a trolley at the end of which is a long rod. The two men push it towards a tunnel-like thing which has a raging fire burning. The body gets pushed into the tunnel, into the fire. Then it shuts and Trish is gone.

That is all there is to it. My Trish is no more. Never will I see her again. Never will I hold her again. Never will she scrunch up her face and get annoyed with me. The pain that washes over me at that instant is unbearable.

It feels like I am burning in that fire I just saw. I feel helpless. I suppress a scream. I want to tell them to stop that fire.

I want to undo the events of the last twenty-four hours.

I am unable to focus on anything now. The lump in my throat threatens to choke me.

I see that her parents are walking out now, and so is everybody else.

In a daze I walk towards my car.

That is when I spot Nidhi.

It's all in the planets—your daily forecast: Darshita Sen

Leo (July 23 to August 22)

… You may have made careful plans and scheduled everything to perfection, but it all comes crashing down. Things do not go the way you want and that makes this a chaotic day. This is temporary, so flow with it as best you can and don't let the instability bother you.

24

ANIKET

Nidhi looks at me and there are tears in her eyes.

'I am so, so sorry, Ani,' she says and she is openly weeping now. I look away. I can't bear to see her like this. And I have no words to comfort her too.

'How did you come here?' I ask her. As hard as I try to make my voice sound normal, it comes out hoarse.

'I don't know this area at all, so I took a cab,' says Nidhi. Then I see her looking over my shoulder and turn around.

I see that Subbu has walked up to us.

'Nidhi, this is Subbu. Subbu, meet Nidhi,' I say and they both nod at each other.

'Do you want me to drive, bro? I took a cab here and I can drive us all back,' he says.

I consider his offer for a second. But no. I want to drive. Driving will give me something to focus on other than this debilitating pain that seems to be shooting through every cell of my body.

'I am okay. I will drive. Nidhi, do you want me to drop you?' I ask her.

'Why don't you drop me on the way to your place, maybe at Dairy Circle, then I will take a cab from there. So you won't have to drive all the way into Koramangala,' she says.

'Okay,' I say. I don't have any energy left to argue or think.

We drive back in silence from the crematorium in Wilson Garden. Subbu gets into the passenger seat in the front and Nidhi gets in at the back.

The only sound in the car is the GPRS guiding us home.

Finally, it is Nidhi who speaks up.

'So, how did this happen, Ani? Weren't you with her? And hey, if you don't want to talk, it's fine, I understand,' she says.

I don't want to talk. I have faced a police interrogation and a funeral. But I can't be rude to Nidhi. Nidhi has only been sweet and kind to me. I force myself to answer.

'She wanted to attend that blasted party and I wasn't invited. That's how all this happened. If I was there, I would have taken care of her. Bloody senseless idiots her friends are. Fuckers.'

I cannot help the outburst. Or the swearing. The rage is simmering along with the grief.

Nidhi nods. Then she does something totally unexpected. She reaches forward and places her right hand over my left hand, which is gripping the gear.

She squeezes it and looks outside as her eyes fill up.

'I am so, so sorry, Ani,' she says and then wipes her tears and says, 'Sorry, I don't want to cry.'

Strangely, I feel comforted.

Subbu, for once, is speechless. He has no wisecracks in coding lingo, nothing to say.

'So how did you two hear about it and how did you know when and where this cremation was taking place?' I ask them.

'It was all over the Internet, Ani. Who called you? How did you get to know?' asks Nidhi.

'Aaah—no wonder so many people turned up. The police called me about it. Then I went with her parents to collect the bo—we had to get her to the crematorium,' I say. I can't bring myself to refer to my Trish as 'the body'.

When we reach Dairy Circle, Subbu asks me if I will be okay and I tell him I will be fine.

Nidhi thanks me for the lift and says that she will call a cab. She asks Subbu if she can drop him off. His place is on the way to hers, and so they both leave.

The rest of the way home, I can't stop thinking about the day's events. I walk into my flat, and I don't bother to switch on the lights. I sit in my living room in silence and the entire house is quiet. The fridge is humming and I listen to the sound. There are some noises coming from the flat upstairs and then they stop.

I feel dirty and grubby and so I decide to take a shower. I open my wardrobe and her T-shirt is right there. I touch it and then I smell it. That Trish smell. Her distinct perfume. An overpowering sensation of fresh pain assaults me again, knotting my stomach. Only last evening everything was fine. Damn that bloody party. Why did she have to go?

I feel faint and, next thing I know, everything goes blank. When I come to my senses, I am lying face down on the floor in front of my wardrobe. I have no idea how long I'd passed out for. There is a dull ache in my temples. My forehead hurts too. I go to the kitchen and drink some water, and then walk to the bathroom. I look into the mirror. There is a large bump on my forehead. It is swollen. I touch it and it starts hurting again. This has never happened to me before. I have never had blackouts like this one. I wonder what the cause could be.

Then it strikes me.

I haven't eaten a single thing since I woke up this morning. I walk back to the kitchen and open my fridge. There is some dosa batter and a packet of bread. I take out the bread, toast two slices and apply butter. I take a bite and then I can't eat anymore, I want to throw up.

I hurry back to the bathroom with bile rising in my throat and I retch. Nothing comes out except the water I just drank.

I feel like hell.

There are beads of sweat on my forehead now and yet I am shivering. I put on a sweatshirt, curl up in my bed and finally sleep overtakes me.

When I wake up I look at the time on my phone. It is five-twenty in the morning. There are at least twelve unread messages. I can't be bothered to read them now. The events of the previous day come rushing back to me. It feels like someone has slapped me. I want to curl up, go back to sleep and never wake up. I don't want to go to work. Trish is gone and that is the reality I have to face. It leaves me with a sinking feeling. How can the end come so suddenly? How can life be so fragile? She is here one day and the next day there is no trace of her. I go to the balcony of my flat and look down. God—my Trish plummeted from a height even greater than this.

Did it hurt, my baby? Did it pain? Are you in a safe place now, my angel? Why did you leave me?

I keep thinking of Trish and me on the beach at Pondicherry. I remember her smiling. I remember our walk on the beach and her feeding the stray dogs. Her being displeased about not having room service. And then I remember that crazy woman, Darshita Sen. What the fuck was that all about? Why did she tell me to break it off? Did she see this coming? What did she mean by that prediction? I wonder how Trish's parents are coping. I scroll through my phone and look at some of the pictures Trish and I clicked on the beach that day. Trish is smiling and my arms are around her waist in the last photo of her. I want to share this with someone. Someone who will get me. The only people I can think of are her parents. I pick up my phone and dial her residence and then I remember that it is not even six o'clock. It's too early and so I hang up.

Within minutes I get a call back. It is her dad.

'Yes, who is this? We got a missed call from this number,' says her father.

'It is me, Aniket. Trish's friend. I am so sorry, I forgot it was this early,' I say.

'It's fine, *beta*, we are not able to sleep. We keep thinking that she will come back. It feels like she has gone on a trip somewhere,' he says.

I know exactly what he means. One part of me still feels as though she will return.

'I have some pictures of her clicked on a trip to Pondicherry. Do you want them?' I ask him.

He says he would be very grateful to me if I shared them.

That brings a lump to my throat. I am unable to speak. I don't want to start crying again.

'Hello—are you there?' he asks, and I tell him to send me a message on instant messenger so that I can send him the pictures.

As soon as I hang up, I get a message from him and

I share all the pictures from the Pondicherry trip. Every single one. Even the badly-taken ones that she said she hated. I leave out the selfies taken in bed, which I have moved to private mode anyway.

After that I decide to read my messages.

There are so many messages of condolences from folks in the office. I didn't even know they knew that Trish and I were a couple. I thought we had kept it discreet. I send a thank-you text to each one and close the chat. The only messages that I care about are from Subbu and Nidhi.

Subbu says that he has spoken to Amit, who has said that he is fine if I take the rest of the week off. One of Nidhi's messages is from before, asking how my weekend went. The other one asks me if I want to hang out with her.

'No thanks, Nidhi. I will be fine,' I type and hit send. I don't want to hang out with anyone.

I get her reply almost immediately.

'Go out and get some air, Ani. Go cycling?' she types.

'Ummm....' I type and then I switch off my phone, and curl up in bed.

I only want Trish.

And there is nothing in the world anyone can do to bring her back.

It's all in the planets—your daily forecast: Darshita Sen

Sagittarius (November 22 to December 21)

*… A friend needs your help and you deliver beautifully.
But do not forget to care for yourself too. Not a good time for
romance or relationships.*

22

NIDHI

Subbu and I have met under the strangest of circumstances.
Now that we are alone in the cab, I feel obliged to make
some conversation with him.

'So have you been in Bangalore long?' I ask.

'Yeah—I've been here ever since I left college,' he says.

'It's a nice city to live in, isn't it?'

'Totally,' he says.

Both of us become aware of the awkwardness of this
small talk. We are pretending as though this is an ordinary,
everyday conversation. But I do not know what else to
say. He too sits in silence.

'Man, what a tragedy,' he says after a while.

I nod. 'I got such a shock this morning when I read about it,' I say.

'I was with her last week when she got drunk and you messaged him,' he says.

'I know,' I tell him.

And then I cannot think of anything else to say.

We complete the rest of the journey in silence, and we finally reach his home and he gets off.

The next morning, I switch on the TV and the local television channel is still covering the story.

Then Vishwa comes on TV and I freeze when he talks as though he was Trisha's boyfriend. I am puzzled. Then I hear the news-anchor saying how foul play has been ruled out and that it was an accident. She says she is now talking to Trisha's fiancé, Vishwa. What the hell? Why are they saying that? I presume that they have made a mistake. Vishwa is now giving an interview and he talks about how devastated he is. He says he and Trisha were to get married in six months.

What? How is that even possible?

I can't believe what I am hearing. Why would he say something like that?

I don't know what to do. I don't want to call Aniket with this news. Yet I want to talk about this to someone. The only person I can think of is Subbu. But how do I reach him?

I look up Facebook and see Subbu is on Aniket's list

of friends. I add him immediately. Then I wait. While I am waiting, I write a blog post.

A Pot of Clay That Holds Gold

Death is a finality that none of us can escape. Yet, we live pretending it doesn't exist. We act as though we are immortal, when today could well be the last day on earth for any one of us. We wake up in the morning, and we go about our daily business, not knowing what lies in store for us.

In case you are wondering why I'm talking of such a morbid topic, I have just come back from a cremation. I am shocked, deeply disturbed and sad. Those of you in Bangalore must have read the news reports of a model falling to her death. Her good friend happens to be my student. I am terribly upset about this, even though I met her only fleetingly.

If today has gone well for you, and you and your loved ones are safe, do send a prayer of gratitude to the forces above. Cherish the happy memories. Create amazing ones.

Live your life in such a way that if you were to go today, you have no regrets.

Apologies for the morose post, but it had to be said.

Take care and smile.

I re-read the post for any typos and then hit publish. I think about how I met Aniket in Chennai and agreed to help him, on condition that he let me write about his and Trisha's relationship without mentioning names. Yet, I had never written about them. That incident seems so far away now. Things had changed so much after that, and now the idea itself, which seemed like a novel one for blogging at that time, seems so silly.

I check Facebook again and almost leap with joy when I see that Subbu has accepted my request. I quickly message him and tell him to call me and I give him my phone number. I add that it is urgent. He replies asking if he can call in fifteen minutes. I say yes.

I am too distracted to work, and so I switch on the television and watch an episode of *Two and a Half Men* even though it is a re-run. Finally the phone rings and I answer immediately.

'Hi Nidhi, Subbu here,' he says.

'Hey Subbu. I needed to talk to you about something.'

'Yes, tell me,' he says.

'Do you remember that guy Vishwa?'

'Who?'

'That tall guy. He was there at the cremation. Trisha's friend. I think she worked with him or something.'

'Hmmm…' There is a pause at the other end. Then he says, 'What about him?'

'He is giving television interviews claiming that he was to marry Trisha in six months.'

'What? What the hell? Trish and *Ani* were together. Ani was … was so madly in love with her.'

'I know. Which is why I find this disturbing. And he sounded genuine too.'

'This is indeed a little strange. Unless … you know…' Subbu trails off, unable to complete the sentence.

I know exactly what Subbu is thinking. It is the same thought that crossed my mind too.

'Do you think she was two-timing Ani?' I ask Subbu. There, I have said it.

He is silent for a while. And when he finally speaks, his voice is low. 'I think it is entirely possible. I always felt she was using him, but I couldn't bring myself to say it. He was ... you know ... so besotted with her.'

'I wish I hadn't found out,' I say.

'We are merely guessing, right? Why don't we speak to Vishwa?' suggests Subbu.

'And what? He will probably say what he told the TV channels,' I reply.

'Let's hear his version. Do you know how to reach him?' asks Subbu.

'No, I have no idea,' I say.

'Okay, leave it to me. I will get his number,' says Subbu.

He calls me back in an hour.

'Nidhi, I have spoken to him. I said we are Ani's friends and that we both wanted to meet him and it was very important.'

'And he agreed?'

'He was puzzled, but he finally agreed when I said it was related to Trisha.'

'Oh!'

This has come as a surprise to me. I didn't expect Subbu to fix up a meeting with him.

'Can you come to Café Coffee Day on 18th Main in

Jayanagar? That's close to where he lives. He has agreed to meet us there.'

I do a quick calculation in my head. It will take me about twenty-five minutes to get there via Hosur Road. It isn't too bad a drive either.

'Yes, I can come there. When?' I ask him.

'Today. I will leave at about four-thirty—he has asked us to meet him at five-thirty. He said he can meet only for ten minutes so we can't be late. He seemed very reluctant but I told him it was urgent. And when he said he could meet today, it wasn't like I could back out.'

'Yes. I will be there Subbu,' I say.

When I reach the place I spot Subbu getting out of a cab. I roll down my window and yell, 'Subbu!'

He turns around, spots me and waves.

There is ample parking by the side of the road and I easily find a spot.

Then Subbu and I walk inside.

'How did you get Vishwa's number?' I ask Subbu.

'I had this girl Ananya's number. She works with Vishwa. I got it from her. Ananya is Trish's friend.'

'Yes, I remember,' I say.

We spot Vishwa the moment he enters the café. He has a dragon tattoo on one arm and some kind of a goddess on the other. He is clearly into fitness. He has large biceps, flat washboards abs and his hair is slightly long. He sports a bandana and dark glasses. He has stubble and he looks striking in his black sleeveless vest and faded blue jeans.

He looks around and I wave to him. He spots us and walks towards us.

He removes his sunglasses and his eyes are red. The guy is clearly grieving.

'Hi, I am Nidhi, and you have already spoken to Subbu,' I say.

'Hi,' he says, and then, 'So, what was so urgent?' The terseness in his tone is evident.

I decide to be direct.

'Vishwa, I saw your TV interview.'

'And…?'

'Was that right? That you and Trish were to get married in six months?'

'Is that what was urgent? You wanted to meet to ask me if it was right? What are you getting at, man?' he asks.

I don't know how to broach this. Subbu steps in.

'Well, Vishwa, Trish had been to Pondicherry that weekend with Ani. You know that she was seeing him, right?'

'What? No way.'

'Yes. I am Ani's closest friend. I know how much time they spent together.'

'But … but she told me Ani was a friend. Just a friend. Come on. She was in love with me.'

Then he takes out his phone and shows us pictures. There are tonnes of them. There is no mistaking from the photos that they *are* a couple. Were a couple.

I can't believe it. Trisha was indeed two-timing Ani.

When was she planning to break the news of her marriage to Ani?

I look at Subbu and he looks at me.

Vishwa looks at both of us.

'What?' he asks.

I shake my head.

'She was two-timing you. She was seeing Aniket too,' I finally say.

'No fucking way. You are out of your mind. Both of you. Trish would never do that. I mean ... see, you have seen the pics. Maybe ... maybe it was a one-sided crush. Your friend Aniket must have been in love with her. There were so many guys who would die for her, you know? But she loved me; and she meant the world to me. And if this is what you came here to tell me, buzz off, both of you,' he says and he stands up.

'Wait, Vishwa. Please sit down. How come these pictures aren't on Facebook? There isn't a single picture of you and her. I checked your profile and all your photos are public. You should take care of your privacy settings, man,' says Subbu.

'She wanted it that way. She didn't want any pictures of us on social media,' Vishwa says.

'Now you know why. She didn't want you to know about Ani. Or him to know about you,' says Subbu.

I can see that this has got Vishwa's attention. He sits back down slowly.

'And have you met her parents?' I ask.

'No, I haven't. I asked her and she said she would introduce me to them, but she needed time,' he chokes on his words as he says it. I can see he is in pain.

But I feel like I have to speak up for Ani. It's like I want to prove to Vishwa that Ani and she were, in fact, a couple. I don't know why I feel I owe that to Ani. Maybe it is because I was so closely involved and was advising him about their relationship.

'Vishwa, if she indeed was planning to marry you in six months, she would have definitely introduced you to her parents,' I say.

'Look, man, it is all over anyway. How does it matter? I loved her with all my heart,' replies Vishwa. His tone is resigned.

'So did Ani,' says Subbu quietly.

Vishwa stands up and says he has to get going. Both Subbu and I watch as he marches out, gets into his SUV and drives off.

'Wow. So Vishwa wasn't lying,' I say.

'Yeah,' says Subbu, and adds, 'You know, Ani would have died for her.'

'I know, I know. He was so in love with her.'

'So shall we tell him today, or wait a few days?' asks Subbu.

'Tell whom what?'

'Aniket. He has a right to know.'

I haven't even thought of this. I am still stunned by the pictures that Vishwa has shown us.

'I guess he does have a right to know. Let's go to his place and check on him,' I say.

'Has he been replying to you?' asks Subbu. 'I have been pinging him and there are no replies. I can see that he is reading my messages though.'

'He gave me a vague reply when I suggested that he get out for a bit. He wasn't his usual self.'

'I guess he needs some time alone. Let's check on him in a couple of days and we'll tell him then?' Subbu looks at me questioningly.

I nod. I tell him that we will go over day after tomorrow in the evening, as I have a few things to finish up at work.

Subbu says that this sounds good. 'I think he wants to be left alone. Let's give him his space,' he says, and I agree.

Since I don't know where Ani lives, Subbu says that we could meet outside Bangalore Central and then go over together to Ani's place.

'Hopefully he will be in a slightly more approachable frame of mind then,' I say and Subbu nods.

I hate doing this. But as harsh as the truth is, Ani does have a right to know. And as his friends, we owe it to him to tell him.

It's all in the planets—your daily forecast: Darshita Sen

Leo (July 23 to August 22)

*Your health causes grave concern to your friends and loved
ones. Your diet will also be a major cause of worry.
You will have opportunities to progress in your professional life
but your health will not permit you to act on it.
Take adequate rest and do not over-exert.*

26

ANIKET

Trish is right here. She isn't dead. It was all a terrible
mistake, she says. I was playing a joke on you, she says,
smiling serenely now.

'Why did you do that, my baby? I was so worried,' I
ask her, holding her face in my hands.

And she laughs. Then she hugs me. God, this feels
so good.

We both sit on my sofa. She lays me down, puts my
head in her lap and strokes my forehead.

'Please don't do this again, okay? You got me so worried,' I say and she nods and bends down to kiss my forehead.

I drift off to sleep in her lap. This is the best feeling in the world. I knew all this was a mistake. I feel comforted, soothed and happier than I have felt in a long, long time.

I am awakened by the incessant ringing of the phone.

'Open the door, Ani,' says Trish, still stroking my hair.

'Ummm… no, this feels so nice. Let me lie down for a little longer.'

'Please open the door. We have been ringing the bell for a while now,' says a voice and it is not Trish's.

Where did that voice come from?

'Open the door, open the door.' I can hear the echoes now. My head is starting to hurt.

'Go, my baby, open the door,' says Trish.

When I stand up, everything spins around. I manage to stagger to the door. Trish wants me to open the door. I turn the handle and bright light assaults me. I close my eyes and I step back.

The next thing I know, I am lying on the sofa and water is being sprinkled on my face.

When I open my eyes, I see Subbu and Nidhi.

'Where is Trish?' I ask.

They both look at each other strangely.

'Bro, we need to take you to the doctor. You passed out. And you are unwell,' says Subbu.

'I am fine, where did Trish go?' I ask.

'Look, let's go to the doctor, okay, Ani? That bruise on your head looks nasty,' says Nidhi.

What is Nidhi talking about? I feel a little weak but am okay otherwise.

'I am fine, I don't need to see any doctor,' I say.

'Ani—I am going to be brutally honest with you. You seem a mess. When was the last time you showered?' asks Nidhi.

'I don't know why you are asking me all these questions. Let me go back to sleep, I want to talk to Trish,' I say as I curl up on the sofa.

'Bro, let's go and after that you can sleep, okay? Please listen to me this one time,' pleads Subbu.

I look at him.

'Please bro, just stand up okay?' he says and I oblige. He helps me up.

Nidhi gets me some water in a glass and I gulp it down thirstily.

They take me to Holy Angel Hospital. Nidhi is driving. I am in the back seat with Subbu. Why doesn't Subbu sit in the front? Something is amiss. But I am too exhausted to think what it is. My brain doesn't seem capable of functioning any more. I need to sleep. I don't know why they are insisting I see a doctor. But I am too weary to argue. If they let me sleep, I will be fine. I try telling them that, but they don't listen.

The doctor sees us almost immediately. Both Subbu and Nidhi accompany me inside the doctor's cabin.

'He lost his girlfriend a few days back. We found him in this state. He fainted and we had to revive him. I think he is hallucinating,' says Nidhi.

The doctor checks my BP and examines me with a stethoscope.

'When was the last time you ate?' asks the doctor.

I rack my head and try to remember. Then it all comes back. Trish's cremation. Her body being sent down that tunnel. The fire. My Trish. She is dead now. She isn't coming back. Ever. I can't see her again. I try to recall her face, and I panic for a few seconds as my mind blanks out.

I don't even know when I have begun to sob. I know I am crying only when I feel a hand on my back. Nidhi's. She is beside me in a jiffy and she strokes my back.

'It's fine, Ani, it's fine,' she says as my sobs subside.

The doctor addresses Subbu and Nidhi now. 'His blood sugar is very low. He has an electrolyte imbalance and this is causing the hallucinations. He has to be put on IV fluids. Is he throwing up?'

They look at me for answers. I am not able to speak. My mind has blanked out again.

'Have you been throwing up?' asks the doctor.

'Yes,' I say finally. 'That's why I haven't been able to eat.'

'Plus, he has been on a diet, doctor. He has been exercising heavily and was on a strict diet before this happened,' says Nidhi.

'Aaah. That explains it. He has severe acidity as well. There is no option but to admit him and start him off on IV. You can either admit him here itself, or you can take him to any hospital of your choice. But I highly recommend he be admitted as soon as possible. He won't be able to keep food down in his present condition.'

Nidhi and Subbu decide to admit me here, in this hospital itself. Subbu goes to fill up the forms while Nidhi and I wait.

An attendant brings a wheelchair for me.

'Look, I can walk,' I say, but when I try to stand, I slump back. It's like my legs don't have strength any more.

'Sir, it is hospital rules. The patient has to be in a wheelchair,' says the male nurse as he helps me sit down and then wheels me out. I blank out again.

When I recover consciousness, I have an IV fluid needle in my left hand. The room is fairly comfortable: large, with white walls and the typical disinfectant smell that permeates all hospitals. There is a cot for an attendant beside mine, and a table and a chair at the far end. A small television faces my bed.

I see Nidhi and Subbu, and both look very worried.

'Hey guys, I am not going to die, okay?' I try and joke weakly. But neither of them smiles.

'Bro, you might have to be here for a few days. It all depends on how your body responds. They have put you on IV now, and they are running some tests. Give me your parents' number. We will have to inform them,' says Subbu.

'There's no need. I will be fine. I don't want to worry them,' I say.

'Ani, I think your parents definitely need to be told. Look at the state you are in. The doc says it is pretty bad, and we brought you in at the right time. Do you even know that you haven't eaten a single thing ever since she died? You are also severely dehydrated. You have had multiple concussions, and there are so many bruises on your face. God knows how many times you have blacked out. And you're asking us to not to tell your parents? What is wrong with you, Ani?' says Nidhi. Her face is flushed and she is trying hard to keep her voice low.

'Okay, whatever,' I say.

'No whatever, tell me their number. Now,' commands Nidhi, and I meekly tell her my dad's cell phone number.

She dials it.

There is no response.

'What is your mother's cell number?' she asks.

'I don't remember it. It is in my phone. Where is my phone?' I ask.

'We didn't bring it, bro. It must be lying at your place. Speaking of which, is this the key to your front door?' asks Subbu, as he dangles a key chain with my house key on it.

'Yeah, that's the one,' I confirm.

'I grabbed it while we were getting you here. It was lying on the side table in your drawing room. I wasn't sure if this was the key or not. If this hadn't been the key, we would have had to break the lock to get back in,' says Subbu.

I nod. My head is throbbing with pain now. I want some silence.

'Subbu, you go and get him his razor, toothbrush, change of clothes and all that. I will wait with him here. Also get his cell phone. Once you are back, I will go home, and get some of my stuff. I will stay the night, tonight,' says Nidhi. She has completely taken charge of the situation and is issuing orders like a commando.

I half-expect Subbu to stand up and smartly salute her.

'All right. Are you sure you will stay? I could stay too,' he offers.

'I will stay tonight, and maybe you can stay tomorrow?' says Nidhi, and he agrees.

'See you soon, buddy,' he says as he lightly touches my hand, gives it a kind of a squeeze and then walks out.

I wonder if I sleep again whether I will be able to see Trish. I close my eyes and lie back. I see no visions of her. All I can see is her disfigured face, and the blood when I first walked into the apartment. I want to throw up now and I open my eyes and make a gesture to Nidhi. She jumps up and grabs a pan which is kept prominently on the stand near the bathroom and I vomit into it. Some of it is on her arm.

Fuck. What a mess. She doesn't even flinch. She walks to the bathroom and flushes the contents and washes her hands and arm. Then she calls the nurse.

I feel helpless with the IV drip. I am unable to move. My hand has begun to hurt now.

Nidhi brings a tissue from the bathroom and tells me that I need to clean my face.

I ask her to give me the tissue; the IV drip is in my left hand but I can wipe my face with my right. But she does not listen to me, and she proceeds to wipe my face.

'It's not like you can see where it needs to be wiped, and hey, it's fine,' she says. Her voice is tender and full of care and concern.

The nurse arrives then and Nidhi tells her I have thrown up and she points to the pan that I have used.

The nurse proceeds to clean the pan. She asks if I have thrown up on the sheet and whether it needs to be changed.

I haven't.

She then pours me a glass of water and tells me to clean my mouth. I do as instructed.

Once again she brings the pan and I rinse my mouth and spit into it.

I feel like an invalid with this IV drip.

'Sister, when will this IV drip end?' I ask.

'What, tired already? This is the first bottle. Doctor has said to give eight more bottles, and after that they will assess,' she says.

'What! How long will it take for one bottle?' I ask.

'We have to adjust the flow. We cannot make it very fast. It should finish in four to five hours. When it finishes I will change the bottle. If you need anything ring the bell,' she says with a heavy Malayalam accent.

Then she turns to Nidhi. 'Are you the attendant staying with the patient?' she asks.

'Yes, I am,' says Nidhi.

'Wife, eh?' asks the nurse.

'Excuse me?' says Nidhi.

'Are you his wife?' she asks.

'No, not wife, just a friend,' replies Nidhi.

'Oh okay. If he vomits again, call me. I will be on duty till eight o'clock, and then my colleague will be here. We have to make a note of all this,' she says.

'I will,' assures Nidhi.

Once she leaves I turn to Nidhi. 'Thanks, Nidhi. I am so sorry. You don't have to do all this. I will manage,' I say.

'I know I don't *have* to Ani, but I *want* to,' she says.

That is when I want to hug her.

'Come here,' I say and she comes closer.

I give her a half-hug with my right arm.

She hugs me back with both her arms.

We stay like that for a few seconds. Then she breaks away and I can see that there are tears in her eyes.

Her phone rings. She looks at me and says, 'Do you want to answer it? It's your parents.'

It's all in the planets—your daily forecast: Darshita Sen

Sagittarius (November 22 to December 21)

It falls upon you to do an unpleasant task which simply has to be carried out. Being an Archer, your trademark frankness carries it off well. Truth is a bitter pill to swallow, but it is best to be honest. A friend will lean on you for support.

27

NIDHI

Good lord—Ani is such a mess. We should have checked on him sooner; not waited for two days trying to give him his space. We did well to rush him to the hospital and it is a huge relief that he is in safe hands.

I feel protective towards Ani. It's like I want to heal him and make him feel better. It is hard seeing him like this. And now he has thrown up. I am glad I was able to hold that pan for him, else he would have thrown up all over the bed. I know he is feeling embarrassed and sheepish, but this situation is definitely an emergency. I hug him and I hold him for a while. Something stirs inside me. It is a feeling hard to define. It's like I want to take care of him. And him being in this vulnerable state makes me want to take charge of everything and makes me want to fix things.

I am also glad I have insisted that we should tell his parents.

My phone is ringing now. It is a call from his dad's mobile.

'Do you want to answer it?' I ask Ani.

Ani shakes his head and gestures that he doesn't want to speak. Then he closes his eyes and sinks back into the pillow. Which leaves me with no option but to answer the call.

'Hello?' I say.

'Hello…. Yes, who is this?' says Ani's dad.

'Hello, Mr Prabhu? My name is Nidhi and I am Aniket's friend,' I say.

'Yes?' His tone indicates it is a question. He doesn't sound friendly on the phone. I wish it had been his mother who had called. Somehow I feel it would have been easier to talk to her.

'Aniket has been admitted to the hospital. There's no reason to panic, he is doing fine. But I thought I should inform you.' My words tumble out in a rush.

'What? What happened? Did he have an accident?' he asks. The anxiety in his tone is painful to hear.

'No, no accident. He has been having blackouts, and his friend Subbu and I thought we should get a doctor to check him. The doctor asked us to admit him for observation,' I quickly clarify.

'What observation?' asks his dad.

How do I tell him that Aniket has lost his girlfriend and is in extreme grief? I know for a fact that Ani has not mentioned Trisha to them.

'I think it's best you speak to the doctors, Mr Prabhu.'

'Let me talk to Ani,' he says.

I look at Ani and he is fast asleep now.

'He is sleeping now.'

'Well, put the doctor on the line,' says his dad.

'He isn't here at the moment.'

'Can you tell me which hospital and who is the doctor?'

'We have admitted him in Holy Angel Hospital and it is Dr. Krishnamurthy,' I say.

There is a pause at the other end and I can hear his dad speaking to his mom in muffled tones. This time Ani's mother comes on the phone.

'Hello, this is Aniket's mother. Is he okay? What has happened? Why did he have blackouts?' she asks.

'He hasn't been eating properly, Mrs Prabhu. He is on IV fluids now. Don't worry, I am staying here and taking care of him,' I say.

It *is* definitely easier to talk to Ani's mom rather than his dad. My hunch was right. She sounds a lot friendlier.

'We are actually in Hyderabad right now. We were attending the wedding of a relative's son. We had planned to spend a few days here, but we can cancel that,' his mother says.

'Oh no, please do not cancel it. His friend Subbu and I will take care of him. They are running some tests and he is definitely recovering. I would suggest you carry on as per your original plan. I will keep you updated,' I assure her.

'Thank you so much. I will discuss this with Aniket's father and let you know. By the way, what is your name?'

'It's Nidhi, Mrs Prabhu.'

'Oh, please don't call me that. It makes me feel like a school teacher. You can call me Aunty. And how do you know Aniket?'

I like his mom already. She seems sweet.

'Aniket is doing a pottery course with me. But I met him first on the train to Chennai. My parents live there,' I say.

Then she asks me where in Chennai they live and when I say Boat Club Road, there is a tiny pause. Then she thanks me for taking care of Aniket and asks me if it is okay if she calls me up every now and then.

'No problem at all, Aunty. I will anyway keep messaging you. Do not worry,' I reassure her.

Once she hangs up, I sit and watch Ani for a while. He looks peaceful when he sleeps. Then Subbu comes back with all that I instructed him to bring. I go back home, quickly pack a change of clothes, and then as an afterthought I make some filter coffee as well, and pour it into a thermos flask. Once I reach the hospital, Subbu asks me if I want to grab dinner. I am starving and say that I would love to. Subbu calls the nurse and asks if we can leave Ani alone for a little while, or whether one of us should stay with him.

'No problem. You can go. It is our duty to see he is safe,' she says.

The cafeteria in the hospital premises turns out to be a fairly busy place, and the food that they serve is delicious.

I tell Subbu about my conversation with Ani's parents.

'Look, I think we should ask them to come. He may well be here for four to five days. I checked with the doctor when I was leaving. Also, he is running a fever and they are investigating the causes for that too.'

I see Subbu's point, but am unsure what to do, since Ani seems reluctant to even talk to his parents. Subbu leaves, and I am still thinking about this, when Aniket's mom calls again. She says she has spoken to his dad and they have decided to shorten their Hyderabad trip and leave for Bangalore the next day. They will come directly to the hospital, she says. She asks me not to mention it to Aniket. 'He will definitely say that there is no need for us to come over,' she adds.

'Okay, Aunty. I will not tell him. Where will you stay, Aunty? Do you want to stay with me?' I ask.

'That's very sweet of you but we do have Aniket's place, right?' says his mom.

'Yes, yes. The keys are with me, and when you come I will give them to you,' I say.

Aniket is still asleep when I get back to the room. I climb into the attendant's bed and settle down. Lying in the dark in the hospital room, my phone beeps. When I look at it, I see a message from Manoj.

'Sorry babe—was swamped. Free now. Wanna catch up for dinner?' reads the text.

That is when it occurs to me that I haven't spoken to him since Trish died. I haven't even thought about him for a second, let alone missed him. I was so immersed in these developments.

I tiptoe out of the hospital room as I do not want to wake up Ani, and I call him.

'Hey, Manoj,' I say.

'Hey, babe—let's go out! I am finally done with this monster of a presentation I was working on. Can I come over and pick you up?'

'No, I can't go out.'

'Why not, and why are you whispering?' he asks.

'I'm in the hospital. My friend is admitted here. He is in a bad state and his family doesn't live here.'

'Which friend?' His tone changes almost instantly.

'I told you about him that day. Aniket.'

'He is the same guy who texted you right? The one you are "coaching"?' The way he says 'coaching', he makes it sound like a sneer.

'Yes, the same guy.'

'What the hell? Where is his girlfriend? Why in the world do *you* have to stay there?'

'She died. And no, I don't have to stay here. I *want* to,' I say.

There is a pause at the other end. He is probably weighing what I said.

Then he says, 'What do you mean "she died"?'

I am in no mood to narrate the whole episode to him. It is too painful and I don't want to think about it now.

'Manoj, it is all over the media. Look, I am busy at the moment. I will talk to you tomorrow, all right?'

'Wait, which hospital is this?'

'Holy Angel. Now good night,' I say and hang up.

Sleeping on the narrow hospital bed is not as bad as I had anticipated and, surprisingly, I get a good night's sleep.

When I wake up in the morning, Aniket is already awake. He definitely looks better today. He sits up now and smiles at me. A wan smile.

'Were you watching me sleep?' I ask.

He has an empty look in his eyes. A look of pain, vacuum, loss.

'Nidhi, you are a sweetheart. Thank you for all you are doing,' he says.

'It's okay, Ani. This is the least I can do. And hey, I have a surprise for you,' I say, and he is curious to know what it is.

I pour out the filter coffee from the thermos flask.

'That's a nice surprise indeed. Thanks,' he says as he sits back and sips his coffee.

There is a knock on the door and Subbu walks in.

'Hey, bro, nice royal treatment you are getting here. I smell filter coffee,' he says sniffing.

'Yes, she makes the best filter coffee in the world,' he says, pointing to me.

'Get your ass to work. Enough of this,' says Subbu to Aniket.

Then Subbu looks at me. I know exactly what is going through his mind. That was what I had been thinking about too. That this is the perfect time to tell Ani the truth. That his angel is not as divine as he thought. Though one part of me feels bad for him, the other part, the practical part, cannot help thinking that this might, in a way, help him. He will stop idolizing her and he might see her selfishness in stringing along two guys who were sincerely in love with her. I decide that he has to know the truth.

'Ani, there's something we discovered,' I say and look at Subbu.

Subbu doesn't miss the cue.

'Bro, look, I am sorry that she died. I feel for you, I do. But Trisha ... she was two-timing you,' he says.

I draw in a sharp breath.

There. He has said it. The words hang in the air.

The colour drains from Ani's face. He is quiet.

'What do you mean?' he asks softly.

'We couldn't believe it either, Ani, but it is true. We ... we saw the snaps,' I say.

He is silent for a few seconds. And when he speaks, his voice is a whisper.

'Who?' he asks.

'Vishwa,' says Subbu. 'We went and met him, bro. Nidhi and I spoke to him. We confronted him and there is no mistaking the snaps he showed us. They were clearly a couple. And he is all over the media. Apparently they were to get married in six months.'

Ani is quiet for a long time. There is nothing left to say. It is like a raw wound that was festering has been exposed with the bandage stripped away. It is ugly, bare.

I feel bad now. Ani looks completely broken.

But we had to tell him. He had to know.

Finally, after what seems like an eternity, Ani speaks. We have to strain to hear him.

'You know what,' he says, 'I always kind of suspected it.'

It's all in the planets—your daily forecast: Darshita Sen

Leo (July 23 to August 22)

Do not hesitate to reach out to others when you need help. You cannot do it all by yourself. Learn to let go of things. You cannot control everything. You get closure on an issue that has been haunting you....

28

ANIKET

There are times in life when you would do anything other than face the truth. The truth has the power to maim, wound, kill. Subbu and Nidhi have just stated what I always suspected. But to hear it as a truth hurts. It's a pain that I have never experienced before. Not even when she died. I feel a massive stab now, an ache that starts in my heart and travels to the rest of my body. To have been suspicious is one thing. But to have to have it confirmed is crushing. Nidhi has said that they have seen photos. I can only imagine what kind of pictures they would have been.

How could she do this? Why?

It wasn't that I was oblivious. The signs were always there. Subtle ones. But the thing is, I had always pushed it aside, refusing to entertain the thought. Anytime I brought it up, Trish would ask me not to be jealous and she would tell me that he was only a friend. And I believed her.

Because I loved her.

And I wanted it to be true.

How blind I have been. What a prize asshole I have been. I think of all the times I went rushing over to the airport to pick her up. I think of the countless times I waited for her, doing nothing on the weekend while she was 'busy'. I want to murder her now. Except she is dead. And that Vishwa … the bastard. How could he?

Although, he is probably thinking the same of me. I can't blame Vishwa. It is Trish who cheated. She was capable of lying so sweetly and so convincingly. How I believed her. I was the puppy dog wagging my tail for every bit of affection she threw my way. I hate myself now.

I am pelted with thoughts. Each one is a torment. Each one unleashes fresh pain. Each one feels like a fingernail being torn out. Or a blow with a hammer to my forehead. Or a knife through my heart.

It is searing.

I am helpless. I am being tossed about in this barrage of torturous thoughts that are increasing in intensity by the minute.

I want to curl up and die. I want this all to end. Why the fuck did I have to pick her of all the women to fall in love with? Why was I so blinded by her beauty?

With a start I realize that Subbu and Nidhi are still around. They look tense. Worried.

I have nothing to say to them. I want to be left alone.

'Guys, can you both please leave? I don't mean to be rude, but please can you leave me alone?' I say.

Nidhi and Subbu look at each other.

'Bro, I am sorry. We thought it was best we told you. Are you okay?'

Ha. What a question.

Would you be okay if you discovered that your girlfriend, who you loved with all your heart, had been two-timing you?

'I am fine. I need some time, all right?'

'Sure, Ani, I will get going. I have some work anyway. Anytime you want me to come back and be with you, call me. I can work from here,' says Nidhi.

'Thanks,' I say and I sink back into the bed.

'Do you think he will be fine?' I hear Nidhi asking, as soon as she and Subbu step out.

'I sure hope so. It killed me to tell him,' he says.

I don't hear her reply as they have walked out of earshot by then.

When they both leave, the hospital nutritionist arrives along with the doctor and the nurse.

'How are you feeling today, Aniket?' asks Dr. Krishnamurthy.

Like a truck ran over me.
Suicidal.
Depressed.
Tortured.
Fucked.
Screwed over.

'I feel better today.'

'Good, good. We will start you off with a semi-solid diet and we will see if you are able to keep that down. If you suddenly eat solids, you are likely to throw up. Your body needs to be slowly coaxed back to its normal functions,' he says.

Then the nutritionist says that if I have any special requests, anything that I particularly crave, she can get it organized.

Yeah right. I crave for the time when everything was all right. When I did not have to deal with the truth that is eating me up now.

Do you think you can fix that? Get that organized for me? Yeah?

'Thanks. Anything will do. I am okay with any food. I leave it to you,' I say.

Once they leave, I close my eyes and a thousand memories wash all over me. Trish smiling. Trish walking on the beach. Trish sleeping beside me while I drove. Her running her hands through my hair. Her voice. Her smell. Her laugh. Her getting irked. Her being silly. Her in my T-shirt.

Was she thinking of him when she did all that to me?

Well done Trish—when were you planning to break it to me? Why did you travel to Pondicherry with me if you wanted to get married to him? Why didn't you end it with one of us? You were the one who was supposed to know me like no one else did. You called me your baby. You loved me, Trish—and I loved you. Was it all pretence? How much of it was the truth?

The nurse comes in and says that I can go to the loo if I want to and that she will disconnect the IV drip. When I'm done, they will connect it again. She says she will have to let the needle remain inside.

'Can't you remove the needle too?' I ask.

'No, it is better it stays in, otherwise we will have to insert it again. This is easier,' she says. 'Are you feeling faint? Please stand up and see?' she requests.

I feel very weak but I walk to the bathroom. My legs feel like rubber but I tell her that I can manage.

'Please do not bolt the door, and if you need anything there is a bell in the bathroom too,' she says.

I finish brushing my teeth. And when I look at my reflection in the mirror, I get a shock. My eyes are hollow, sunken. My hair has started to get matted. Now I have a beard, not a stubble. And the fat seems to have melted away from my body. I have definitely lost weight—it is obvious to me even in this state. I don't have the strength or energy to shave, though. And I don't think I can shower with this IV needle in my hand.

I go back to the bed and there is a piping hot breakfast waiting for me. It is some kind of a thick vegetable soup. I am able to eat half of it and then I feel queasy again, so I push it away and lie down.

Now I do not even want to sleep. I don't want to think of Trish again and if I sleep I might dream of her. So I switch on the TV and flip through some sports channels, pausing when one of them catches my eye. It is a surfing competition going on in Fiji. The guy who is surfing is brilliant. I watch in amazement as he rides the waves.

A little later, the nurse comes and asks if I want to finish the rest of the soup, and I tell her I am feeling nauseous.

'Don't force yourself to eat, it is fine,' she says. Then she hooks me up once again to the IV drip and leaves.

I am alone now with my thoughts for company and the surfer on television. I think about Darshita Sen. What was she trying to warn me about? Did she see through Trish's ways? Why did she tell me to break it off? Can she genuinely read faces?

My phone is beside me on the bed, and I look her up online. She doesn't have a website, but there are many articles about her, and in one of them she talks about how she got into face-reading and tarot. When she was very young, her mother had committed suicide. Darshita had had no idea her mother was depressed, and that guilt drove her to study micro-expressions in the face. After that she was drawn to tarot and then astrology, and she trained under many gurus. In interviews she has stated that her mission is to help people get clarity about their lives and alleviate their suffering.

I am overcome by a sense of urgency to speak to her. I want to ask her a few things. I wonder if she will speak to me.

I think about how to reach her and it occurs to me that my best bet would be to try through Priyanka. She and I are connected on Facebook.

I compose my message:

Hey Priyanka,

Remember me? The guy who agreed to do a strip-show in order to get a reading from your boyfriend's aunt? Well, guess what—turns out she gave me a reading after all, without the strip-show. I met her in Pondicherry recently and she kind of gave me a reading. I am desperately trying to contact her.

I am in a hospital right now, and hence have all the time in the world. (I am doing okay—recovering.)

Could you please, please do me a favour and give me her phone number?

Aniket

Then, as an afterthought, I add my phone number. I read it twice. I like how it sounds. It sounds nice and normal—not like the wreck that I am at the moment.

I keep checking to see if she has replied and finally, after two hours, I hear from her.

Hi Aniket!

Yes! I do remember you.

I am getting married soon. I guess you already know that as Shomo's aunt must have told you. I spoke to her, and she says she will call you at three-thirty. I have passed on your phone number to her.

Peace man! Hope you recover soon.

Priyanka

PS: I still laugh thinking about the strip-show.

'Thanks a ton, I owe you,' I type and hit send.

Then as an afterthought I type, *'Good luck with the wedding!'*

Darshita Sen calls at exactly three-thirty. I almost leap out of bed when the phone rings.

'Hello, Aniket,' she says.

Her voice is deep. Calming. In a strange way, comforting too. It feels like a balm to my soul. Like I am talking to an old friend. This is the weirdest thing I have ever experienced.

'Ma'am, hello. Thank you for calling me,' I say.

'I had to. I saw impending disaster that day. I tried to warn you. The disaster is on a scale of a huge magnitude. It has destroyed or claimed a life,' she says.

Oh. My. God. So she knew all along.

'I am stunned, ma'am. So stunned. I still cannot believe this has happened. Trish ... well, she died.'

'It was bound to happen. It's all in the planets,' she says.

'I am still reeling under the impact though.'

'Priyanka told me that you are in the hospital. What happened? Are you okay?' she asks.

'I am recovering. It's just that her death, well, let's say it hit me badly. She went to a party, and then she fell to her death. I keep thinking that, had I been there, I could have stopped her. But …' I trail off.

I am not able to bring myself to tell her that Trish had been two-timing me, and that revelation has come as a nastier shock than her death, even though I suspected it.

'You should not take it badly. It was a liberation for you. Your life will take a better turn now. She wasn't good for you. Your soul had lessons to learn from her. The karmic cycle is complete and now she has moved on. That day, when I looked into her face, I saw another male energy. A very strong one. And it wasn't yours. It was surrounding her. She was absorbed in it. I also saw death and destruction. Had you stayed with her, it is you who would have died, instead of her. Your karma saved you.'

That sends a chill down my spine. I shudder involuntarily. I am taken aback at what she has said. It all seems so surreal to me.

'Ma'am, I am astounded that you could foresee all this.'

'I do not foresee, Aniket, I only sense the energies. Your energy field—it is very pure. You loved her with all your heart. You were besotted by her aura. And the only way your soul could liberate itself was if she severed all ties. And her death—it was something that she brought on herself. These things are not in our control, Aniket.

You did your best. Be at peace now. Rest and heal. Your body needs that,' she says.

Her words soothe me. They are like medicine. They feel like a cool compress on a forehead that is burning hot. I do not know if what she says is the truth or not, but it brings me such peace. For the first time in days, I feel calm.

'Thank you so very much, ma'am. You have no idea how comforting your words are. I would love to make some kind of payment for … for your time and consultation,' I say. I am so grateful to her.

She laughs. 'You can't afford me, Aniket. I charge way too much and I have a celebrity clientele on a waitlist. But how about a strip-show in exchange?' she says and laughs again.

And for the first time since Trish died, I manage a genuine smile.

It's all in the planets—your daily forecast: Darshita Sen

Sagittarius (November 22 to December 21)

There is finally some clarity with regard to a situation that you have been struggling to accept. Karmic connections cannot be suppressed. It is best you make peace with whatever it is that you are feeling. Do not try to fight it.

29

NIDHI

A Pot of Clay That Holds Gold

Is it possible to peg down the exact moment when you know for a fact that you are in love with someone? It is hard to define. But you know. You start off as friends, and somewhere along the way, over a cup of coffee, a text exchange, the way they laugh, the shape of their nose, something they say—it makes you fall in love with them. And once that happens—boy, does it get you in its grip!

Everything becomes clearer. Brighter. Better. Your heart

sings when you hear from them, sinks when you don't. You hold on to each word of theirs.

When they reciprocate what you feel, a certainty like never before sweeps over both of you. You are elated, euphoric, ecstatic.

Love has that power to transport you both to a place where nothing matters but the two of you.

That is the magic of love.

When was that exact moment YOU realized you are in love?

A web-portal that deals in jewellery wants me to write a few real-life love stories for them. If you have stories that you want me to share and want to get featured on their site, do get in touch with me. There are goodies to be won. My email is on the right-hand corner of this page.

Till next time—adios and keep your heart full of love.

The post is something that I have written totally from the heart. I can feel every word that I have said in it. Ever since the day of Trisha's death, I have been thinking constantly about Ani. The more I think about him, the surer I become. I don't know how it happened, but it has. I am definitely in love with him. I know this for a fact now. It excites me and horrifies me at the same time. People who are engaged do not have feelings for anyone other than their betrothed; they have time and eyes only for them.

How could I go and fall in love with someone else? This is not how it is supposed to happen. Manoj and I are supposed to get married and live happily ever after. When did I fall out of love with Manoj? He isn't a bad guy. Yet, I don't feel the same way around him as I do with Ani. I don't feel protective towards Manoj at all. I don't want to hold him or take care of him. This is most certainly love that I am feeling. There is no mistaking this.

I have to speak to someone about this. Automatically my finger scrolls down my contact list and settles at Tara. I dial her number and she cuts my call with a text.

'Anything urgent? With clients,' it reads.

'No ... we can talk later,' I reply.

Then I scroll through my contacts again. It has been a while since I spoke to my girl pals. I look at my instant messenger and see that Mary is not even on it. Sujata is there, and her 'last seen at' is ten minutes ago. Priya's 'last seen at' is two days back. So it is Sujata that I reach out to. I ping her.

'Hey! How are you doing?' I ask.

'I'm good. How are you? Long time! You seem to have vanished. When are you coming to Chennai next?'

I smile. That's typical Sujata for you. She floods you with questions, barely giving you time to answer. She calls me then and we catch up on what is happening in each other's lives. She is busy juggling a home, two kids and her career. She gives me details about a new project she is working on and how she is finding it increasingly difficult to manage both home and career.

Then she asks about me.

I pause for a minute, wondering how much I should

tell her. Finally I decide not to reveal anything. So I ask what I wanted to in a roundabout way.

'Hey—a quick question for you. What would you do if you are no longer in love with the guy you intend to marry?' I ask.

She catches on immediately.

'Ha! I sensed it from the way you spoke when we met last time. I couldn't put my finger on it then, but you were so hesitant to talk about the date of your wedding. Usually people are excited. But with you, that spark, that joy was missing,' she says.

'What do I do now? I don't love him anymore. I thought I did. I was in love with him at one point. But not anymore.'

'Does he earn well?'

'He does, but that was never my consideration. I was earning well, too, at one point.'

'He is nice to you, isn't he?'

'Yes, yes. I told you, he isn't a bad guy. He is pushing for the marriage very hard. In fact, he wants me to shift to the US with him as soon as we get married.'

'Nidhi, do you want my honest advice?'

'Yes! Why do you think I reached out?'

'Look, this love and all that—it runs its course. I have been married long enough to know that for a fact now. It changes. Everything changes when the kids come. Then you become practical about it. All that early yearning-for-each-other goes out of the window. But there are other things. Like a stable environment to raise kids, the financial security as you pool in incomes, plus the advantage of having a team that will root for you always.'

'So you mean you don't have to be in love with a person to marry them?'

'Grow up, Nidhi! That's only some romantic idealistic notion that you are holding on to. If he is nice to you, earns well and you are looking for marriage and he is very eligible, grab the guy and settle down. Love does not last. But that joint property in your name—boy, is that a high!'

I am a little taken aback by Sujata's candidness. I tell her that I will think about it and I thank her for the honesty. I tell her that I appreciate it.

Then I make myself an iced tea, and switch on the TV. I think about what Sujata has said. Are marriages all about compromise? How can love *not* matter to her?

The phone rings and it is Tara.

'Hey, beautiful sunshine. How are we doing today?' she asks.

She is such a sweetheart. So dependable. Always there for me.

I tell her about Trisha dying, about Subbu and me attending the funeral, about my staying in the hospital and looking after Aniket.

'Oh no—I am so sorry to hear that. In fact, I did read about it in the papers. But I never even thought that you might know her personally. Poor you. Please offer my deepest and heartfelt condolences to your friend Aniket,' she says.

'I will. And Tara … um … one more thing I wanted to talk to you about. Do you have the time? Do you have to go back for some meeting or something?'

'I have all the time in the world for you, my sunshine. Shoot,' she says.

'I … I think I'm in love with Aniket. No. I *am* in love with Aniket.'

There is a pause and then she says 'Oh … okay… and?'

'What do you think I should do, Tara?'

'Is this why you say you don't want to get married to Manoj?'

'No—the marriage thing was making me distinctly uncomfortable. But I wasn't able to put a reason to it till now. This morning, when I got back from the hospital, I knew the depth of my feelings by the intensity with which I was missing Ani. I feel warm and happy around him. With Manoj, I feel lifeless.… Look Tara, I don't know if I am even making sense here. I seem to be blabbering wildly.'

'No, no, sunshine. You are making complete sense. I get you. I hear you. And I think finding love is one of the greatest feelings in the world. People seek it all their lives, but only very few find it.'

'Yes. But am I being practical here? I spoke to my friend Sujata. You remember her right? She went to school with me?'

'Yep. I do remember her. She lives in Chennai if I recall? Isn't she the one you met along with some other friends last time you visited us?'

'Yes, yes, the same. I had a chat with her and she says love doesn't last after marriage. She advised me to be practical and get married to Manoj.'

'Ha! What does she know? And why are you talking to her, sunshine? Can't you see me and your dad? We are so happy. I was around your age when I got married to him. I wake up every morning feeling so lucky to have him in my life. I love sharing my days with him. And you know he feels the same way too. Do not listen to people who ask you to be practical and "settle" for whatever they think is the best option for you. Ask yourself what you feel. Listen to your heart, and the answers will come to you.'

'Thanks, Tara! You know I always feel good talking to you?'

'It is mutual. You ought to know that by now. By the way—have you told Aniket how you feel about him?'

'No, Tara! The guy's girlfriend died a few days back. He loved her very much, you know.'

'Yes. Give him time. Let him heal. And if you are certain about what you feel, break it off with Manoj. Sooner the better. Why keep him hanging in false hope?'

'Yes, I will. When are you coming to Bangalore next?' I ask.

'Let's see. Something may come up soon. Take care, darling,' she says.

I call Subbu as soon as she hangs up. I am desperate to see Ani. And I know Subbu will want to visit him too.

'Hey, I'm planning to visit Ani later today. Do you want to come along too?'

'I do. Can you pick me up? I can meet you outside Intel,' he says.

'Yes, I will. And all these free rides you are hitching— you ought to pay me for it.'

'I can redesign your blog for you. Give you a great header and your own website.'

'Oh! I was only kidding. But hey, that would be great!' I tell him, and he promises he will help out.

'Subbu, do you believe in God?' I ask.

'Why? Why this sudden question?'

'I wanted to visit a temple. The funny thing is, I have never wanted to before. But now, somehow, I want to pray for Ani. There's a temple on the way to the hospital. So if I am picking you up, you can either wait in the car while I pray, or you can come along with me.'

'I will go along with you. I was raised in a very religious household. I think you can tell what kind of beliefs my parents had if they named me Subramaniam,' he laughs.

'Great, see you soon,' I say.

Once I hang up, I know what I have to do. I have to tell Manoj.

There is simply no delaying it any more.

It's all in the planets—your daily forecast: Darshita Sen

Leo (July 23 to August 22)

… Your family is very supportive and tries to help you but you want to be left alone. Be a little more appreciative of their efforts. However, take some time off for yourself too.

30

ANIKET

There's a knock on the door and I look up to see the nurse smiling at me.

'Aniket? There are visitors for you. See who is here.' Her grin is wide.

I wonder who it is. Then I spot my mom and dad. Hell, no. This is the last thing I wanted. I don't want them here. Damn. I should not have given Nidhi my parents' number.

'*Kanna*, how are you?' asks my mom as she walks in. Her eyes fill with tears.

I hate this. I am fine. I don't want my mother getting emotional. I hate to see her cry.

'Ma, it's fine. I am okay,' I say as she puts her arm around my shoulders.

My dad nods at me, and then sits down on the attendant's bed.

'Look at you, you have become so thin. And you haven't even shaved,' says my mother.

'And what is with the hair? Are you growing it? Looks like a goat,' remarks my dad.

Funnily, that is comforting. He is being himself. One would not get any melodrama or tears from him. If he is worried about me, he definitely isn't showing it.

'I need to get a haircut, but I don't think the hospital has barbers,' I retort, but the sarcasm is lost on my dad.

'So what happened?' asks my mom.

'Long story, Ma,' I say.

'Who is the girl who called us up?' asks my dad.

'Her name is Nidhi. I learn pottery from her,' I say.

'Hmmm.' He nods but doesn't say anything.

'So how come you guys decided to land up here? Weren't you supposed to be going to Hyderabad or something?'

'Yes, we attended the wedding. Ushakka's son was getting married. You remember him, don't you?'

'How am I supposed to remember him, Ma. How old was I when I last met him?'

'I think you were around five. You used to play together all the time. Then they shifted to America.'

'How in the world will I remember someone I have last met when I was five?'

'He is your age, Ani, and see, he has found this very pretty girl. Such a nice couple they made,' she says.

'Ma—is that all there is to marriage? He looks nice, she looks nice and so they make a good pair?'

'No, no, they met two-three times. Their parents are very open-minded,' says my mother.

'Ma—that is precisely my point. How can you decide to get married to someone based on two or three meetings. Honestly, I think you ought to get to know the person.'

My dad looks up sharply when I say that.

'So is that what this is? With your friend who called us? Are you … er … getting to know her?' he asks.

'Dad—please, she is a friend.'

'What is this friendship that you young people have, I do not understand. Either you like her or you don't. How old is she?' asks my dad.

'Look Dad, you won't get it. How does it matter how old she is?' I ask.

'No *kanna*, please answer your dad. If she is your friend, I think we ought to know a bit more about her.'

'Ma, just leave it okay?'

'Why? What is the problem?' asks my dad.

'No problem, Dad, that's why I am asking you to leave it.'

'It's high time you decide on your marriage, Aniket. If you have someone in mind, please tell us. Your dad and I will go and speak to her parents,' says my mom. When she calls me Aniket and not Ani, I know she means business.

Please Ma—not now, I want to plead. I want to tell her that I want to get over Trish first. But I can't speak in front of my father.

'Ma, look. I don't have anyone in mind at the moment, okay? And can we talk about this later,' I say and throw a glance at my dad.

My mother understands.

Dad and Mom sit down for a while. I can see Dad is getting fidgety and restless.

Then he says, 'All our luggage is still in the car. If you give me your house key and your address, I'll go keep the suitcases there and come back.'

When I first rented the apartment, I had planned out my parents' visit. I decided I would see to it that they had a grand time. I thought about how I would give them a guided tour of my residential apartment complex, which has a pool, a sauna, a gym, tennis courts, basketball courts and all the modern amenities that builders these days throw in. My parents have lived in an independent house all their lives, and all of this would be novel to them.

This is the first time they are coming to my place and ideally I would have liked to do all of that.

But now I am stuck like this, in this hospital bed.

'Dad, I wanted to show you around my apartment complex,' I say.

'Yes, but I guess now we will have to find our own way. It is not like we have a choice here. Don't worry, when you get discharged, you can show us around,' says my dad.

The key is lying on the side-table where Subbu left it. I point it out to my dad and give him directions to get to my home.

Once he leaves, Mom and I are alone.

'Tell me now, *kanna*. How did all this happen?' she asks as she strokes my forehead tenderly.

No kindness, Ma. Not now. I can't take it right now.

I blink away the tears that are threatening to rise. There is a lump in my throat.

'Nothing, Ma. She died,' I say.

My mother looks at me for a few seconds. Then she understands.

'Oh no,' she says.

'What is worse, she had been cheating on me,' I say. I cringe as I say it. I don't think my poor mother is capable of understanding the dynamics of modern relationships.

'Cheating? Means what?' she asks. She is genuinely puzzled.

'I don't think she loved me, Ma. She had another guy who she was planning to get married to,' I say.

The pain is back now. I thought I had managed to tame it, suppress it. It rises now like a monster and grips my throat hard. I lie back on the pillow and I cannot fight the tears any more. My mother watches me as I helplessly sob. I think the last time she has seen me cry was probably when I was seven or eight.

'*Kanna…*' says my mother as she hugs me and holds my head to her chest. She kisses me many times on my forehead and holds me till the sobs subside. Then she wipes my tears.

'Ani, it was not meant to be. Let it go,' she says.

'I know, Ma, I know. But it still hurts,' I say.

'It will hurt for a long time, Ani. But remember, as each day goes by, the pain will lessen. Its power to hurt you will reduce with every day. Do you know what my mother used to tell me about death?' she asks.

'What?'

'It is a saying in Konkani—*Aaji meleri phayi doni*. It means, if you die today, tomorrow is the second day of death, the day after tomorrow is the third day, after that is the fourth and so on. It is another way of saying that life goes on. Life waits for nobody, Ani. We have to grab it and ride it.'

I think about what she has said. She is so right. I never knew my mother had this philosophical side to her.

'You are sad now. But this will pass. One day you will be happy, and I am not saying this to make you feel better. Do you know how old I was when I had you?' she asks.

I have never even thought about my mother's life before she had me. I shake my head.

'I was nineteen. They got me married to your dad at eighteen. I wanted to study further,' she says.

'Why did you agree?' I ask.

'You know how it was, Ani. I had no choice. And I was in love at that time. Not with your dad. With another guy. And you know what—he loved me too. He was in my class.'

'Why didn't you tell your parents?'

'He was a Christian. His name was Biju Tharakan. He was good-looking and kind.' She has a faraway look in her eyes now. 'He died the year after my marriage in a bike accident. I kept thinking about the number of times I'd ridden on his bike with him.... I couldn't go for the funeral. It was in Kerala and your dad and I were in Baroda by then. I would rock you to sleep and then cry in the bathroom. Then, in front of your father, I would pretend everything was fine. But, to this day, I wonder what might have happened had I married him. I don't know. These things, Ani, they are fated. You cannot fight them. No matter what you do, your destiny unfolds in the way that it is meant to.'

I nod. This is the second time I am hearing this. First it was Darshita Sen, and now my mom. Maybe there *is* something beyond our control. Things may not turn out the way we want them to. But how we deal with it is what matters.

Dad calls from my place and says that he is tired and will rest for a while. He asks my mom if she is fine with that, and she tells him to go ahead and that she will manage.

My mom and I talk for a long time. She tells me so many stories from her childhood. She makes me laugh, she makes me think and, most importantly, she does not let me wallow in self-pity. How I love my mother. She is a remarkable woman. I would never have thought that my mother might have, at some point in her life, been in love with someone other than my dad.

Subbu and Nidhi arrive in the evening.

'Hey bro, we came to check on you,' says Subbu, and then he spots my mom.

'Oh, hello, Aunty! I am Subbu,' he says.

'Hi Aunty, I am Nidhi,' says Nidhi, and my mom hugs her and she pats Subbu on the shoulder.

'I have to thank you both for looking after Aniket so nicely. I am very grateful to you,' she says.

'Don't even mention it Aunty. He is our friend,' says Nidhi.

I can see that my mother instantly likes Nidhi. I can tell by the way she is looking at her. Nidhi is wearing a salwar kameez, something that I haven't seen her wear, ever. She is also wearing some kind of dangly earrings and a bindi. She seems to have done something to her eyes too. They look bigger. And she looks stunning.

'Both of you coordinated your coming here, is it? How did you manage to land up together?' I ask.

'Yeah, I picked him up on the way here. He waited at the Intel junction and hopped into my car,' says Nidhi.

'You look great, Nidhi,' I say.

She smiles and looks away. 'Thank you. You know, we went to a Venkateshwara temple on the way here,' she says.

'Oh! I didn't know you go to temples.'

'Well, I kind of miss those Buddhist temples I used to go to in Sri Lanka, so today I decided to go to one. I prayed for you, Ani. I prayed for your peace of mind.'

'Thank you, Nidhi. I think your prayers worked. I am feeling more peaceful,' I reply.

Dr. Krishnamurthy examines me when he comes on his evening round and says that I can be discharged the next evening, provided I am able to keep food down. He says they will start me off on solids for dinner today. If I don't throw up, they will give me solids at breakfast tomorrow. And if I am able to keep that, and lunch, down, I should be okay for discharge.

He says all the test results have come, and everything is clear. My mother is relieved to hear that, and so are Subbu and Nidhi.

My mother and Nidhi are talking to each other now and they are getting along well. My mother is asking Nidhi a lot of questions, and I am surprised at some of the things Nidhi is saying; things even I didn't know about. I am beginning to feel a little jealous now!

Subbu tells me that the team misses me and they wanted to visit me today, but there was someone from the UK coming into the office and hence Amit kept them busy. After that we don't have much to talk about, and so we sit and listen to Nidhi and my mum chatting.

My dad comes back late in the evening, when Subbu and Nidhi are on their way out.

'Dad, this is Nidhi and Subbu,' I say.

Dad is nowhere as friendly towards them as Mom.

'Hello,' Nidhi says. 'We were on our way out. We will come tomorrow and help with everything when Ani is being discharged. Looks like he will be able to go home tomorrow.'

'Okay, thank you,' my dad says. And once they leave, he pounces on me. 'Oh, so that is Nidhi. Tell me—how old is she?'

I sigh. This is one thing he simply will not let go of.

'Dad, she is thirty-two,' I say.

'Aniket. You have considered that she is too old for you, haven't you?'

I look at my mom helplessly. She tries to intervene.

'See, it is not like that between them,' she says, but my dad does not let her speak.

'Aniket, it is high time you start thinking about these things. Look, I have got four marriage proposals for you. I have the photographs and their matrimonial bios with me. All good families. I think you should at least start meeting these girls. And this girl who just left, forget her. It is best if you marry someone who is twenty-four, twenty-five. That will be a good match for you.'

'And what makes you an authority on who is a good match for me, Dad?' I ask quietly.

But my anger is lost on him. How can my dad barge in here and decide that Nidhi isn't 'good enough' because she is thirty-two. Firstly, I haven't even thought of marrying her or anything like that. Secondly, I think it is for me to decide how old the woman I ultimately marry should be. Not my dad or mom.

But my dad has launched into a full-fledged explanation now.

'Ani, if a girl is around twenty-five, she will be ready to have children by the time she is twenty-eight or so. You would have had time to get to know each other. You will be thirty by then. Just the right age to start a family. See, by the time you retire, your son or daughter will be twenty-eight, which means they will be entirely independent of you. Many people do not plan their retirement or having kids early enough.'

'How do you know what will happen tomorrow, Dad. What if one of us dies? Who has seen tomorrow? It is entirely possible, you know.'

'Ani, we operate on the presumption that nothing untoward will happen. The chances are slim, aren't they? Look, please meet and consider these girls. Your mother and I will be very happy. Meet them once, will you? And please stop associating with Nidhi. It's best to close all those friendships when we proceed with marriage alliances. We don't want complications later.'

What can I even say to my father? I don't want to meet any girls. And what do I tell Nidhi? 'Buzz off. I now want to get married and I can't meet you?' No way. I *like* Nidhi. Nobody is going to stop me from meeting her. But I don't have the energy to explain to my father why I don't want to meet girls. Not now. Not ever. If I ever get married, it has to be to someone with whom I have a connect. Someone who cares deeply for me. I have been burned once in love. I don't think I have the strength to go through it all again.

I want to forget Trish. I want to put this all behind me. Love is too painful. As much as it can elate, it can also kill. And if you do survive its aftermath, you would still feel the searing pain each time a memory creeps up. I want to start anew. And I definitely do not want to complicate my life at the moment by going and meeting girls that my dad has fixed for me.

But I know my father is in no mood to back down.

So I say, 'Dad, okay, let me get discharged first and let me recover. Please give me some time, will you?'

'Okay, Ani,' my dad says, and then he does something that he used to do when I was a child.

He smiles and ruffles my hair.

It's all in the planets—your daily forecast: Darshita Sen

Sagittarius (November 22 to December 21)

Beware of being coerced into something you do not want to do. Unless you stand up for yourself, you will always be forced into agreeing to do something that you did not want in the first place. Walk alone if you have to, and stick to your resolve.

31

NIDHI

'It was nice to meet Ani's parents, wasn't it?' I tell Subbu on the way back from the hospital.

'His mom is sweet but his dad is a grouch,' says Subbu.

'Ha ha—yes. Fortunately Ani takes after his mom,' I say.

Subbu simply smiles.

Once I reach home, I make myself some coffee and work for a while. But I am unable to focus on work. I know I am stalling for time here. Better to get it over with, I finally tell myself. I can't put off calling Manoj any longer.

I dial his number.

'Hey, can you meet me? There's something I need to talk to you about,' I say.

'Sorry babe, I have this important conference call tonight. No can do,' he says.

'It's urgent, Manoj.'

'Okay, then tell me what it's about now.'

'Look, I would rather tell you in person. When is the earliest that you can meet?'

'Umm … let's see, I have this presentation tomorrow afternoon. I should be done by about four. Can I meet you after that?' he asks.

I don't want him to back out from this meeting so I tell him that I will meet him at the Café Coffee Day opposite his office.

'That way you don't have to drive all the way to meet me,' I say.

'That will be nice. And, hey, this is indeed a pleasant surprise!' He sounds relieved and there is a cheerful note in his voice.

If only he knew what I was going to tell him.

The next morning I call Aniket's mom to ask her how he is doing.

'You know what, he managed to eat two idlis. And he did not throw up. So that is a good sign. Fingers crossed. The IV drip is likely to be taken off after lunch,' she says.

I smile. Then a thought strikes me. When you feel happy listening to details of what that person ate, and how they did not throw up, then you know it is love.

'Oh, that's good, Aunty. Will he be discharged today then?'

'It looks like that. He has to be able to eat lunch also and keep it down. Are you and Subbu coming today?'

'Yes, Aunty. We will come and help you with all the discharge formalities. I will be there by about five-thirty or so. I have to meet a friend first.'

'If you are busy, do not worry. Uncle and I will manage,' says his mom.

It takes me two seconds to figure out that by 'Uncle' she means Ani's dad.

'Never too busy for a friend, Aunty. And Aniket is a good friend. We will definitely be there,' I say and hang up.

I am too restless to focus on my work anymore. I keep watching the clock, wishing time would speed by. I check my blog, and I am pleasantly surprised to see seventeen comments for my last post. Seventeen! They have all shared their love stories and talked about that moment when they knew that their partner was The One. Each of the stories is unique. One talks about a bad haircut that she gave when she was interning at a salon, and how that turned into love. Another talks about how she actually slipped and fell, right into his arms, at a bar when she missed a step, and how they both felt the electricity between them. Yet another relates how he was tutoring his girlfriend's brother, and how she kept making excuses to ask him things and how their love blossomed from that. Each of the stories is beautiful. Whoever came up with this marketing idea for that jewellery company sure has struck the right chord online.

When I finally look up from my computer, I realize it is almost time to leave. I was so absorbed in those stories, I have even forgotten to eat lunch. There is no time now. I don't want Manoj to wait for me and then vanish saying I am late. I look around and slip into the same sleeveless yellow salwar kameez that I wore yesterday. I quickly do my eyes, run a brush through my hair, and wear a sparkling lipstick, all in less than five minutes.

Then I hurry out and drive to the Café Coffee Day, zig-zagging through Bangalore traffic. I'm relieved when I reach, as I am on time. I park my car and walk in and there is no sign of Manoj. I take out my phone to text him, when I see him walking in. He is wearing a pale cream shirt, grey trousers and a deep red tie.

'Hey, babe, so good to see you,' he says as he plants a kiss on my cheek and sits down.

I freeze and instantly stiffen up.

Hell. This is going to be harder than I thought.

A waitress comes to take our order. Manoj orders a watermelon cooler for himself and asks me what I will have.

'An Iced Eskimo please,' I say.

'Good choice,' he says and smiles.

I can feel a knot in my stomach.

'So, to what do I owe this visit? What a pleasant

surprise, Nidhi! And you're wearing a salwar kameez. You look nice!' he says.

'I went to the temple yesterday, so I wore the same thing today. I didn't feel like pulling out another outfit,' I say.

Tell him. Stop talking about your choice of outfit. Tell him. Tell him. Tell him. Come to the point.

'When did you start going to temples? You have never gone to a temple since I met you! Must say, though, that this Indian look suits you.'

'Thanks.'

Tell him. Enough stalling. Deal the blow. Show some courage here.

I draw in a deep breath.

'Manoj.'

'Yes, babe.'

'There is something I need to confess. Something I want to tell you.'

'What? You are coming with me to the US, aren't you? I knew it! I knew you would change your mind.'

'No, Manoj, I am not.'

'Oh,' he says. He takes a moment and then says, 'What is the surprise then?'

How do I say it? This is awful. But there is no choice here. I have to tell him.

Tell him. NOW.

'I am … well … Manoj, I am sorry, but I am not in love with you.'

'What?'

'I am sorry, Manoj. I can't get married to you. Our engagement … it is off … I can't do this.'

'What?'

Then it sinks in. His face sags.

His expression slowly changes before my eyes. His face is clouded now. Dark. His brows are knitted. There is a frown across his forehead.

'Tell me you are joking. You don't mean this do you?'

I am unable to meet his eyes.

'I mean it … I am sorry. I can't get married to you. The engagement is … off,' I repeat.

'There is someone else, isn't it? Who?'

'Look—it is not like that.'

'Then what is it? Can you make me understand what is going on?'

'I … I can't do this, Manoj. I simply cannot get married to you.'

He leans over and he has gripped my arm now. He begins twisting and squeezing it.

'You cheated on me, didn't you? You weren't at that hospital. You … you … were with him, weren't you?'

'Manoj, please let go. It hurts,' I say.

His grip tightens.

'You can't do this to me. Two years. You led me on for two years.'

I can feel his breath on my face now. His grip tightens further. It is beginning to hurt badly.

'Let go,' I say. 'Please let go.'

He doesn't. I am frightened now. I look around frantically. There is an ashtray on the table. I could pick it up with my left hand and hit him.

'You can't leave me,' he says.

'Manoj, if you do not let go of my hand, I am going to…'

'What are you going to do, eh? What?' his mouth is a grimace. His jaw is clenched. The expression in his eyes—it is steel. It terrifies me.

I am frantic.

'Let go…. Otherwise, I will call for help and make a scene here,' I say.

'Bitch,' he hisses and loosens his grip.

I am shaking now. I am scared. The waitress brings our order.

Walk away. Walk away. Walk away. He is not in control of his emotions. Stay away from him. Go. Run.

He calmly sips his drink. I grab mine. I am so shaken that I need to calm down before I can drive.

I close my eyes and take deep breaths.

'Who is he? He is the bastard who texted you, isn't it?' he asks.

My heart is beating like a drum roll. Boom. Boom. Boom. My palms are cold. There is a thin film of sweat on my forehead.

It takes all my effort and all my courage to look him in the eye.

'None of your fucking business,' I say without flinching.

Then I walk out without looking back.

It's all in the planets—your daily forecast: Darshita Sen

Leo (July 23 to August 22)

To find the balance between the past, present and future is hard. Living in the moment is highly advised, but the past casts its shadow. Break free. A conflict is on the cards. Go with your gut feel. Success comes through creative thought, recapturing past talents. Enjoy life with youthful enthusiasm—and only embracing the most passionate of loves.

32

ANIKET

My mom says that, surprisingly, she has slept well in the attendant's bed.

'You know, Mom, Nidhi said the same thing. The bed must be comfortable.'

'Oh, did Nidhi stay over?'

'Yes. They both took good care of me. In fact, Subbu was supposed to stay over last night, but then you and Dad arrived.'

'Your friends are extremely nice, Ani. You are fortunate to have them. And Nidhi—she is a good girl. Did she tell you that she lost her mother when she was fifteen? Poor girl. And her dad remarried when she was twenty-two.'

'Yes, she told me. I have met her step-mom. Not actually met; I just saw her. They are very close.'

'Oh, is it? When did you see her step-mom?'

'When I travelled with her to Chennai on my last visit home.'

'Oh, I see. She is a sweet girl,' says my mom.

The doctor comes on the morning rounds after my breakfast and asks me how I am feeling. I feel a little weak, but I am fine. The best thing is that I haven't thrown up. The doctor says that he will come again after lunch to check if I am doing all right. And then he will instruct the nurse to remove the IV and initiate the discharge proceedings.

Once the doctor leaves, I lie back on my pillow and think about my exchange with my dad.

How easy it is to placate parents. Do exactly as they want you to. Listen to everything they say. Put aside your hopes, your ambitions, your individuality, and they are happy.

When we are young, they control us by praise and punishment. 'Finish your milk, if not you are a bad boy.' 'Study for your engineering entrance exam, otherwise you won't do well in life.' 'You should forget about enjoying.

You can enjoy later.' 'When I was your age, I walked five miles to school.' 'Nothing in life comes easy.'

When we are older, they control us, but with emotional blackmail. 'Just meet these girls. After all we are getting older, and we want to see you settled. You can choose to marry any one of them. There is bound to be someone you like. You will be happy. We have been through your age.'

Parents think that marriage is the magical solution to everything. Or at least my parents do. Subbu's parents too have started asking him to 'settle down'. I know that Nidhi's parents are pretty chilled out, but then, her father isn't exactly a conventional one, and she has a great relationship with her step-mom.

I wish I could explain things to my dad. How much it hurts to have your heart torn out. To have been cheated twice over—once by her death, and then by the things she did. I wish I could tell him why I am not ready for marriage to some girl I barely know. Dad seems to think that there are only two criteria to determine if someone is a 'good girl'. One: her family has to be 'good'; and two: she has to be around twenty-five.

My mom at least understands. She knows what it feels like to be in love. I don't think Dad will get it. Ever.

It's best to simply play along. Once I get discharged, I decide that I will stall for time. Find some excuses. Anything to avoid meeting those girls.

Dad arrives after lunch, and when the doctor comes, he has a lot of questions for him. I have managed to keep my lunch down too. They have served some kind of khichdi with pickle and it is delicious. I can feel my appetite slowly coming back. The doctor asks me to take plenty of rest for the next few days. Then he turns towards my mother and says, 'Give him a lot of TLC and nice, delicious home-cooked food.'

My mom is puzzled.

'What is TLC, doctor? Is it some kind of tablet?'

'It is the best medicine, but you cannot buy it. It is Tender Loving Care,' he smiles.

Then the doctor signs the discharge slip and tells us that we can proceed with the paperwork for discharge.

'Let's wait for his friends to come. Nidhi spoke to me this morning. She said she is coming with Subbu and they will do all the formalities,' says my mom.

'I can go and do it too,' says my dad.

'The queues are long and you will have to go to different departments to collect all the reports and other things, Dad. It will be easier if you let them do it. Between the two of them, they will take care of it,' I say.

'All right, then,' says my dad grudgingly, and he opens his *Financial Chronicle* and begins reading it.

The nurse comes in and she removes the IV drip. It feels great to finally have my arm free. She says she will leave the needle inside, as there is one more medicine that has to be administered through an injection. 'Once we give that, I will take off the needle too,' she says.

I sigh.

'It's okay *kanna*, it's only a couple of hours, and then we will be going home,' says my mom.

Subbu and Nidhi both arrive on the dot, like they did yesterday.

'Bro, so how is the agile software development progressing?' he asks as he high-fives me. I smile. The old Subbu is back.

'Cleared two levels. Breakfast, lunch, tick tick,' I answer.

Nidhi looks at me quizzically.

'It's a software term we use in coding. It basically means that you build a small succession of parts with simple functional codes and test it as soon as they are ready. We don't focus on delivering one large application. Instead we focus on clearing these little bits, so that it all works together beautifully when we finally integrate it,' I explain.

'Interesting,' she smiles. 'Oh, the IV drip is off?'

'Needle is still there,' I grimace.

'Why?'

'They will take it off soon. One more medication to be given intravenously. After that I am a free man.'

'Welcome back, bro!' says Subbu.

Then they greet my dad and mom.

'Hello Aunty, how are you doing?' Nidhi asks. Then she turns to my dad. 'Hello Mr. Prabhu,' she says.

My dad grunts a reply but my mom immediately starts chatting.

My mother admires Nidhi's silver bangle and asks her how much she paid for it and where she got it from.

'Ma! Please don't embarrass me. You can't ask her things like that!' I say.

'No, no, it is fine. I don't mind telling her at all,' says Nidhi. 'Aunty, if you like silver jewellery, I will take you shopping in Bangalore. They have amazing designs in this jewellery store on Commercial Street. I buy all my jewellery from there. This one cost me around three-and-a-half thousand rupees. Isn't it worth it?'

My mother says that for the workmanship involved, it totally is.

Suddenly there are footsteps and a clean-shaven guy dressed formally in a red tie and grey trousers comes charging in. He looks at me and then he spots Nidhi.

I see the colour drain from Nidhi's face.

'What the hell are you doing here, Manoj?' she asks.

He doesn't reply.

In that frozen second, I see his eyes dart towards me.

'Is this the bastard? Asshole,' he says.

It takes me only a second to register who this gigantic idiot is. Manoj. Her fiancé. The guy who caused her that bruise. The bastard who hurts women.

'Watch your mouth, you fucking idiot. How dare you hurt her,' I say.

'Who the fuck are you to tell me what to do, you asshole. She is my fiancée,' he says.

'No, I am not. I made that amply clear to you,

didn't I?' says Nidhi and her hand automatically goes towards her arm. I look at it and I see it. A reddish purplish bruise. And her arm is swollen.

I know what has happened then.

I recall my conversation with Nidhi in her house and it makes me erupt in fury. I feel pure hatred towards this worm of a guy who is standing before me.

'You heard her, you fucking prick. Now leave,' I say.

He lunges towards me with his fist raised. But before he can land a blow I hit him with my right hand, on his jaw. His eyes lock to the roof and he stumbles and collapses to the floor. I see only red now. Blind fury. I want to kill this guy. I jump off the bed and the bed slides. The IV drip stand tumbles down. I am too angry to care. I kick him hard on his face. There is a *thwack* sound on impact. It feels like kicking a brick wall. I want to kill this guy.

'Stop, Ani. STOP,' yells my mom and the nurses come rushing in hearing the commotion. Manoj is doubled up on the floor now, blood spurting from his face.

'Get the first aid kit,' yells the nurse as she crouches down.

'Ani, it's fine. Let him be. It's over—I broke it off with him,' says Nidhi.

I am breathing hard and I sit back on the bed.

The other nurse straightens the IV drip.

'Sir, are you okay?' she asks.

'Yes,' I answer.

My parents are shell-shocked by what has just happened. Manoj is being helped up now by the nurses.

He manages to stand up, his hand to his nose.

My dad walks up to him. 'Look, son, I don't know what the deal between you and this young woman here is. But when she says she is no longer interested in you, my suggestion would be to leave her alone. You cannot force someone to be yours,' he says.

The nurses escort Manoj out of the room.

Then he looks at Nidhi and says, 'I don't know what is going on between you and my son, but I know he cares for you. Very much. And that is always a good thing. That's a great place to start,' he says.

He turns to me and tells me, 'Son, I am proud of you.'

The last time Dad had said that was when I finished first in the hundred-metres sprint on sports day in Class 9.

I lie back on the bed and look at all the people in the room—my dad, my mom, Nidhi, Subbu—and think how fortunate I am that I have people who love me so much.

A memory from my childhood, when we all celebrated Diwali with fireworks, comes to mind. I remember the million sparkling colours lighting up the dark sky as they exploded, far, far away, above the ground, bringing joy as we watched. I was with my family then.

I feel the same way now.

EIGHT MONTHS LATER

It's all in the planets—your daily forecast: Darshita Sen

Sagittarius (November 22 to December 21)

You become very certain of what you want. The events of the past few months have reached a culmination now. There is clarity on a situation which has been peaking and reaching its crescendo. Good tidings are in store.

33

NIDHI

A Pot of Clay That Holds Gold

Remember the cyber-biber? He kidnapped me again. Actually, I am still in his clutches. But oh, what a delicious feeling! I love being with him. I guess love does that to you. No road is too hard, no path too long and nothing is too much trouble when you are in love.

You wake up with thoughts of them. You go to bed with thoughts of them. And throughout the day, you are reminded of them in a million little ways. The skies are bluer, and everything is in technicolour. There's a constant smile on your face. The very thought of them is comforting.

If you know what I am talking about, then you have been touched by the magic of love.

On the professional front, the next batch in my pottery course is starting soon. My previous batch has graduated with honours. Each of them has made at least twelve projects now, and they are all so beautiful. You can judge by the pictures here.

Any of you wanting to take a demo class, please use the links on the right-hand side of this blog to sign up.

I hit publish and, within a few minutes, Ani calls out to me. 'Hey! Why are you calling me a cyber-biber? I never kidnapped you!'

'Oh, you so did. You stole my heart.'

'You gave it to me on a platter. You should make the guy work for it!'

'You did all the work, Ani. Only, you did not know it.'

'Did I? How?' he asks as he comes towards me. The he pulls me closer and tenderly kisses me on the lips. He stops and kisses me again. And again and again.

I go insane with desire.

'Don't stop, Ani, don't stop,' I say as I reach for him.

His hands encircle my waist.

'Ani, I love you,' I whisper and he silences me with yet another kiss.

'A minute,' he says and I wonder what he is doing, moving my centre table aside.

Then he pulls out the sofa-bed and lies on it and says, 'Come here, you. You irresistible thing.'

I climb onto the bed. Into his arms.

He gently pushes my hair away and kisses me on my forehead and on my eyelids. His eyes are so dark, and I lose myself in them. I love looking at him. It is like I disappear into his eyes. He can't break away the gaze.

We end up making love. Gently. Slowly. Unhurriedly.

It is the best feeling in the world.

When we are done, he says, 'You know, I have a confession to make.'

'What?' I ask.

'Do you remember the first time I came here to stay? That night?'

'Yes.'

'You looked so good that day, and I checked you out. I wanted to tell you that. But I was too shy.'

'Ha! And look at you now!'

'For a second that day, mind you only for a second, I wondered what it would be like to make love to you. But I squashed the thought immediately. There was no way I was cheating on her.'

His face clouds with the memory.

I kiss him and say, 'Let go, Ani. You can't hold on to things that never were.'

'Yes,' he says. 'It was a different time. And I am

beginning to believe now that it's not in our hands. Darshita Sen was right. It's all in the planets.'

'Yes. We are dealt cards. That is fate. But we do have free will. What we do with the blows that land on us is up to us. We can fight and emerge stronger than before. Or we can give up.'

'Wise old owl,' he smiles.

'Do you want coffee?' I ask.

'Have I ever refused any offer of coffee that you make? You are the best, Nidhi!'

'That I am,' I say as I walk towards the kitchen and brew it.

We sit on my sofa-bed, sipping our coffees, our arms entwined, and he kisses me again on my cheeks.

'I love you,' he says and I rest my head on his shoulder.

It is a gigantic effort to tear ourselves away from each other. But he has to go, as his parents and sister are arriving today. Once he leaves, I lie for a long time on the sofa-bed, content, happy and blissful. How is it possible to miss a person this much?

For the last eight months, we have been talking non-stop to each other. Mails, chats, phone-calls. It is like we never run out of things to say. I know that he is still healing. He is not yet completely over the pain she caused. But I am in no hurry. I will wait.

After a while, I take out my laptop and, though I have two pieces of commissioned work, I can't resist composing a mail to him.

My love, my darling, my baby, my precious, my life, my Ani,

No terms of endearment suffice. Trying to fit in terms of endearment to address you is like a human looking at the entire cosmos, the thousands of galaxies, several hundred billion stars, where he is not even a speck, and trying to capture this feeling in words.

The longing for you is now a constant companion I carry in my heart. It surrounds me like a cloak and everything that I see is through this filter. It permeates every cell in my body. There is no waking moment that goes by without you on my mind. And if I could control my dreams when I sleep, I would dream only of you.

I stare at pictures of you, memorizing every detail, every curve, every line on your face. I want to soak you in my eyes, keep you there. I could look at your picture for hours, and still keep staring endlessly.

I lose myself in you. And I find myself in you.

If happiness could be measured in electric current, the joy I feel when I hear your voice over the phone, or see you, would easily cross a million watts. If the disappointment I feel when we are finally forced to hang up the phone, or part from each other, could be measured in sound waves, it would easily beat the 400000-watt speakers at rock concerts. Except here, it is the sound of silence. Stillness. With you being so close one moment, and so far away the next when we part. Parting is agony.

I long to be with you physically, inhale your scent, nibble your ear, run my hands through your hair, and I long for you to rest your head in my lap. I crave to hold you in my arms, to lay my head on your chest, to hug you so tight that I can feel every contour of your body and your hands wrapped around me. I would be happy if I could stay that way for the rest of my life.

The time we talk feels like a few minutes, even if it is many hours. It is never enough. The moment we stop, I want to speak to you, yet again.

The millions of broken pieces inside me sing together in perfect rhythm and harmony, the most melodious symphony because of you. You make me feel alive.

There is no day and night any more. There are only moments that painfully tick by till I can connect with you again. Everything else has ceased to matter.

My life was like a jigsaw puzzle and I got by with a piece missing. For many years, I looked for the missing piece. Nothing felt right. And now that I've found you, I feel complete. Whole. Loved. Cherished. Valued. Treasured. Adored. The void in my life—the missing piece of the jigsaw—takes the precise shape of your body, your soul, your spirit.

We fit.

And I live—for you.

Will you move in with me?

All my love,

A wise old owl

I wait for his reply. It comes within a few minutes of sending out the mail.

It's a single word that has the power to change our lives forever: Yes.

ACKNOWLEDGEMENTS

Some authors like to put everyone's name they know in their acknowledgments. Some like to skip it altogether. And for some, this is the 'truest' thing they can write, the 'highest honour' they can bestow, and years later, when they look back at what they have written, they remember every memory associated with the people whose names are mentioned. I won't tell you to which category I belong, because I think you already know.

So here goes:

My dad, K.V.J Kamath, as always, and my mom Priya J. Kamath too. I know you are proud.

My readers—who shower me with love, cover me with care, and wait eagerly for all that I write. I am ever so grateful to you.

Purvi Shenoy, for being my early reader, critic, Instagram- and Snapchat-manager, and my fashion consultant number one.

Atul Shenoy, for the praise that is so difficult to earn from him, for being an early reader and for the fitness advice.

Satish Shenoy and Lostris. If these were Oscar credits, they would get the award for the best supporting roles.

Anukul Shenoy, for all the inputs and the questions.

Naveen Vadakkan, for the kindest words, quickest response, unconditional support, laughs and friendship.

Mayank Mittal and Suresh Sanyasi, for being there, always. My ever-reliable, rock-solid pals.

Sooraj Barjatya and Rajkumar Barjatya, for believing in my stories.

Deepthi Talwar, my wonderful, brilliant editor, with whom I love to work.

Saurabh Thakral, for answering all my questions patiently.

My lovely women friends who understand when I disappear into my hidey-hole, no questions asked— Rathipriya, Shabina Bhatti, Jayashree Chinne, Vani Mahesh, Shinie Antony, Madhuri Banerjee, Dipa Padmakumar, Suma Bhat, Vinoo John, Nishu Mathur, Prathibha Rajesh, Shalini Raghavan.

To Dr. Oliver Rodrigues, for the medical inputs.

To my friends from the writing world—Nikita Singh, Kiran Manral, Sachin Garg, Durjoy Datta, Meghna Pant, Nandita Bose and Milan Vohra.

To the fantastic team at Westland—Gautam Padmanabhan, Krishnakumar, Satish Sundaram, Sarita Prasad, Preeti

Kumar, Gururaj, Satya Sridhar, Neha and others who are always a pleasure to work with; Jayanthi for being super-efficient; and Semy Haitenlo for a great cover.

To the fabulous Indiblogger team—Vineet, Renie and Anup.

To J.K. Bose and Arup Bose for recognizing my potential.

A big thank you to Narasimha Murthy, who clicked brilliant photos of me.

Thank you to Pranav Shah for my website.

And to Manjula Venkatswamy, for managing the stage behind the scenes.

It Happens for a Reason: Vipasha was a teenage mom; she is now 34, holding two unusual jobs, trying to raise a 15-year-old as a single parent, and hoping to find true love, when the one guy she cannot get over—the father of her child—reappears in her life.

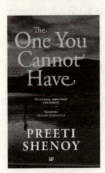

The One You Cannot Have: Two years after the break-up of what he thought was a near-perfect relationship, Aman is still struggling to get over his now-married former girlfriend, when a new girl enters his life.

The Secret Wish List: Bound by social stigma and parental pressure, trapped in a marriage long gone stale, Diksha is struggling to break conventions and discover her true calling, when an old crush comes back into her life.

ABOUT THE AUTHOR

PREETI SHENOY, among the top five highest-selling authors in India, is also on the Forbes longlist of the most influential celebrities in the country. *India Today* has named her as being unique for being the only woman in the bestselling league.

She has been awarded the Academia Award for Business Excellence by the New Delhi Institute of Management, which is given to distinguished professionals for innovative best practices for their contribution to their field. She has also given talks in many educational institutions, including IITs and IIMs, and corporate organisations, such as KPMG, Infosys and Accenture.

Preeti is also an artist specialising in portraiture. She has a very popular blog and writes a weekly column in the *Financial Chronicle*. She has a huge online following and is very active on social media. Her other interests are travel, photography and Ashtanga yoga.